Praise for

Spoiled

"These nine stories are less concerned with the fabulous than with something altogether more demanding and substantial. . . . They are exquisite character studies: urbane, assured and filthy rich in smart observations." —*The New York Times Book Review*

"Laser-sharp . . . probes the heartbreak of high expectations, the self-hatred that can go hand in hand with a ferocious sense of entitlement. Read it and squirm." —*O: The Oprah Magazine*

"Macy has a gift for revealing characters who remain blind to themselves." —*Newsweek*

"Sharply insightful." —*The New York Times*

"Macy shows that, in addition to penetrating, witty insight, she shares a more important trait with the chronicler of the Golden Age [F. Scott Fitzgerald]: a deep empathy for her subjects."

—NPR

"Wickedly smart, unwittingly timely . . . [Macy] attains a wonderfully transgressive Cheever-like honesty." —*Vogue*

"Husbands, wives, nannies and children orbit one another in the cold moral vacuum of the uptown Manhattan. Caitlin Macy's stories dissect the lives of the rich and miserable with tender but surgical precision. This is what happens to gossip girls twenty years down the line." —*Time*

ALSO BY CAITLIN MACY

The Fundamentals of Play

SPOILED

SPOILED

Stories

Caitlin Macy

RANDOM HOUSE TRADE PAPERBACKS

NEW YORK

2010 Random House Trade Paperback Edition

Copyright © 2009 by Caitlin Macy

Published in the United States by Random House Trade Paperbacks, an imprint of The Random House Publishing Group, a division of Random House, Inc., New York.

RANDOM HOUSE TRADE PAPERBACKS and colophon are trademarks of Random House, Inc.

RANDOM HOUSE READER'S CIRCLE and Design is a registered trademark of Random House, Inc.

Originally published in hardcover in the United States by Random House, an imprint of The Random House Publishing Group, a division of Random House, Inc., in 2009.

"Christie" was originally published, in different form, in *The New Yorker* and in *The O. Henry Prize Stories 2005* (New York: Anchor, 2005).

"The Red Coat" was originally published, in different form, in *This Is Not Chick Lit,* edited by Elizabeth Merrick (New York: Random House Trade Paperbacks, 2006).

ISBN 978-0-8129-7172-9

Printed in the United States of America

www.randomhousereaderscircle.com

2 4 6 8 9 7 5 3 1

Book design by Victoria Wong

For Jeremy

with the usual disclaimers

"Mrs. Spragg had no ambition for herself . . . but she was passionately resolved that Undine should have what she wanted."

—EDITH WHARTON
The Custom of the Country

Contents

SPOILED

Christie

WHEN YOU MET Christie for the first time, it took only minutes to learn that she was from Greenwich, Connecticut, but months could go by before you got another solid fact out of her. After a couple of years in New York, she realized that she had to give people a little more information to stop them from digging, so once she'd mentioned Greenwich she would quickly add that she'd gone to "the high school," meaning the public one. The first time she said this, you'd find her forthrightness refreshing—disarming, even, in the midst of so many pretenders. You'd be prompted, perhaps, to admit something about yourself—the fact that you were doing Jenny Craig, for instance, and had to sneak the packaged food into your office microwave when no one was paying attention. But then you'd overhear Christie making the same confession to someone else, and it would lose its charm. It was just Fact No. 2, which, added to Fact No. 1—her childhood in Greenwich—represented the sum total of what could be stated about Christie Thorn's background, about her entire life before college and New York, where I met her.

Plus, you couldn't help being suspicious of her motives in revealing Fact No. 2. If, at a party, a group of people were standing around, sharing a corner of a room, and someone made an opening bid—mentioning Hotchkiss or St. George's, say—Christie would always pointedly interject, "Oh, I wouldn't know. I went to public school. Greenwich High. That's right—I was a good old suburban kid." Of course, Christie and the person who had mentioned boarding school were doing the same thing—preemptively defending themselves against attack—yet rightly or wrongly you were tempted to give the Hotchkiss guy a free pass. With him you could figure that his parents had divorced badly, or his mother was an alcoholic, or his brother had committed suicide (or perhaps it really had been an accidental overdose), or that in keeping with the family tradition Dad had gone crazy and now spent his days in slippers and a robe shooting intricate, archaic forms of pool. On account of one or more of these family problems, the young man felt insecure about himself as an individual, and so, in moments of social anxiety, he mentioned boarding school a little too early, and a little unnaturally, to shore up his resolve. Still, whatever his problem, whatever the big bad family secret, it was just the slightly burned edge on a cake that everyone still wanted to eat. How bad could those family problems really be, you'd asked yourself more than once, if, at the same time, you had the house in Edgartown? How bad—if you had the gray shingles, the weathered shutters, the slanting attic roof, the iron bedstead, the needlepoint pillow on the wicker settee proclaiming "A woman's place is on the tennis court!" the *batterie de cuisine* of lobster pots and potato mashers from the forties, and the octagonal kitchen window, through which you could glimpse the dunes and smell the salt air—could anything really be?

Meanwhile, you'd assume that Christie had more to protect, that her history was more embarrassing, somehow: a chronological downsizing of suburban homes (all of them, albeit, technically in Greenwich), a cheapness in things like bedding and glassware, or four people sharing one bathroom with a stand-up shower. And you wouldn't be wrong. The real story was simple, of course, and if it was sad, the sadness lay only in the gap between it and Christie's grand expectations. Christie's father had gone into business for himself and had cash flow problems. That was all. No one had murdered anyone; there wasn't a whiff of incest or abuse, embezzlement, or even tax fraud. Mr. Thorn had owed money his whole life, but he paid his bills more or less on time, and when he died, his life insurance policy would pay off the mortgage on the house. He was an honest man with a clean conscience.

Yet Christie's conscience was not clean, and seemed never to have been. In a typical scenario from her adolescence, her father would plan a nice vacation for the family, then wouldn't be able to swing it, Christie would throw a tantrum, and her mother, who spoiled her, would charge the trip on her credit card to appease her. Christie would go on the vacation, but she would go alone, with a similarly spoiled friend. She and the friend would go helling around Key West, say, or Miami Beach, feeling worse and worse and worse and laughing harder and harder. And then, and this was the kicker, Christie's mother would pick them up at LaGuardia (the friend's mother could never be bothered) and would want to know—would have been anxious about, primordially concerned about—whether they'd had a good time.

On the way back from one of these vacations, when she was sixteen or seventeen, Christie and her friend checked in late and were bumped up to first class. They were separated and Christie was seated next to an affluent-looking older man. The man drank Scotches and read a golf magazine, and, when the flight was delayed, the two became partners in peevish complaint, the man turning to Christie to include her in his "Can you believe this?" glare. Eventually, he asked her where she was from, and when she said, "Greenwich," he looked at her with a kind of absolute approval that Christie couldn't recall ever having inspired before. After that, whenever a flight of hers was delayed she'd shake her head and say, "Time to spare, go by air," as the Scotch-drinking man had, and when she met people, she liked to make sure that they knew where she was from.

After college (four ambitious yet misguided and ultimately obscure years at Colgate), after a prolonged phase of running around New York while drifting through a series of support jobs at big firms, and after she had slept with fifty-five, or was it sixty-five men, Christie found someone to marry. We spent a lot of time speculating as to who would be invited to the wedding (only a strange, angry girl named Mary McLean, who had made some Faustian bargain with Christie long before any of us met her, considered herself one of Christie's *real* friends), but in the end everyone was invited—to the Pierre, no less. Throughout the evening, Christie wore a look of incurable dissatisfaction. Her face was gaudily made up, as if for a school play or an ice-skating competition. At the reception, her parents seemed frightened. It was as if they had been instructed to keep their mouths shut at all costs. A guest would shake Mrs. Thorn's hand in the receiving line and say, "Hi, I'm Jen Ryan. Christie and I were roommates at Colgate?" and Mrs. Thorn would nod, grim-faced, and say—literally—nothing, a strange gravelly noise sounding from the depths of her throat. The groom's name was Thomas Bruewald, and he was gawky and tall, with an oversized head and a unibrow. His parents were never identified; perhaps they were not in attendance. Apparently they were foreign. He had grown up half over here and half over there—in Bavaria, was it? Or Croatia? At any rate, it wasn't Umbria or Aix or anywhere worth trying to lock in the invitation for. Bruewald had gone to one of those Euro institutes with the word *polytechnical* in the name. The champagne at the reception was a little too good, and some people had more than their fill and, by the end of the night, were making rude remarks. One guy said that Christie's parents must have taken out a second mortgage to pay for the wedding. "Didn't know you could get a second mortgage on a trailer," a yet unmarried, embittered young woman said. And then, of course, you got "Hey, wait a minute! There are no trailers"—the crowd in unison—"in Greenwich,

Connecticut!" But nobody said that the groom was funny-looking. You could pick on Christie for trying too hard, you could note the moment when Mr. Thorn said, "Fuck it," took off his tuxedo jacket, and started doing body shots with the bridesmaids, but you didn't pick on the groom's looks. You just didn't go there.

Christie herself was quite pretty. Her features were large and unflawed, her hair was dyed only a shade or two lighter than it would have been naturally, and, in an age when Manhattan had been overrun by the kind of chain stores you'd find at a suburban mall, these attributes had kept her in dates for a decade and the word *beautiful* had been lobbed over her head with surprising—to some of us, disturbing—frequency.

The groom had some kind of science-related job—engineering? drug research?—that required a reverse commute to New Jersey. And once the wedding was over, once the gift had been ordered (they had registered for everything but the kitchen sink, in anticipation, evidently, of dinners for sixteen at which oysters would be served and finger bowls required), once the thank-you note from Christie—Christie Bruewald now, of course—had arrived, it seemed that only the sparsest smattering of social interactions was indicated, a coffee or a drink with her perhaps twice a year. There was even some thought that the newlyweds would move out of the city. Christie had long anticipated children (little trophies, one presumed, to fill up that bottomless pit of dissatisfaction), and the suburbs had been held up as a superior way of life even, as I recall, when she was still single.

Christie's new thing, at our biannual meetings, was to brag about her visits to see Thomas's family in Europe. It was mystifying—one would not have thought an "in" in the former East Germany particularly bragworthy, and, in any case, everyone at the wedding had seen how cowed the young man was, how classic the trade they had made. Did she think we didn't see her boasts for what they were? She started to slip into conversation the fact that

Thomas's uncle had a title, or had had one—she was vague on the details—and she mentioned straightfacedly that there was a castle in the family. Her Christmas card (sent yearly to all of us, even though we had not sent one to her in years) introduced the Bruewald family crest. It was all so ludicrous and pathetic, really, when they were living in a studio in a high-rise on York Avenue.

"So why do you even see her?" my husband would ask. (I was married now, too.) "If she's so awful, why don't you dump her? Just don't call back." Like most men, he had no patience with these pseudo-friendships between women that drag on for years. The question troubled me, and in my head I came up with three reasons that I continued to see Christie Bruewald, née Thorn, at six-month intervals. First, in an anthropological observation sort of way, I enjoyed taking note of her pretensions. I enjoyed seeing how far she would go. In a way, I had exulted in the family-crest Christmas card. I had put it up on the refrigerator and shown it to everyone who came over. I was just dying, now, to see what would follow. When I met her for coffee, I went prepared with a mental tape recorder to catch her appalling lapses in taste—not so much for myself as to pass on to everyone else. Second, there were, and this was harder to admit, sparks of humanity in Christie's pretensions, and in her desires, that were missing from my life. She had coveted *a huge diamond ring.* She had hoped *to land a guy with money.* She had wanted her wedding to be an extravaganza, *a day she'd remember for the rest of her life.* She wasn't "over it." She wasn't over anything. She knew what she wanted, and she wanted the kinds of things that the marketers of luxury goods describe as "the best"— Jacuzzis; chandeliers; access to the tropics in the middle of winter. Third, and finally what got me, I suppose, were the indications of humanity in Christie's life that had nothing to do with the pretensions. The family crest on the Christmas card had been embossed onto a picture of the Bruewalds and their new baby, all three of them in matching red-and-green velvet outfits. The little girl looked exactly like Thomas—an odd-featured, brown-haired older man. She wouldn't have the advantage of her mother's looks, and, for someone as entranced by the superficial as Christie was, that must have been hard to take. You could say that I felt sorry for Christie.

STILL, DESPITE HAVING my reasons for keeping in touch, a year or so after my own wedding I went through a period when I decided to burn the fat from my life. Christie had begun to represent all that was wrong with New York. Of course, this really meant all that I was tired of in myself, but I didn't see that then. I wrote "Seeing people like Christie Thorn" on a list of things that were a fatal waste of time, and when she called and left a message to start the back-and-forth that would culminate in our having lunch a few weeks later, I didn't call back.

Perhaps I ended it then simply because the interesting part of Christie's story seemed to be over. Though my own life still seemed to me a fountain of infinite promise, hers felt blandly curtailed. I realized that there was a part of me that had almost wanted her to make it, on her own terms, whatever they might be. The somewhat sad thing about Christie's wedding was that it hadn't been outrageous at all; it had been just another overpriced New York wedding spearheaded by a bride with too much makeup on. I found it all too easy to imagine how her story would continue, how, inevitably, it would end. I lived with that story, kept the thread going in my mind, amending or extending from time to time, when some event in my own life recalled Christie's unhappy mixture of envy and drive, of self-promotion and apology.

My version (wholly fictional) went something like this: Having married for money, Christie quickly discovers that she hasn't married for enough. Realizing her mistake only deepens her underlying dissatisfaction, and, in order to convince herself that things can still change, she has an innocuous little affair in the first six months after the wedding. A year later, the second affair—with a secret dedicated cell phone; a pregnancy scare perhaps—is not so innocuous nor so little. Thomas is doing as well as he ever has, but this is New York, and after their second child is born (also looking—phew—just like Daddy) the Bruewalds are unable to afford a large apartment in the city and they make that move to the suburbs. (For Christie, the outer reaches of Brooklyn, or a bohemian setup with the baby in a dresser drawer, has never been an option.) They buy a starter house in one of the less well-known towns of Westchester. They socialize a lot and their favorite friends are people like themselves, but who make a little less than they do, and are jealous of them for some other reason as well—Christie's having lost the weight after her pregnancies, say. The children are the usual product of a marriage like the Bruewalds'. They suffer from Christie's frustrated ambition and their father's subservience to it, and they end up angry and self-hating beneath a surface of entitlement. But the European influence helps to normalize them somewhat, and at least they know how to ski. When the children are grown and out of the house, Christie starts spending most of her time down at the time-share in Cancún, befriending other "party people," whose spouses turn a blind eye. She and Thomas never divorce because she's afraid to be alone.

That would be about the size of it. It would end in a grasping old age, marked by an incivility to service people (flight attendants, doctors' secretaries) and a dye job that wasn't what it used to be.

It was what she deserved, wasn't it? There is order in things; what comes around, as they say in my hometown, goes around, and people who spend a hundred and fifty grand on a wedding they can't afford simply so they won't lose face will someday have to stare down the demons that drove them. Who was she kidding?

IT WILL BE clear from my iteration of Christie's excesses that, as a couple, my husband and I have always prided ourselves on living within our means. When the time comes for us to move into a slightly larger apartment, we understand that staying in the city will mean living at the back of a building, in interior rooms that open onto shaftways. So it's only for kicks, just to see what we're missing, that we ask our broker to show us something fancy. We go prepared to look, to smile wistfully, and to depart, understanding that by any reasonable standards we have more than enough, and by any other standards we simply don't measure ourselves. When, high up in Carnegie Hill, on our way into one of those hushed old buildings that face the park, our two-year-old daughter falls in love with the doorman, we take it, laughing, with endless hope for the future, as a sign that the girl knows quality when she sees it. "You can see him again on the way out," we promise. "He'll be waiting for you." Yet when we fall in love with the apartment itself, we cannot take it as a sign of anything at all. It is smaller by a room than the others we've looked at; and costs more by oh, about a couple hundred grand. Where are our wistful smiles now? Where is our comfort in reasonable standards? It is clear that we—and only we—are capable of fully appreciating the charm of this place. Who but we would actually enjoy the fact that the stove and the refrigerator appear, like the building, to be prewar? Who but we would *keep* the sixties-style wallpaper in the maid's room? (The ghost of Christie Thorn shakes her head impertinently at the broker: "Total gut job in the kitchen!" "No closet space!" "No wet bar!") And then there is our daughter and the doorman, who is pretending to play hide-and-seek with her, while we stand slack-jawed in the marble lobby, looking out at the green of the park, doing sums in our heads, reconsidering decisions of the past, decisions that might have netted us this apartment, pure and simple.

Because now nothing else will do.

The apartment is at the breaking point of our price range, and though on paper we can nearly—almost—sort of swing it, our broker calls that night with bad news: He's "shopped" us to the board, and they are reluctant to consider anyone whose liquid assets are as low as ours. That fast, it's over. We have been slotted into position. We know (and can laugh bitterly at the notion that this knowledge, in other circumstances, is supposed to be comforting) exactly where we stand.

A week after getting the bad news, I walk by the building, daughterless this time, and find myself slowing, then stopping in front of it. A man emerges, then two schoolgirls in uniform. I put my sunglasses on to hide the fact that I am staring in an ugly, covetous way. How tortured and unpleasant I must look compared to the woman my age who comes out next, well dressed, smartly coiffed, followed by two children, a girl and a boy, who are tailed by two Tibetan nannies. For an incredible moment, I mistake the woman for an older, more sophisticated Christie Thorn. Out of habit I am pretending not to see even this twin of hers (the way you ignore a man in a bar who resembles your ex-boyfriend), when the doorman's greeting rings out—yes, as if in a dream—"Mrs. Bruewald." "Hi, Lester." He asks how long she will be, and the woman says, "Oh, an hour or two. We're just going to go to the park and do some shopping before Daddy gets home."

In a vile moment only Darwin could love, I paste a smile on my face, and I call out, "Christie?"

WE WENT TO that Italian restaurant on Madison that people are always forgetting the name of. Kids and nannies were dispatched to the park. It was an off hour, three or four o'clock, and I remember I almost hated to dirty one of the white linen tablecloths that were set for dinner. We started with cappuccinos, then moved on to glasses of the house white—that fruity Soave you can always count on. When we got hungry later, the waiter, who clearly knew Christie, brought a plate of pecorino and some bread, and to wash it down I had another glass of the white and Christie switched to red. I was longing for a cigarette, and eventually I asked her, "Do you still smoke?" "My God, I'm dying for one," she said, and took a pack out of her purse. It was just after the smoking ban had gone into effect and there was giggling when the waiter slipped us an ashtray. Feeling happily illicit, we each smoked two.

I should have mentioned before that it was one of those surreally springlike days at the tail end of winter, the kind of afternoon when you flirt with the mailman, the coffee-cart man, and the busboy, when you long for a new pair of open-toed sandals and a good excuse to sit in a café all afternoon, ignoring your responsibilities, rousing that old pleasure-seeking self of yours, and getting drunk. Well, we certainly had the excuse. There was catching up to be done—husbands, children, careers, in a nutshell.

From the beginning, I was drinking rather fast. All the information sharing, I realized, was making me uneasy. I, who used to rattle off insouciantly all the good things that were happening, was the guarded one now. I had something to protect, it seemed. I held back, forming half-truths for every potential question Christie might pose—asking myself, "Will I tell her about that or not? Will I act as if everything's fine or will I level with her?"— while she was expansive with me, as she now could be. The family crest was not a joke; it was not a sham. In some little town in the former East Germany, the Bruewalds were evidently a big deal. "All the money was tied up in this castle in Saxony—this huge, horrible house—and, the minute Onkel Guenther died, Thomas and I looked at each other and we were like, 'We're selling!' It was like, before he died we couldn't mention it, and the minute we got the news we never looked back. It was a done deal." They had inherited the lot: sold the *Schloss,* auctioned the furniture, started up trusts for Hildie and Axel. (Although Hildie still resembled her

father, her appearance would be seen, later in life, as distinguish-
ing. I could see that now. People would seek ownership of those
peculiar looks—how could I have missed that before?) In addition
to the ten rooms on Fifth Avenue, the Bruewalds now owned a ski
lodge in the Arlberg, a country house in New Jersey, and a man-
sion in Solln, which Christie cheerfully described as "the Greenwich of Munich."

The sheer mass of the good luck was making me dizzy, but
when she mentioned Greenwich I sat up and did her the one cour-
tesy I could. I fed her the line. "That must be nice," I said. "It
must feel just like home." She drained her glass of wine, though
she had already drained it once, and then she put it down and unexpectedly met my eye. "You know," she said, "when we got the
money I went out and got myself a two-hundred-and-fifty-dollar-
an-hour shrink. I used to think I was a horrible person." She
wasn't a horrible person, the shrink had told her; in fact, there was
nothing wrong with her at all.

We split a third glass of wine and then split a fourth, which
made the waiter laugh. I told her why I had been loitering outside
her building. I wasn't hoping to get something out of telling her,
I just wanted to ante up with something real of my own. It seemed
secretive and creepy *not* to mention it. Christie laughed, the way
you laugh at something you find absurd. "Oh, for Christ's sake!"
she said. I stared stonily at the table, the way I do when I'm both
drunk and mortally offended—that's how defensive I felt—and
she had to talk me down. "No, no—listen. Thomas is on the
board, and they *so* owe us. This is no problem, no problem at all.
Don't believe what they say about the liquid assets. It's just a way
of keeping people out."

I was still suspicious.

"You know what I'll do?" she said. "I'll tell them about your
Mayflower ancestor."

"I told you about my Mayflower ancestor?" I said.

"Yup." She smiled. "The first time we met."

There was nothing I could do but turn bright red and finish my wine.

Christie went to the bathroom, and I sat at the table, flipping a matchbook over and over in my hand. I felt giddy and keyed up, as if I were waiting for a date to return, as if we might be planning to go back to her deluxe pad and make out on her and Thomas's king-size bed. People had always said that Christie had a great body, and that's the kind of body it was—firm, relentlessly fit—offered up as a commodity for others to comment on. In the early nineties, she had been an aerobics queen, logging two, three hours a day at the gym; now, of course, she was into yoga and Pilates, but, "to tell you the truth," she'd confessed to me earlier in the afternoon, "I kind of miss the screaming and the jumping up and down."

We had moved to the city at the same time—ten years ago now—and sitting there, playing with the matchbook and waiting for her to come back, I tried to get a handle on what those ten years had amounted to. We had been single. Now we were *married* women with *children.* But, despite the italics in my head, I couldn't seem to take it any further than that. My thoughts drifted to the apartment, trying in some way, I suppose, to notch the progress we had each made. If my husband and I got the place, we'd be cash-poor for a few years. With both of us working, we could bring in x amount per year, put y aside, and contribute z to our 401(k)s. But, even considering promotions and raises, there was a limit to x. X was fixed, and there was only t—time—to increase it. But time ate up your life. You could say "In ten years" or "In twenty years," but the problem was that then whatever it was would be *in* ten years, or *in* twenty years. A decade, two decades of your life would have gone by before you attained it. The fixity of x was the most bittersweet thing I had thought of in ages. Of course, it was comparing myself to Christie that had brought on all these thoughts. When she came out of the ladies' room, look-

ing as happy and drunk as I had felt a minute before, her innocence struck me like a storm. And I realized that what separated
us, and perhaps had always separated us, was the understanding
that I had only just reached and that she—she would never have
to: In life you can only get so far.

I WALKED HOME with the good news for my husband and
daughter. It seemed that Christie and I were going to be friends
again—friends after all. My husband would be dubious, to say the
least. "The same Christie Thorn you told me you would never have
coffee with again?" Nor would he like the idea of her getting us
past the board; it would take a week to make him understand
what had changed in the course of an afternoon and why it wasn't
the case that we were simply using her. Then again, I deserved a
dose of his skepticism. I had carried on about her—had laughed in
my best moments, but from time to time had been disdainful, and
even indignant. I asked myself, now, how I truly felt about all
those pretensions of hers. I went through them one by one—that
wedding, the Christmas card; then little things, little remarks
from her single days, her obsession with going to the "in" restaurant every year, for instance. I came to the conclusion that none of
it was worth getting worked up about. None of it was profound.
As the shrink had evidently made clear, none of it had anything to
do with Christie herself. On the contrary, I told myself, it was your
problem.

Bait and Switch

"OH, GOD, ELS, it's that nightmare German guy I was telling you about." Louise shuddered, pleasurably, in the doorway of the beach house, and rejoined Elspeth on the terrace. "I told him we'd have lunch with him tomorrow in Riva Bella."

"Why?" Elspeth said, her voice flat to mask her alarm. Despite the fact that the two sisters had been squabbling nonstop since she'd landed at Fiumicino two days ago, Louise's finding the need to make plans beyond themselves worried Elspeth. It was so nice, in Europe, to ride Louise's long coattails; intolerable to have to cope on one's own, getting by, like any tourist, with foolish smiles and an ingratiating overuse of the formal "you" form.

"He keeps calling me. . . . It's so *funny*." Louise tucked a lock of black hair behind her ear with a coy little shake of her head, as if protesting a too-lavish compliment. "I can't *imagine* what he wants."

"What—is he on vacation here, too?" said Elspeth shortly. Lately, she felt she was on a one-woman mission to combat all outward manifestations of Louise's moral shortcomings: this habit her sister had, for instance, of speaking aloud yet seeming to consult herself.

Louise looked blankly at Elspeth for a moment, as if puzzled to find her sister sitting across from her. "No, haven't I told you?" She faux-cringed and murmured significantly, "He's actually *moved* here."

"Has he," Elspeth said neutrally—pointedly obtuse. She knew, of course, what Louise was hinting at—knew that she was meant to say "Gosh, do you think this guy is in love with you or something?" Oh, she could see right away where all of this was going. But she pressed her lips grimly together, refusing to be complicit. Louise called out nervously to Annie.

"What are you doing, Anz? You having fun?" The little girl was squatting, a few yards from the table, beside a puddle the outdoor shower had made in the dirt, a trove of plastic Pollies and Polly accessories arranged around the bit of water as if the dolls were sunning themselves at the beach. It was nearly ten o'clock but the light lingered still, and Annie, like an Italian child, stayed up late.

"It's my fault, I guess. I've let it get out of hand," Louise went on, topping up their glasses with the last of the trebbiano. They'd been nursing the wine since supper ended, both unwilling to desert the terrace. The lapping of the Maremman sea, just visible through the row of umbrella pines, and the lasting evening light, which never lost its novelty for Elspeth, seemed to entrap them there each night, while Louise unburdened herself to Elspeth. "We were all sort of friends in London. His wife worked with—" Here Louise raised her eyebrows to avoid mentioning "Robert" in front of Annie, and Elspeth rolled her eyes, for it was a habit she disapproved of. "It's not like he's dead, Louise! You ought to mention him all the time—in a very natural way," she'd instructed Louise, on the way home from the airport. "What do you think you're saying to Annie by pretending her father doesn't exist?" Last night's temper tantrum, too, had provided an opportunity for reproach, or rather not the tantrum—now impossible to impute to the child's absorbed, industrious mien—but the spanking it had resulted in.

"My Polly's all wet," Annie announced.

"Is she, sweetie? Let me see." Louise swiveled in her chair, more quickly solicitous, because of the topic of their conversation, than she would have been normally.

("I would never hit a child," Elspeth had sententiously pronounced when Annie had been put tearfully to bed, to which Louise had replied blackly, "Call me when you have a kid.")

"Bring her here, Annie."

Annie stood up, frowning, and walked carefully to the table, the doll's fibrous hair springing from her fist. "She fell in the water and her hair got wet."

Picking up the child, Louise drew her into her lap, her mass of black hair descending around her daughter. There was no denying that Louise was striking. Unlike Elspeth, who was more hit or miss, Louise had the kind of looks that could withstand photographs, which announced beauty and then carelessly bucked the scrutiny that followed. In the iconic maternal pose her sister's face looked a little unnatural, Elspeth thought, as if it withstood the softening maternal glow as well. A petty thought, for now it was Elspeth's turn to sip her wine and look away—left out. "Shall we dry it with this special spa towel?" Louise said, pretending, with a cloth napkin. "Will that help? I think she'll be all right, don't you?"

After Louise's failed marriage to Annie's father, an Englishman named Robert Dennis (or more likely, Elspeth suspected, though she shrank from any precise dating, the affair had overlapped with the end of Robert), there had been the brief, Parisian interlude with Jean-Marc. That had ended when she met the quasi-divorced Giacomo in a chairlift in the Dolomites, and moved herself and Annie in a rental van to Tuscany. Elspeth was still single—free as usual, she thought with vexation, to vigil through eight hours in coach to Europe for the annual homage paying *à* Louise.

IN NEAR DARKNESS Elspeth wiped down the table while Louise did dishes in the tiny strip of kitchen at the back of the house. Elspeth sponged the oilcloth irritably, a vision of tomorrow's luncheon, with herself in the role of chaperone to Louise's flirtation, coming rapidly into focus.

"He's always had this . . . thing for me, I guess you could say,"
Louise had said as they cleared the table, now speaking in the
lockjawed murmur she used when she didn't want Annie to follow
the conversation. Two or three trips inside were required, to return
the plates and serving bowls to the kitchen, the oil and wine, the
salt and pepper, the tablecloth and napkins. Louise believed in
nothing if not the keeping up of domestic standards. "They split,
too . . . As a matter of fact, it was just around the time we did."

"What does Giacomo think of—what's he called again?" Elspeth felt a perverse, self-preserving loyalty to Louise's current
boyfriend, who had after all rented them this beach house. ("If," as
Elspeth had said in the one e-mail to a pseudo-boyfriend in New
York she had managed from the Internet café in town, "it's not too
misleading to refer to a semidetached, postwar, cement condo-
minium as a 'beach house.'") Giacomo had laughed at her gushing
encouragement to try to drive out from Florence and join them for
a few days. "No, no, Spee," he had said, his short Tuscan accent,
the severity of his manner, making the family nickname both
funny and touching. "I cannot 'find' time. I must work." In the
driver's seat, Louise was silent behind her large sunglasses. Nevertheless, she managed to convey a supreme derision at this claim.

"Werner Stechel?"

"It sounds familiar—I think I have met him." Louise sounded
tentative when she finally came up with the man's name, as if she
was a little embarrassed that this was all she had to offer, after so
much buildup. Elspeth responded as she did simply in order to
keep herself in the conversation—remain part of tomorrow's plan;
she couldn't, at the moment, distinguish the man in her mind
from the dozens of Louise's Euro-acquaintances who had been produced for her in the last decade, from the first summer Louise took
the au pair job in Brittany, abandoning Elspeth to a hateful summer alone with their mother and her shame. Nearly all of them,
acquaintances over the years, had seized upon Louise's little sister

as the ideal person to whom to show off their English. (Elspeth had fantasized about delivering a lecture to the lot of them. "The Present Progressive," she was going to call it. "Not a Tense You Want to Use a Lot Of.") Werner Stechel, though, she thought suddenly, rinsing the sponge under the outdoor tap at the side of the house and meditatively wringing it out. He did sound familiar.

"You like this stuff?" Elspeth said as she came inside. Her niece was standing before the large, squat TV. Onscreen, two men caught up to a third, pinned him against a wall, and began to knife him.

Annie neither concurred nor demurred but, tucking a foot underneath her, settled into the fat, tapestry-covered sofa—thumb in her mouth, her index finger hooked around a strand of perfectly straight black hair. The joke when she was born—Robert's own self-deprecating one—had been that while Annie's father had not contributed any genetic material to his daughter, "at least she'll understand cricket." Funny, it had been at first, Elspeth recalled.

"Do you think she ought to be watching this?" she muttered, as the knifed victim's knees buckled and he sank slowly down the wall, streaking it with lines of blood. But she didn't repeat the question loudly enough for Louise to hear over the running water. Her niece had seen it all—sex, murders, the beheaded horse in *The Godfather.* Instead, still holding the sponge, she sat down reluctantly beside Annie in the hope that her presence might mitigate the violence.

Elspeth got it—she wasn't dumb. The television free-for-all was Louise's answer to their childhood—their own PBS-only, no-sugar-cereal Vermont childhood that had, nevertheless, managed to go so dangerously off course. The TV, and the spankings, and the packaged chocolate cookies for breakfast, even the Bain de Soleil tans: It was all an elaborate way of saying "I will not be like her." Noel. Fat and pathetic—so Louise had called her, anyway, to her face, Elspeth following suit soon enough. And red-faced and unkempt, they might have added—half-dressed most days. After the divorce, their mother's incapacities were simply staggering. Yet Noel, who might have started by trying to help herself (blue-collar, she had put her husband through grad school), instead bled all over everyone else. Her ten-dollar checks to CARE and UNICEF and the cleft-palate people: Louise would steal them from the mail and rip them up. "We're not letting her send them till we get color TV goddammit." When the Jehovah's Witnesses came to the door, in the strange acrylic clothes of the poor, it was Louise who turned them away—"I'll deal with this, Mom!" Or the child getting smacked in the supermarket: Tears would come into Noel's eyes as she asked her older daughter in a choked voice to take the grocery cart and her wallet and go and pay—"I just need to get control of myself. I'll just be a minute. I'm sorry. I'm sorry, girls. Take Elspeth, too—oh, God, you really shouldn't see me like this."

"The bad man is back, Mama—look! *Il cattivo!*"

Louise hung up her apron tidily, on a hook under the spiral staircase that led up from the kitchen, and came and perched on the arm of the sofa, watching the television distractedly, a fake, merry look on her face. Presently, Elspeth felt her sister's eyes on her. Louise said touchily, "You know, Spee, you don't have to come tomorrow. You really don't. I should have said that before." Louise folded her arms over her chest and tried very hard to look interested in the cop drama. "You can stay here, obviously—relax—or whatever. I can take Annie with me. I'll go by myself. It's fine."

"No! No, Mom! *Absolutely not,*" said Annie, aping Louise's stern voice. "Do you understand me?"

"That's okay," Elspeth said, relenting. "I'll come." She was on the point of adding, "Do you know, I figured it out—I have met that guy," for she had finally connected a flash of memory with the name. Or rather, not a memory, but a sensation—like a half-recalled pleasant dream that puts one, rather stupidly, in a good mood. She couldn't picture his face, and in her mind the setting was not Louise and Robert's terraced house in Clapham but Louise's first apartment in London, the ground-floor flat off Marylebone Road, where she had lived when she'd moved to London after college, on some vague premise of studying art history. "And I'm never coming back." And that setting, of course, made no sense. But what Elspeth could recall was a warm, blondish man, of about her height (she always liked that, unlike Louise, who liked to be towered over), who—despite her disdainfulness when they met (she automatically dismissed any admirer of Louise—protecting herself, one might have assumed, but it was really a priggish moral isolationism that prevented her from entering the fray)—could not take his eyes off her. That unexpected occurrence of instant chemistry—for she had immediately felt it as well, though she could barely look at him—and the knowledge that a man (of whom there had historically been a few noteworthy examples) had quite particularly preferred her over Louise had stuck with amazing tenacity in her consciousness. With an embarrassed dip of her head she realized that she had probably thought of Werner Stechel in the abstract within the last few weeks. "What am I going to do here all day?" she said, trying not to grin.

"It'll be fun for Annie—he's got a little girl," Louise said quickly, as if seconding the motion. She stood up and brushed off her striped cotton housedress, pleased, clearly, that everyone was falling into line. "We'll all come back here for a swim. I think that's what he's been hinting at. It's insanely hot in Siena now. I'll get rid of him quickly—don't worry."

Annie took her thumb out of her mouth and addressed the television set. "I don't like that little girl," she said.

THE LITTLE GIRL was called "Julia," with the soft German *J.* "Annie!" she screamed as their party appeared, Louise and Elspeth tense and bickering because they were late, having parked at the entrance to the wrong *bagno,* and then having had to walk to the next one, down the relentlessly shadeless midday streets.

Annie stopped dead and shrieked, too, rather theatrically, Elspeth thought, and ran to meet her friend.

"There he is," Louise said. Her eyes narrowed with bemused in-decision. A man had emerged from the restaurant—Elspeth had seen him first: wheat-blond and sunburned, Hawaiian shirt but-toned over swim trunks. Biting off a chunk of roll, he gestured with the rest of it, waving them forward. His eyes seemed to flicker on Elspeth. "Come in! Come in! We are eating inside." Ve ah eating.

Elspeth, dragging her heels, suddenly couldn't face the meeting. Louise turned to her sharply, holding the door. "What's going on?"

Inside they stood blinking in the dim, mercifully cooling light, as Werner's voice boomed through the darkness.

"The terrace was too full!" He came up behind Louise and put his arms around her. "I couldn't be bothered." Startled, she turned her head and he kissed her on the lips.

Louise gave a hearty, scornful laugh at this. Craning her neck after the girls, who had disappeared, she distractedly introduced Elspeth.

"So, you live in the States?" said Werner, eyeing her with a puz-zled, and yet not inconfident curiosity. "Where, East Coast?"

With detachment she remembered now, as she took in the flar-ing nostrils, the appraising eyes that lingered frankly on her breasts, that he had the sort of looks only a teenager could love—one who would see the shaggy shock of bleached blond hair and beachcomber stubble as romantically iconoclastic, not the signs of dissipation they were. She recalled Louise's lovingly scathing as-sessment on the beach this morning: that in London he had smoked pot all day and sunbathed nude in his garden while his wife held down the law job and a Filipina came in to clean up the kitchen and iron his shirts. And was now supposedly thinking of starting up an *agriturismo* at the run-down farmhouse in the Val di Merse he'd bought with God-knows-whose money.

"New York," she said, meeting his gaze.

"Manhattan, yes?" Werner sounded doubtful. His focus shifted minutely, from one of Elspeth's pupils to the other. He was looking at her, she realized, the way a man looks at a woman whom he can't be sure he's slept with, but can't be sure he hasn't, either. Unable to keep a straight face, she cracked a grin. "Brooklyn."

Louise, who was beckoning Annie and the other girl away from the windows, shot her a "don't be difficult" look, to which Elspeth responded, "What? It's where I live."

The faintest points of recognition glimmered now, behind the bloodshot blue of the man's eyes. "Ah, yes, the Brooklyn Bridge." Elspeth smiled again, embarrassed as she always was in front of Louise when she took up any time or notice. "One of the great engineering feats of the nineteenth century." He gave a victorious chuckle and seized her elbow and Louise's and steered them awkwardly, three abreast, through a bevy of small tables to a larger one that stood slightly separate from the others, though not in a privileged way, but rather as if the staff used it.

"I wanted to wait, Louise," he said, gesturing to the half-eaten bowls of rice on the table. "But Julia wouldn't let me!"

"Oh, no, no, no, no—you shouldn't have waited," Louise said contemptuously. The sisters sat down on each side of Werner, who took the head. Louise pushed a used plate from before her as the two girls appeared, Julia's hands on Annie's shoulders, thrusting her forward through flanks of indulgent diners.

"We'll get some more wine—"

"Stop! Stop!" Annie was afrenzy with giggles.

A look of impatience crossed Werner's face. "Sit down, Julia!" He reached out his arm, batting it ineffectually in the direction of the girl, as a harried, indifferent waiter appeared with menus. Louise got Annie settled in the empty chair beside Elspeth. "All right?" she said to Elspeth—meaning, "Will you do the lion's share?"

"Fine," said Elspeth. "Fine."

"Julia, stop making that disgusting face! Sit down and eat your pasta!"

"Pasta, pee-sta! Poo-sta!" Julia said, still standing, and punctuated the comment with a resumption of the silly face.

"*Sitz dich jetzt hin, um Gottes Willen!*" Werner lunged for the girl, yanking her into place. Shocked, Elspeth averted her eyes but Louise, as if nothing out of the ordinary had just happened, took her seat and said vivaciously to the little girl, "It's *so* nice to see you again, Julia—*bist du gross geworden!*"

Julia looked very solemn for a moment, then, in a whisper, said to Annie, who was watching, enthralled by all this, "Pasta, pista, poosta."

Werner shook his head and wiped his face with his napkin. "Raising kids is hell, eh, Louise?" he said. He swallowed some wine and his eyes strayed cautiously once more to Elspeth. She put a skeptical but not uncharmed expression on her face, like that of an undeceived but indulgent parent. Abruptly, Werner summoned a different waiter—not their own—and demanded two more glasses and another bottle of the vermentino in a serviceable if graceless Italian.

"How long is she visiting for?" Louise said. "Julia," she asked as she turned coaxingly to the girl, "how long are you visiting your father?"

"Visiting? No, no. She lives with me now. You remember what it's like, Louise," Werner said, now addressing his plate with a crust of bread. "She and Sally don't get along."

At the other end of the table Annie took out her Polly and the two girls began to strip her naked.

It was as if he were talking about a pair of sisters, thought Elspeth. But diagonally across from her sat the six-year-old in question. The girl had her father's wheat-blond hair, cut rudely—hacked, almost—as if around a bowl. Her clothes, too, were the sort of clothes that looked as if the parents were trying to make a statement: the artsy smock, striped socks, funny pink hat. Around the child's own mouth was a second, larger mouth, a faded pink clown's smile, as if she had been playing with markers a day or two ago.

"Sally is not like you, Louise," Werner was saying. Louise let this pass, as if it were beneath comment. Werner pushed a plate of bruschetta in Elspeth's direction, not looking at her. "Have some," he said under his breath, so that she couldn't be sure he had addressed her. "She's not content shuttling the kiddies back and forth to playgroup. She should never have had a child. She came last month and, well—dropped her off!

"We are stuck with each other now, eh, Julia?" Werner reached across Louise to give the girl a squeeze and was promptly whacked at. "Oh! Oh! Oh! Don't hit me, please! I am so scared!"

A young woman, a redhead, quite obviously American, in a peasant skirt and the inevitable unisex sandals, seemed to have some business at their table. An inconvenience, Elspeth read now in her sister's face: the jejune tourist, newly abroad, who has failed to understand that class divisions remain intact overseas—who had never been made to understand, more likely, that such things existed at all. The young woman was looking with such intensity from Louise to Annie that Elspeth steeled herself for the compliment—although more typically it was a man, seeking to get through to Louise by exclaiming over Annie.

"Your daughter is beautiful!" the girl gushed. "And she looks just like you!"

Annie glanced up quickly not at the redhead but at her mother, whose reaction, she had obviously learned, would indicate where on the spectrum of significance the compliment fell. Louise acknowledged the young woman with a nod, lips pressed into a line of forebearance, as the latter continued, "You didn't tell me she had a *daughter,* Werner, jeez!" and plopped into the empty chair at the end of the table.

Elspeth *felt* the pause that passed between her and Louise. She opened her menu again, bent her head to it, feeling ill. "I'm Melissa," the girl said. She extended a hand down the table. Louise had to rise to shake it, which she did belatedly—Elspeth couldn't watch.

"We met each other a week ago—crossing the Ponte Vecchio, can you imagine?" Werner announced, as if the girl's physical presence demanded an explanation; whereas, Elspeth sensed, had she failed to return from the bathroom, he would not have felt compelled to mention her. "I've offered her a job: She's going to clean the apartments when I get my *agriturismo* going. Sleeping with the help is the way to go, don't you think, Louise?"

"Yes. I mean—I would think so," Louise stammered. "That's right." The flustered, undecided note, so rare in Louise, made Elspeth cringe; her own assumptions she had kept private, thank God. Anyway, the idea of herself and Werner (in one image, from the night before, swimming together in the ocean and then collapsing into a sand-screw, *From Here to Eternity*–style) seemed like a joke. Despite the insult to Louise, it was clear—this struck Elspeth at once—that Werner and she were in fact the true intimates at the table, the old comrades from London, from divorce; the partners in parenthood, in the complicated disappointments of grown-up love. Still, Elspeth's fantasy had been vivid; she reeled silently, as one does, from the juxtaposition of that vividness with its farfetchedness.

"Papa!"

"Julia, you don't have to shout! I'm right here, for God's sake."

"What about my gelato? Can I have it now, Papa?"

The half-English, half-German girl's accent reminded Elspeth of a grade school production of *Oliver—Ken oy hev it naow.* "*Bitte, Papa! Ich wille ein Eis!*" Julia looked up beseechingly at Elspeth, as if the latter's silence had bestowed impartiality on her. From this grotesque coda to her flirtation with Werner, Elspeth looked hurriedly away. She felt trapped by the child's eyes, with their wildly indiscreet announcement of need.

"Do you know, Elspeth," Werner said kindly, misinterpreting her stricken expression, perhaps, "I love to walk across the Brooklyn Bridge at midnight. Whenever I am in New York you will find me doing this."

"Is that right?"

"It's nice, isn't it?"

Louise and Elspeth had spoken at the same time, overeager, and each was more embarrassed than if she had interrupted someone else. Then neither of them could think of anything more to say. Oblivious, or at least pretending to be, Melissa began an overture to Louise. "You just have to come and visit us." Elspeth could feel Julia's eyes boring into her but she refused to engage the child. An outraged exasperation with expat life seized her suddenly—its unearned pleasures, its pretensions to assimilation, the children invariably the zenith of this ambition.

"Oh, good!" Louise fairly cried as the food arrived. She and Elspeth finally dared look at each other. "*Ecco la fritto di paranza,* Annie!" Melissa went silent at Louise's perfect Italian. The waiter who, Elspeth fancied, shared her exasperation, unloaded several dishes rapid-fire onto their table. Werner poured more wine. As the adults turned back in on themselves, Julia's spoon flew through the air and hit the floor.

"*Ju*lia!" cried Annie. Guilty in her admiration, perhaps, she glanced at Louise.

"It's okay, Werner, I got it." It was Melissa who leaned down and retrieved the spoon, holding it out toward Julia with an idiotic expression of hope. The girl, arms crossed over her chest, put her nose in the air and refused to take it.

"Of course," said Werner, at last raising his eyes to Elspeth's again, "I don't know when I'll be back in New York now—with this house to fix up . . ."

"I hate that fucking house!" Julia spoke up.

"Eh—it is not so bad, *liebchen,*" Werner said wearily. "Just look: You have your friend Annie only one hour away."

"So?" said Annie, suspicious at the introduction of her name. "So, what?"

"That *will* be nice," Louise said sharply, glaring at Annie. "She and Julia can play together."

"Yes, actually," Werner began, his mouth full of fried fish. He seemed to have regained his spirits suddenly. "I was going to ask you about that." He swallowed and gulped some wine. "Would you mind if they played together today?"

Elspeth, silent in her chair, sensed immediately what he meant—was impressed he had the nerve. But Louise (who had remained the more innocent, despite the divorce, of the two) said blithely, "Yes, I was thinking you all might want to come back for a swim."

"Wherever you like," Werner said cheerfully. "It doesn't matter to me! Melissa and I are going to get some sun, maybe walk around. She's never seen Castiglione before. I'll come pick her up around suppertime or a little later. Eh, Annie? Won't that be fun? A day with your friend?"

"Suppertime," Louise repeated. She fixed Werner with a freeze of a smile. "I see." Elspeth saw Melissa lean down to pick up Julia's spoon, again cast to the floor. The young woman held it aloft uncertainly for a moment, then tucked it with a shameful grimace under the lip of her plate.

ON THE CRAMMED service road that wound through the blocks of beach houses, the young women circled around twice, not speaking. Normally Louise would have gotten annoyed at the dearth of parking spots and sworn; today, she remained, through the stop at the grocery store, the gas station, the purchasing of gelatos for the girls, irreproachably calm. Elspeth glanced at her a couple of times, willing her to crack, but Louise stared ahead, her face a neutral mask. Finally, she created a spot, painstakingly wedging the station wagon between two Fiat Multiplas, a good fifty yards from their gate. The sisters lugged the bags of groceries and bottles of water; the girls ran ahead dripping the last of their gelatos. They all stopped off at the house to trade the groceries for towels, beach toys, sunblock, and magazines and made their way slowly down the path to the beach.

Elspeth tripped on a root and cried out. "Are you all right?" Julia was at her side immediately. "I'm fine!" Elspeth said, forcing herself to smile. When the girl insisted on taking her hand she was overcome by a kind of peevish dismay. "It just doesn't seem fair," she said aloud, glancing at Louise over Julia's head. "That we get stuck—you know . . ." Her voice trailed off bitterly when she saw that Louise wasn't going to respond, wasn't going to be her partner in complaint. "Whatever could you mean?" her bland expression seemed to say.

"Stop at the edge, Annie, do you hear me?" Louise warned as she and Elspeth set up camp on the cramped unprivate row of chairs and umbrellas that was the European beach.

"Mama, can we go in the water now?" Sensing her mother's mood, Annie was polite, judicious, fastening on her arm floaties.

"I don't need those!" Elspeth heard Julia saying. "I know how to swim already."

"You want me to take them in?" Elspeth was surprised to hear herself volunteer.

Louise gave a shrug: *Do what you like.* Without the girls to perform for, her face had gone flat with disdain.

"What's your name again?" asked Julia, shielding her eyes to look up at Elspeth, as Elspeth dropped the sarong Louise had produced to replace the ratty cotton shorts she had arrived with. *Wots your nime.* "You can call me Elspeth."

"Yay, Auntie Elspeth!"

"She's not your aunt," Annie said.

"It's *fine,* Annie!" Elspeth half-shouted, making Annie look at her curiously, for she, too, had bristled at the word on the girl's lips.

She took each of them by the hand and brought them down to

the water. Though it was ideal for swimming here—shallow, with friendly waves breaking near the girls' chins, Elspeth's waist—the Italians never seemed to go in, standing instead in unambitious clusters on the sand like congregating birds, clucking and gossiping among themselves. There seemed to be seven or eight grandparents for every child, giving their own party, Elspeth thought, an impermanent aspect—making them seem "fringe."

Elspeth meant to take them in for ten minutes and then plead changing-of-the-guard, but each time she inched closer to the sand Julia said, "No! Turn around! Turn around at once, do you hear me?" and, taken aback, Elspeth obeyed. After half an hour Annie got bored and went to play with her sand toys at the water's edge.

Louise's conscience must have pricked her, for she stood up and called to Elspeth and Julia, "There's a little baby here, girls— come see! A little *bambolattina*!"

"No!" Julia protested. "I want to play the turtle game again." She clung to Elspeth's arm, pulling her back toward the water. "You and *I* can play all day if we want! There's no one to stop us."

"I think I'd rather say hi to the baby. You should come, too," Elspeth suggested weakly, reasoning, like a fool, with the child instead of simply telling her what to do.

"Oh, babies!" Julia made a face. "They're incredibly tedious and all they do is cry and shit all over the place. It's hardly worth the bother."

"I'm getting out now," Elspeth said. She was appalled by the desperation in her voice. "You really should come, too, Julia. We've been in a long time!"

On shore, she shook out a towel and lay down on the sand a few yards from Louise's chair. Julia danced around in the water, pretending for a couple of minutes to continue the game alone. She got out, presently, and came up the beach toward Elspeth.

"I think I'll take a nap," the little girl said. Purposefully, Elspeth did not look up from her book. Julia got a towel out of the beach bag and spread it out right next to Elspeth's. Out of the corner of her eye, Elspeth could see her pinching the two towel edges together to make sure no sand stuck through in between. "Auntie Elspeth? Could you put sun cream on my back, please? I wouldn't want to get a burn."

"Oh, all right. Fine." Elspeth opened the cream, but then she said, handing it back to Julia, "You know what, Julia? I'm reading now. Why don't you ask Louise?"

"But she's reading, too!" protested the girl—logically enough.

"Louise? This *is* your fault, after all!" Elspeth called, her voice cracking with frustration.

Louise didn't so much as nod. "Okay, Louise is going to do it," Elspeth said loudly and went back to her book.

"What are you reading?"

"It's—nothing."

"Is it a grown-up book?"

"Yes!"

"Are you a grown-up?"

"Yes, Julia. I'm a grown-up."

"Do you have a husband?"

"No," Elspeth said.

"Are you divorced?"

"Could you just leave me alone, Julia? I'm really trying to read."

"Did you never have somebody fall in love with you and want to share your bed and go snog-snog-snog-snog-snoggy with you?"

"For Christ's sake!" Elspeth sat up. *"Louise?"*

"It's your fault." Louise laughed meanly and turned a page. "You shouldn't have played with them. Raises their expectations."

Annie, sensing drama in the air, abandoned her bucket and shovel and drew close to the chairs.

"You shouldn't say 'Christ,' you know," Julia said. "Are you trying to attract attention?"

"Yes!" Elspeth cried. "As a matter of fact, I am! Louise, can you just—?"

Louise put down her magazine and fixed Elspeth with a belittling stare. "What? *What's* your problem now?"

Trembling, Elspeth hesitated. "Never mind." She picked up her book and towel and had toiled halfway up the beach before she turned around and shouted, "Next time you make us all eat lunch with some guy you think is in love with you, you might at least find out if he has a girlfriend!"

By the time she got up to the house she had a splitting headache. She drank several glasses of water and a glass of blood-orange juice and stretched out on the sofa, her forearms covering her face.

She tried to summon her indignation, but as soon as she felt better physically, her foul mood subsided, as well. Lying there in the impersonal house, with its furnishings familiar to beach houses the world over (the dumpy sofa that the owners always felt compelled to protect with a tapestry; the driftwood-framed flower and sailboat pictures), and with the ceiling fan whirring overhead, and snippets of a mama's litany of complaint floating over from the house next door (*Basta, Paolo, basta!*), she felt surprisingly content—humbled, as always, before Louise, who had given her the real Europe, which the Melissas of the world would never see. She picked up her towel again and went out, heading back down the path to the beach. She met them coming up—Annie leading the way, with solemn, measured giant steps, Louise carrying Julia in her arms. Julia was whimpering.

"Spee!" Annie broke out when she saw Elspeth.

"Too much sun?"

"She cut her foot," said Louise.

"Cut it very badly," the little girl said, and lifted the appendage in question to show a blood-soaked T-shirt tied around it, tourniquet-style—Louise's white one from the Prada outlet, Elspeth noted with mild titillation.

"I tied the bandage!" Annie announced.

"God."

"There was a broken bottle in the sand. They ran right over it."

"God," said Elspeth again. "So, are we . . . ?"

"Yes, we *are*!" Louise raised her eyebrows, imputing some significance. "We're running up to call Papa *right* away."

"Oh, *right*. Of course."

"No! No! I don't want to call my papa!" Julia struggled, kicking in Louise's arms. "I don't want to go home!"

"I know you're disappointed, Julia. But you actually have a very serious injury and we don't want it to get worse." Louise looked at Elspeth. "She's going to have to go to the emergency room."

"It does look pretty bad," Elspeth said seriously. It came easily to her to sound—even to be—concerned. In Louise's eyes, too, she read joy behind the solemnity: They were going to be rid of the girl after all.

Elspeth offered to go down and collect the things that were left on the beach. "Annie, why don't you come and help me, so Mommy can tend to our patient."

"Hey! *I'm* the patient!" Julia said. "You're talking about me!"

ON THE BEACH, aunt and niece were gay, Annie seeming to have caught something of the relief that was in the air. Elspeth let the little girl prolong the packing up of the toys, let her put one last, two last, three last toes in the water. It had long been assumed—acquaintances had often remarked—that because Annie was an only child, and because her parents were divorced, she must have a particular desire, more acute than most children's, for friends her own age. But seeing her with the various playmates that had been inserted randomly over the years Elspeth got the sense that Annie saw them as supernumeraries. She seemed to feel pressure to act more like a child with them than she would naturally; her giggle, in play, sounded self-conscious. Once they left for the day, she would relax, and as she was now, would act more like a kid.

Elspeth let Annie drag her heels up the path, even encouraging a forbidden detour that skirted the neighbors' yard: If they took long enough, there was the faintest chance they might miss Werner Stechel altogether, find he had already come and gone by the time they came in.

Outside the door of the house, she and Annie slid off their flip-flops. They tapped the sand off and lined them up neatly along the doormat as Louise required. "Did you get in touch with Werner?" she couldn't stop herself from calling from the door. She couldn't hear what Louise said. "What?"

Inside Julia was lying on the sofa watching television—a dubbed action movie was on; Schwarzenegger, in a jungle.

"Hey!" Elspeth heard Annie observe, as she joined Louise in the kitchen. "You're still here!"

"So, did you call him?" Elspeth murmured.

"Yup." Louise seemed to be concentrating very hard on counting out the forks and knives. "He's not coming."

"What do you mean he's not coming?" It had crossed Elspeth's mind that even if he left right away, Werner might be tied up in traffic for a quarter of an hour—it was peak season on the Maremma, after all.

Starting on the spoons, Louise said, "He says she'll be all right." She took a tray from a low cabinet and piled the silverware on it. "He'll be over ''round nine or ten, as planned.'"

Annie came into the kitchen, scuffing her feet. "Can I have some Coke?"

" 'Could I *please* have some Coke, Mama,' and no, not before dinner, Annie, you know that. Can you help me by carrying this tray out to the table? *Careful,* Annie—don't drop it."

"I don't even know where the *pronto soccorso* is near here," Louise said when Annie left. Elspeth watched her sister take the supper things out of the fridge and cupboard. Her efficiency, hard-won, in the kitchen was soothing.

"There must be something, though," Elspeth said finally. "People are always hurting themselves on the beach."

"Yeah . . ." Louise began to chop onions, irritated. She wiped her forehead with the back of her wrist. "Can you take her up and put a proper bandage on her? There's Bacitracin in the medicine cabinet. It's the white tube with the brown stripe."

"Careful!" Julia cautioned as Elspeth labored, with the girl in her arms, up the tortuous spiral staircase to the second floor. "You've got to be careful, you see, because I'm hurt rather badly."

Elspeth ran a bath and made Julia sit on the side of the tub and soak the injured foot. She ran some water in the sink as well, to soak Louise's T-shirt, though there was hardly any chance the stain would come out. Through the open door she could see into the bedroom the two of them were sharing, as they had shared a room growing up. In the corner, near the cheap French doors that opened onto a little Juliet balcony, stood the ironing board, hungrily poised for its daily supply of wrinkled cottons, seaside vacation notwithstanding. Elspeth had made fun of Louise for it—had commented condescendingly on the first night, "Still ironing the underwear, I see." Louise's twenty-year habit of when-in-Rome-ing had long been an easy target: the joint-and-two-veg she had learned to put in the Aga on Sundays when married to Robert; the sudden penchant for "football," and the out-of-character repudiation of shaving that had appeared with Jean-Marc. Now she felt a taste of remorse—for despite being ridiculed, Louise had done Elspeth's skirts and shirts as well. And it was nice to have one's clothes ironed.

As Elspeth was running the tap over Louise's shirt, turning the water up high so it would pulse out the blood, she remembered something else Louise had once done for her: She had washed out her underwear for her. When they were eight and seven, Elspeth kept wetting her pants because she couldn't get to the toilet on time. It must have been summer because she could picture Louise wringing out her underpants and spreading them to dry on their mother's old Chevrolet. She could almost see the unappetizing cans collected for the Goodwill food drive filling up the backseat, the recycled plastic toys for the Cleary's Corner children, the brooms the blind had made . . . "We can wash them in the sink and dry them out here and she'll never know," Louise had said, as if even then they had both instinctively wanted to protect any part of their private lives they could—even a private sickness—from their mother's metastasizing woundedness. How long had they kept it up? Two weeks? Three? Eventually the mother of a friend, a neighbor of theirs, had noticed Elspeth running for the toilet and called Noel. She had been taken to the hospital; an advanced-stage urinary tract infection; an outpatient operation; a course of antibiotics—and everything was fine.

And for Louise, too, there had been the interventions of friends' mothers—a string of friends' mothers, then boyfriends' mothers—most notably one Mrs. Janocek, who had pointed out how good Louise was at languages; suggested looking into a job as an au pair one summer; going abroad.

She had no idea what Louise had done in situations that would have required *her* to wash out her underwear, though. Elspeth turned off the tap, screwed it tight so the faucet wouldn't drip. Louise had picked out her clothes every day, told her how to wear her hair—figured out French braiding, when that was the style. But Elspeth had no idea whether anyone had told Louise, even offhandedly, as Louise had mentioned the fact to her, when they were driving somewhere in high school together—now at fifteen and sixteen—that just because someone wanted to have sex with you didn't necessarily mean he wanted to date you. "You should be careful about that," she had said simply, not elaborating, Elspeth not asking her to.

Louise never complained. It wasn't her style. And when she alluded to it, the allusions were oblique, couched in signature Louise-style bravado. She would say, "You know, I was showing Giacomo some pictures of me when I was little, and you know what he said? He said (here Louise would slip ruthlessly into Giacomo's accent), 'Your part is not straight. Your part is never straight. And why do you wear such mismatched clothes? Your mother had you! (*Had* would come out *ed.*) Couldn't she take care of you, too?'"

WHEN JULIA'S FOOT was dressed and bandaged, Elspeth carried her back downstairs. She sat her on the sofa beside Annie and propped her leg up on pillows—two little girls watching Arnold.

In the kitchen, the sisters conferred. "I found out there's a *pronto soccorso* in Grosseto."

"How far's that?"

"In the car? Twenty minutes . . ." Louise gave the broth on the stove a stir. "It's so annoying, I just put the rice on . . . I wonder if we really need to take her."

They looked at each other impassively. Then Louise gave a big angry sigh and turned off the flame under the saucepan. "So much for that."

"You want to get them ready? I'll get the car."

Elspeth walked along the service road till she saw the first of the two purple Multiplas. She was glad she was alone, wrenching the car out of the tight spot. Louise would have teased her about her driving. "While we're young, Els, while we're young," she would have said. "Can't find 'em, grind 'em." When she got out of the spot she drove carefully along the service road until she saw them, standing at the foot of the path to the beach house, Louise propping Julia up, with Annie beside them, the latter holding Louise's oversized straw bag.

Louise's whole life, people had been telling her how beautiful she was, had stood in awe of her talent, her phenomenal taste. There had been the expectation, in the family and beyond (old teachers, old neighbors), that one day it would all come to brilliant fruition. Running Sotheby's. Or married, at least, to some count with a crumbling castle. "Three kids by thirty"—that, Elspeth recalled suddenly, had been Louise's own, more modest plan. She hadn't counted on divorce. Seeing her sister with the two girls now, Elspeth had a glimpse of how things might have gone, if she hadn't married Robert at twenty-five—if she hadn't married someone to stay away from home. The fantasy held her for a moment—Louise as the head of a growing brood, married, stateside, to some big investment banker, moving out to Larchmont when number three came along . . . Something struck her about the threesome just before she pulled up. Whether it was Annie's studied look of solemnity or Louise's chilly, un-American poise or even Julia's Oscarworthy impersonation of an invalid, she didn't know, but it was as if they had each had to become slightly more professional than their real-life counterparts would have, as if in fact, Elspeth were seeing three people who had been hired to play a mom and two kids. Then Elspeth was upon them: her sister, her sister's daughter, and Julia Stechel.

"All right, guys, into the car we go," Louise was saying.

Elspeth put the car into neutral and cranked on the emergency brake, feeling underneath her for the lever to slide the seat back. Louise drove like a teenage boy, with the seat so far back she could barely reach the clutch. And although Elspeth had now had her driver's license for fourteen years, there was never any question as to who would drive.

The Secret Vote

ONE EVENING NOT too many years into this century, at a closing dinner for an IPO she'd worked on, Alice was seated next to one of the bankers on the deal. Alice made a mistake early on—mechanically using the phrase "your wife"—and had to spend the first half of the evening coming up with remarks that showed she understood the man was gay.

To her left sat the biotech start-up's CFO, soft-spoken and seemingly diffident. Alice had thought she had better draw him out, with the result that "Don" was now mortally preoccupied with making sure she realized that, despite his divorce, he was dating someone seriously ("Sarah," whom he had re-met at a business school reunion). Implied reproach on either side of her made for static exchanges over the salad. It wasn't until the pasta arrived that the conversation cracked open. Alice refused wine. "Really?" The banker hesitated politely with the bottle over her glass, his lips pursed with concern. "Not even a drop of red?"

"No, I really can't," said Alice. And after an annoying internal debate in which there seemed to be two losing sides, she admitted, "I'm pregnant." Don's eyes flew, somewhat indignantly, to her left hand, only now of course registering the ring on it.

"How many months?" He reached for his back pocket to draw out a wallet-size snap.

"Four," said Alice. "Seventeen weeks." She turned her lips up at the photograph of grade-school twin boys; she wasn't, actually, particularly interested in children.

"No sushi for you, huh?" Don chuckled, replacing the picture.

"Or wine or coffee or unpasteurized cheese—it sucks, doesn't it?" enjoined the banker. Despite the impudence of the remarks, Alice laughed. The truth was she was grateful to be talking with two men, who wouldn't know the significance of the number of weeks—wouldn't think to ask her, "Yeah? You gonna get amnio?" as a female colleague of hers had earlier tonight. She had had it—amniocentesis—barely a week ago, after a blood test came back showing increased risk for Down syndrome, and she was so bored and anxious waiting for the results she had actually been glad of her required attendance at this work dinner, any distraction better than none.

"We're trying, too," the banker said warmly.

"Really." Alice was afraid she looked at him rather blankly.

"We should be getting going by the summer."

"That's great," said Alice, feeling a politically correct prod somewhere in her conscience.

"We're excited."

"I bet." It was inane. She had no idea what the man was talking about. She forked some penne.

"We've already gone out to Texas twice to meet our surrogate," continued the man—Julian—over the sea bass. A belated-but-not-very-embarrassed exchange of names had come with the main course.

"Oh!" He seemed to want to talk about it, assumed, evidently, that she—and Don who was listening in—would want to know the details. "So, she . . ." Alice tried. "I mean, this woman . . . ?"

Her companion leaped, however, to the generalizing plural: "These women are the most amazing women in the world," he said, and his tone, which was quite aggressive, startled Alice. As if she'd been caught out, she put a perky, nonjudgmentally interested look on her face as she studied his: the sardonic brown eyes and long, elegantly tapering nose; the pleasingly aligned cheekbones and defiant shock of blond hair. "They feel it's their calling to bear children." There wasn't the slightest hesitation when he said this—the slightest concession to a possible demurral on her part. Instead, his words to Alice seemed to presume a shared faith.

"Their calling," she said slowly. "You mean—religious?"

He was nodding before she finished the question. "They're all Catholic—or fundamentalist Christian or whatever. The woman we're interested in has already done it three times. Experience was important to us," he added, as if they were discussing—as indeed a pair of analysts across the table had been a moment ago—the latest in LASIK surgery.

The waiter insinuated himself, proffering a sauce boat. Both Alice and Don pulled their hands up out of the man's way with alacrity, as if a little too happy to have something to do. "So, have you guys picked out names?" Julian asked cozily, her new best friend.

"Yes," said Alice slowly, still trying to absorb what the man was saying. "But I've learned not to talk about it. Whatever you say, it turns out the person had a dog named that."

Don gave a coughlike bark and Julian beamed—indulging her with the smile, Alice realized with a prick of indignation. He was not truly amused. "I'll keep that in mind."

"My ex had to do IVF," Don said hopefully, but the other two had moved on to a safer topic—a subject an earlier generation might have avoided—politics; the upcoming election, in which it was assumed everyone would be for the challenger, the patrician Democratic senator, the thinking man's candidate. "Anyone but who we've got," Julian said, and Alice said she couldn't agree more.

"BREEDERS!" ALICE CRIED when she got home, yelling into the bedroom as she hung up her coat and scarf. "Isn't that what *they* used to call *us*?"

She jammed the closet door shut and crossed the tiny, book-lined living room to the cramped bedroom. "Isn't that just too weird, Mark? Isn't it so *Handmaid's Tale?*" she said impatiently. "Screw fifty people in a sex club and now I'd like a child, please!"

Mark was lying on the bed on his stomach, reading *The Economist.* "It's not a lifestyle choice, Mark!" Alice said. "It *takes* a man and a woman. There's something actual there—there's something real. It's called Nature, you know? As in, eighty million years—hello?"

Now Mark dragged his eyes up from the magazine, the election coverage; he looked happy, simply, that she was home. Alice shook her head pityingly. She warned him direly, brushing her teeth a little later, "Cloning'll be next!" She was talking with toothpaste in her mouth and had to stick out her jaw to prevent it from running down her chin. "I'm telling you, Mark! Mark?!" she cried, fearing he had fallen asleep. "Are you gonna care then? When they start cloning people?"

HURRYING INTO THE elevator the next morning, Alice caught a glimpse of her tired, stricken face in the reflective doors. She was still smarting from Mark's bemused, even reply: "You're always the last to know, Alice."

In her office, Alice sat down at her desk and clicked on her computer screen. She peeled the lid off her tea and had begun to scroll through the overnight load of e-mails, when the phone rang. Alice picked it up hopefully, eager for a distraction. "Good morning—Alice?" Dr. Rand, her obstetrician. For a second she actually thought he was calling to see how she was holding up during these nerve-racking two weeks that followed the test—some new civility initiative at the hospital in keeping with the movement to demedicalize birth. There was an oddly placed silence and then the doctor asked her, "Do you have a moment to talk?"

As he went on she read and reread a paragraph in the contract before her:

The securities offered hereby involve a high degree of risk. See "Risk Factors" beginning on Page 4 . . . The securities offered hereby

The moment lengthened endlessly—beyond the call, the day, beyond her thirties—a decade that, she now saw, had been characterized by a profound and blissful naïveté. Beyond the rest of her life, even.

"Dr. Levien and I have reviewed the results of your amniocentesis, and I am very sorry to have to tell you."

It took Alice a second or two, when Dr. Rand had finished, to find the civil reply that would let the man off the hook, release him to his quotidian obligations—calls like this a—what? monthly? biannual?—nuisance . . . Some women more composed than others—the odd unhinged one who attacked his graceful, practiced phrases, not having any—neither "great disappointment" nor "painful decision." Alice managed to keep her voice low—her office door was wide open—as she agreed to consider all of her options.

(If one wanted to be honest, though, wasn't it better to admit that there was no choice to be made? Wasn't it the case, not unlike the upcoming election, that you'd always more or less known which way you would vote?)

She even—the martyr in her sensing a once-in-a-lifetime opportunity—thanked the man for taking the time to let her know personally.

Then the call was over. Alice got up and pushed the door shut. She sat staring at the gray expanse of steel that separated her from the bustle of the corporate corridor, her eyes narrowed, like someone concentrating very hard to remember some fact or sequence of events, gone all of a sudden from one's memory. After a moment she picked up the phone and dialed the hospital, mindful of how busy her schedule was next week (a new deal starting, with a partner she'd never worked for), and made the appointment for her only available window—election day, when she could use the excuse of having to vote. When that was finished, she dialed Mark. He didn't pick up at home; his cell phone went straight to voice mail. He was getting ready for class, probably; he had the big freshman poli sci lecture Wednesday mornings. A little later she could try him at the department. It didn't really matter *when* she told him, did it? *Conveyance* of the fact was not the issue now.

MAUREEN, TOO, WOULD have to be told. Alice put her head in her hands as the last conversation she'd had with her mother came back to her in sharp, shameful recollection, the hindsight irony of it almost more than she could bear. Maureen, in the confusion of her general daily anxiety, had misunderstood a message Alice had left on her machine earlier that morning. "Increased risk for Down's, I said! Increased risk!" Alice had stood on the corner of Park and Fifty-third shouting into her cell while the flood of rush-hour pedestrians broke around her. "That's why I have to have the amnio! Jesus, Mom—you think I'd leave that on a message?"

Maureen sounded as if she'd been shot. "Well, I was going to say, they *are* very lovable, you know."

"*Mom.*" Alice struggled against the adolescent impulse—to scream and dash the phone against the pavement. "Why would you say that?" she pleaded, as she walked the last half block to her office building, an eighties homage to chrome and glass. "In what way does pointing that out now . . . help me? It's a *routine* test. People—everyone thinks I'm nuts to be at *all* worried!"

Inside the building, Alice had been able to hear the long pause that followed. Maureen seemed to be clearing her throat, but in the distance, as if she was holding the phone away from her. Then she asked Alice, "I hear you're going to see Brenda and Kev this weekend?" These were Alice's Long Island cousins; Maureen was the younger sister of Brenda's mother, Roberta.

"Mom, you always change the subject."

"I'm sorry."

"Yeah . . . I think so." Alice tried to feel mollified, tried to end the conversation on a good note so as not to jinx the amnio; she was going in for the appointment tomorrow. That was why she had called Maureen in the first place—she felt she should let her know. "Probably. They invited us out for a barbecue on Sunday."

"Mm-hmm."

"What?" Alice said. "What exactly are you saying, Mom?"

"Nothing, I just—" Her mother hesitated. "I wouldn't say anything about it, Alice. I wouldn't mention the—the test to them."

"Mom." She had not felt able, Alice remembered, to put sufficient disgust into her voice.

Maureen had tried to defend herself. "I'm just saying, if—later on—you had to make a decision—"

"You mean if I had to abort the hell out of it, Mom? Is that what you're getting at?"

SHE AND MARK had gone out to the Healys' that weekend— to Brenda and Kevin's. They had taken the train from Penn Station, as they always did, Alice irritated when Mark seemed to jump at the idea of their having concrete plans to help them get through the one weekend before they got the results. It wasn't that he shared her worry, not at all—the odds were with them—she was the one who was torturing herself for no good reason; Mark took comfort in statistics, as rational people did. He just didn't want to have to deal with her touchiness, her overactive imagination all by himself.

The Long Island Rail Road outbound on a Sunday morning was soothing. It was sleepily optimistic, the scene—single men and women, mostly, taking up a whole seat with their duffel bags and the *Times*. Alice had cast an indulgent eye around the car as she slid into the seat beside Mark. Many a weekend she had been one of them, down to the newspaper and the little paper bag of coffee, before she met Mark. The ace up her sleeve it had been, on slow lonely weekends, to escape to her cousins' in the burbs. Brenda and Kevin had seemed to take satisfaction in her needing them in that way, seemed gratified that Alice had turned to them—she who might just as easily have gotten on without them. "Whenever you want to get out of the city," Brenda would make Alice promise at the end of every visit, "you give us a call. We're here for you, Al." That they were still getting together, that the Healys' invitations and her acceptances had continued apace after she got married, was unexpected: Alice acknowledged this in the rare moments of disabusing clarity she allowed herself. She supposed she'd assumed that her cousins were another comforting but indefensible habit that Mark would call a halt to—not directly, of course; he was far too evolved to dictate actual behavior, but that his presence would demand a reckoning of some kind, instead of which, Alice would let herself drift apart from Brenda, with geography's help. Instead, the frequency of their pilgrimages to the Healys' had increased slightly, from once a season to every couple of months. There had been the pleasant, unpredicted fact of Mark's getting along with Kevin, of his approving of Kevin, though the two men had little in common. "We're here for you," Brenda still maintained, though perhaps now the subtext had shifted: an established family, she might have meant, on which Alice and Mark going into their child-rearing years could model themselves. Brenda herself was pregnant with her fourth. A mistake, she freely admitted when she called Alice with the news— "Mom said Kevin should get a vasectomy."

Once the train had gotten under way, Alice turned to Mark and said casually, "So what did you mean, you 'can't argue viability'?"

She was referring to a comment he'd made Friday night, among friends of theirs, apropos of an election issue. She posed the question with a careful neutrality of tone, as if it were motivated by intellectual curiosity alone, but Mark asked sardonically, "Do you really want to discuss this *now*? I mean, like, three days after you have the fucking test?"

"No time like the present," Alice said chirpily. It was the fashion, among her old roommates from Yale—tomboyish and cynical, eschewing the maternity shops for as long as they could by passing around a pair of large-waisted Levi's cords—to belittle one's pregnancy, to treat it as an absurd moment in their otherwise genderless lives, to define themselves expressly against the women (their secretaries, certain girlish women who had married the guys they knew) who spent hours on websites charting the growth of their unborn children. There was no vocabulary in their witty bitterness—without which they had nothing—for the pure elation Alice felt in odd, solitary moments when she thought about the creature growing inside her and thought she might have it in her to be a good mother.

"Look, it used to be thirty weeks, now it's, what, twenty-six?" Mark said wearily. "They keep moving it back. How can you say something's not immoral at a certain point, when the point itself keeps changing? It's ridiculous. It's indefensible." Mark picked up the section of the newspaper he had been reading, the Week in Review, and proffered the rest to her.

"You *know* I can't," Alice said huffily, enjoying the melodrama of refusing the paper, taking out a novel instead. "He makes me too mad."

As the election neared and her first trimester came and went with no sign of the promised abatement of nausea, Alice had developed an intense personal hatred for the president. Cocksure and charismatic, it was as if he were a young man she had despised in high school, instead of just being like that young man. Helped along perhaps by her physically incapacitated state, Alice had quickly internalized the futility of protest, assuming everyone would do the same. Yet, as if anything could be done about the polls from here, an earnestness had overtaken the city. Toiling up the subway stairs, Alice had been stopped not once, not twice, but four separate times by a clipboard-wielding volunteer for the Democratic National Committee and pegged for a donation. She felt spiritually weak when she gave, as if she were being taken in, as if, as in the aggressive panhandling in the city of a decade before, she were half-knowingly supporting a drug habit.

When Maureen had visited Alice in the city then, Alice's mother had always stopped to look through her purse, no matter how offensive the approach (once a homeless man, in what was practically a mugging, had come running toward them on Broadway near Columbia demanding "Real money! Real money! None of that quarter and dime shit!"), take out a dollar, and apologize—through Alice's seething disapproval—if she found only change. "I can't turn my back on someone like that!" Maureen would plead with her as they walked on. "Not when I have so much more!" Poor Maureen had never discovered that a new morality had overtaken the old, and the former was all about maintaining personal boundaries—talk to the hand, dump that addict friend, wash that problem person out of your hair, and congratulate yourself afterward on your inner growth.

ALICE AND MARK'S friends had all stayed in the city when they got married, moving out to Brooklyn when they had kids, an idea they themselves had recently begun to pursue. Her cousins were the only couple Alice knew who had bought a bona fide starter house in the suburbs: 1960s construction, one level, with a basement they'd half finished by the time John, the second boy, was born, and they sold it and bought their current house.

The new house, as the Healys still called it, was narrow; the living inside it was very up-and-down. Conversations, usually involving the location of objects, were conducted in an aggrieved shout from floor to floor ("So, is it down there or *not?*"). No question it was tight for a family of five. Robbie and John slept in bunk beds. The baby, as far as Alice knew, was still in with Brenda and Kev, and she couldn't imagine what arrangements would be made for the new addition—Brenda was due with Number Four in May, just a month after Alice. But despite the feeling one had, inside, of the house's being ramshackle and bursting at the seams, there was something classy about it that the starter house had lacked. Simply its age, perhaps—it was a village Victorian, one street over from the train—and in keeping with its age, the proper-feeling configuration of the rooms; the absence of the oversized family room that Brenda coveted. Brenda had decorated it with what Alice thought of—and not bitchily, the way it sounded—as "classy touches": photographs of Tuscan streetscapes and catboats on Nantucket, with colorful sails, things Alice had once aspired to hang on her walls but that, somewhere between her junior spring in Paris and the Upper East Side walk-up, she had bypassed, but that looked nice, anyway. Alice was always glad to see the pictures again, just as she was always glad to be reminded that Kevin was a scratch golfer and had won the club championship two or three years running. She would feel herself relax a little on seeing them, or on noticing Kevin's clubs leaning up against the back door, and she would say something that to an outsider might suggest it had been a long time since she had seen her cousin: She would ask, as she did now, withdrawing from Brenda's bosomy, freckly, strawberry-blond embrace, the surfeit of clunky gold—earrings of crossed nine-irons, the chain with the pendant in the shape of the east end of Long Island—a leading question in order to flatter: "So, does Kevin still have his own parking spot down at the club?"

They were only cousins, after all.

"No, he does not," Brenda said belligerently, licking her fingers as she returned to the batch of instant brownies she was mixing up.

"What, he lost?" Alice said, flushing because she feared a faux pas.

"Hello-o?" said Brenda. She wiped her index finger along the spatula and licked it. "He's got three kids at home? And he's hanging out down at the nineteenth hole with retired guys twice his age?" She held out the spatula to Alice, who shook her head. "When I found out I was pregnant again, I'm like, 'You know what? No. Bullshit. You stay here with me, or you go and you take the boys with you—and not just John because he's good; Robbie needs the practice, too.'" She gave the bowl a final scrape and tossed the spatula into the sink. She then set the timer on the stove. "Twenty minutes—don't let me forget."

She drank a glass of water at the sink, surveying Alice. "Jesus, *you* look good. You don't even look pregnant."

Alice flushed again, speechless, and Brenda said impatiently, "It's *okay*! I know I'm fat. *I* look like shit! But what am I supposed to do about it?" She opened the fridge and took out a half-empty bottle of the *vinho verde* she and Kevin liked to drink. Alice watched her yank out the cork. "Not gonna tell on me, are you, Al?" Brenda said. Cracking ice into two tumblers, she topped the wine off with club soda and pushed one over the counter to Alice. "I'm not allowed to diet when I'm pregnant. It's bad for the baby."

"You know, you're right." Alice was disgusted by the sycophantic tone she relied on with Brenda but never quite seemed to find another. "You're absolutely right, Bren."

"My friend Ellen gained sixty pounds with her twins and she lost it all, every single effing pound, can you believe it? On Atkins. That's what I'm gonna do." Brenda picked up a paperback off the counter and tossed it to Alice, who, with only one hand free, caught the edge of it and had to lunge for it as it

dropped. "Oh, right, I've heard this is good." She frowned to herself as she examined the book's cover, annoyed that she had forgotten the proscription against big, sudden movements after the
amniocentesis. Minor physical humiliations were a staple of visits to the Healys'. The hot water in the bathroom off the kitchen
scalded one's hands; the screen door that led out to the deck,
through which Alice followed Brenda now, was hung too tightly
on its hinges, as if to make people jump when it slammed shut on
them.

"I hear breast-feeding helps, too," Alice said without thinking,
as they came out onto the deck.

Brenda stopped and scrutinized her in a way that made Alice
have to swallow. "Guess I wouldn't know, would I?" she said. She
set her drink down on the picnic table and shielded her eyes to
where Robbie and John and a Chinese kid they palled around
with—adopted, Alice recalled—were whacking one another with
clubs in front of some sort of golf game: a patch of Astroturf that
ended in an oversized net. "You guys play for real or I'm gonna
lock that thing up!" Brenda hollered.

Kevin, who was fiddling with the grill, grinned when he saw
Alice. "Hubby and I have been talking, Al," he called, gesturing
with the barbecue tongs to Mark. "We figured three more and you
guys'll be right on track!"

"Yeah, right," Alice said lamely, pretending to drink from her
spritzer, stymied as usual by Kevin's easy banter, his comically
good hair—dark and wavy, just now graying at the sides.

"Says he," Brenda grumbled good-naturedly as the two women
tugged out facing benches from beneath the teak table. Guests at
the Healys' were expected to sit outside since the completion of
the deck a couple of summers ago, even on a nippy, late autumn
day like today, with Brenda's Halloween cutouts fading in the
windows and the last of the brown crunchy leaves clinging to the
maple in the corner of the lawn.

"So, my doctor thinks I should get amnio," Alice said, shivering a little.

"I mean it, John!" Brenda half rose to yell at the boys again. "Doesn't it make you sick?" she said, turning back to Alice, and Alice, mesmerized by the physical aggression of the preteen boys, had to concentrate to remember what they'd been talking about. Brenda had a way of speaking that seemed to indict nuance and qualification—to take pleasure in exposing both as the weenie-ass conversational tics they were. "Doesn't it just *disgust* you?" She pushed a silver bowl of nuts toward Alice. "And it's all just for their own benefit, you know, so they don't get sued and have their malpractice go through the roof."

Frowning mistrustfully, Brenda withdrew a plastic baby monitor from her apron pocket and held it up to her ear.

"No, but come *on*, Kevin," Alice heard Mark say, "if the administration cared about terrorism . . ." She looked quickly at Brenda, hoping her cousin hadn't heard. Why, with the election a week away, did Mark have to go there? But Alice's husband would have considered it condescending *not* to mention the election—to dance around it the way Alice would with Brenda. Mark's politics, an extension not of passion but of an unforgiving moral logic, didn't allow for fury, for disappointment, for attraction and repulsion. On their very first date, he'd told her that no white, upper-middle-class, college-educated woman had legitimate fear of getting AIDS. "So much for that excuse," she'd said, giggling, happy to be debunked.

"They wanted me to have it with Tyler, amnio-CVS-nuchal-cord-blood shit crap whatever, 'cause I was over thirty-five, and I'm like, 'Bullshit. I'm having this baby no matter what, thank you very much,'" Brenda recalled, satisfied.

There was a guffaw and then a scuffle as Robbie, in braces and with an unattractive new haircut—high on top, with the sides shaved—was interrupted from teeing off by one of the boys making a loud farting noise. Brenda watched them, expressionless. "I swear if I don't have a girl this time *I'm* going over to China to adopt." Alice laughed aloud and was surprised at how good it felt. "Yeah, so they all act like I'm making a big mistake and I might regret it. Oh, *crap.*" Brenda gave the monitor an aggrieved shake. "I forgot to turn the fucking thing on!"

"Yeah," said Alice slowly. "I know what you mean." She hesitated as Brenda pressed the device to her ear. "I mean, to be fair, I'm not sure I see the harm in just *having* the test . . ."

A look of alarm crossed her cousin's face and Alice flinched. But then she, too, heard the noise coming from the monitor: Upstairs, the baby had woken up. Brenda's face sagged with the realization.

"Do you want me to go get him? Let me go."

Brenda scowled in the direction of the men. "Never on his watch. I swear to God he plans it."

"Let me," insisted Alice, halfway to her feet. "You relax."

"No, no." Brenda reached across the table and gave Alice's forearm a squeeze. "You've got to enjoy it while it lasts, lady!"

She had always been like that. Disarming gestures of warmth, even in adolescence, had confused one's belief that Brenda didn't, fundamentally, like one; eventually one began to realize it was nothing personal, the abrasiveness. And Alice's cousin really believed that thing she and her mother, Roberta, were always saying, that family were the only people you could count on. Their attitude couldn't have been further from what Alice had learned growing up. Her own mother's example, even within her immediate family, had been social affability to a groveling extreme, followed by endless private litanies of complaint, of remembered insult, of minor unfairnesses—an overlooked younger sister's lot, perhaps.

Brenda took her time about getting up: taking another handful of nuts, crunching them in her mouth, staring vacantly out at the men. As she sat there, the way her cousin looked—defeated, knowing she had to go get the baby, but bent on procrastinating nonetheless—moved Alice unexpectedly. She had to turn away and bite her cheek.

"All right, all right!" Brenda got heavily to her feet, draining her glass, as the wail intensified. "I'm coming already!"

WHEN SHE WAS gone Alice got up and went inside and poured her spritzer down the sink. She was hunting in the cupboards for the club soda when the timer went off on the brownies. She couldn't find pot holders in the mess on the counter so she doubled over a dish towel and took the pan out of the oven one-handed. The smell was intoxicating. Before Alice could stop herself she had gotten a knife and dug out a corner piece. She ate it, gobbling it down as it burned her tongue and the sides of her mouth; she cut off another piece and ate that, looking out the kitchen window past the deck at the guys. Kevin was having a go at the tee, and even with her total ignorance about the game, Alice could see his swing had something that the others' lacked. A head shorter than Mark, he had the lean, careful kind of physical fitness that suggests control. Alice would find herself paying her cousin's husband the tribute of being "well preserved," forgetting that Kev was only three years older than she. But Kevin had had a mortgage and a child and another on the way at twenty-five, when people like Alice were basically still in college—getting trashed in Village bars.

Now Mark was having a go, clowning, playing it for laughs—nothing at stake.

Alice sliced the rest of the pan into squares, slid the brownies out, and arranged them on a ceramic pumpkin plate. She wiped her mouth vigorously with the dish towel and ran her tongue carefully over her teeth several times.

When she heard Brenda on the stairs, she turned around

guiltily and then was confused for a moment, unable to recall the source of the guilt.

"Had to change him," Brenda said. "Sorry." With a practiced gesture she thrust the baby into a plastic stand-up play circle on the floor.

"Can I do something?" Alice said as her cousin started to mix up a bottle. "I put the brownies on a plate." The little boy had Brenda's strawberry-blond coloring. He was robust, rosy-cheeked—cuter than Alice remembered from the christening. Feeling useless, she knelt down and waggled her fingers at him. "Hi, Tyler, how're you doing?"

Brenda held up the empty glass Alice had left by the sink. "You ready for another?"

"Actually, you know—I think I'm good," Alice said, straightening up.

Brenda nodded. Then she got the bottle of wine out of the fridge. "There's not much alcohol in it, you know."

"No, no, I know. I just—" Alice gave an inarticulate, impatient shake of her head. "I'm trying to be good."

Brenda studied her impassively for a moment and then she gave a little nod. "I remember that," she said. "First kid. You think every little thing matters."

OF COURSE, IT had come to Alice on the train back to New York—what she could have said when Brenda asked her, when they were dumping the paper plates, plastic cutlery, and ends of hamburgers into the trash, why anyone would ever get amniocentesis. "To be ready," she could have said. "They say it helps to be ready." She'd heard people say that before. Why couldn't she have thought of it in the moment?

It was late afternoon—getting dark, and the train was drawing close to the city; passing rows and rows of the red-brick, barracks-like housing of some cemented-over neighborhood, unknown to

Alice and Mark but for its proximity to the Long Island Rail Road. On one block, in each of the houses' windows that faced the tracks, the president's name blared forth from the familiar oblong red campaign signs.

Alice made a strangled noise. "God, will you look at these people?"

Three or four beers in, Mark leaned over and gave her an atta-girl pat on the thigh. "Give it twenty minutes, babe, the signs'll change color."

"No, but Mark, it's insane!" she said angrily, shrugging him off, his cozy mood. "He's a total . . . he's a fucking asshole!"

"Ye-e-es," Mark said, in a voice that made the pretense of placating her, but was really a laugh cue to the imagined audience that attended their marriage.

"Don't say it like that," Alice said ferociously. "Don't you dare fucking condescend to me."

Mark studied her face. He wasn't angry, just unimpressed. "This really isn't a fun ten days, is it?"

"This isn't about the amnio! For Christ's sake, not everything is about that fucking test!"

After a pause, Mark shrugged and said, "It's really not that bad."

"How can you say that? How can you say that when he's going to win—again—and we're going to lose? I just can't bear to think about it, Mark. All the money we've given, and the time people have spent—and it's all so . . . wasted. Months and months—when you think about the *work*—and it's all just wasted!"

Mark sat back in his seat, withdrawing to some remote place, his expression unreadable; perhaps he was simply disappointed in her, by her display of emotion when he preferred solutions. "Neither one's going to put an end to the war," he said finally. "Neither one's going to outlaw abortion."

She looked at him quickly but just then the train ran underground, creating that momentary sensation of intimacy among all of the passengers, so she didn't dare to speak. It wasn't until they had pulled to a stop and people were clogging the aisle, trapping them in their seats that she turned to him and said in an urgent murmur, resuming the conversation they'd begun the trip with, "I don't understand, all right? I don't get it. If it's got nothing to do with viability . . . ? I mean, where exactly do you draw the line?"

"Oh, Alice." Mark raised his eyes to the ceiling before he spoke. "I think the only consistent argument," he said slowly, "is that sometimes it's okay to kill a kid."

A FEW MINUTES after she hung up with Dr. Rand, Alice took the elevator down to the ground-floor atrium of her office building.

She sat down with a paper cup of tea at one of the chrome café tables, dunking the tea bag, then fiddling with her cell phone, clearing her throat and practicing her "hello"—gearing up to try Maureen. She sipped her tea and looked around the open-air space at the random assortment of people who'd come in off the street to kill time with a cup of coffee in this strange, corporate charity— the atrium was open to the public—and it wasn't rage or a sense of injustice that came over her, but weariness, a profound weariness, for the time in which she lived, and a longing for the past, when you had to wear a coat and tie at the Yale Club and there were no free agents in baseball, when people still put four hundred thousand miles on their cars and jury-rigged fifteen-year-old toasters to go another season. Whereas nowadays, she thought, appliances were so expendable.

She dialed home and when Maureen picked up, cheerful and expectant, Alice's voice cracked.

"Mom?"

SHE WAS AN educated, successful woman.

Oh, sure, given some other context, a different context, there was no question Alice would have gotten something out of it. One of her mother's cousins, Danny (didn't every family have one?), had presided over every extended-family function these last thirty years. He gave the speech everyone remembered at Brenda and Kevin's wedding—the most heartfelt, the least self-conscious, even through the stutter and the nasal tones—a moment of grace in an otherwise, let's face it, pretty tacky affair. Tears had come to Maureen's eyes, to Alice's eyes. When Alice's great-uncle died and her great-aunt was ailing, Roberta and her mother and their brother had looked around for a group home for Danny outside of Boston. The one they found was a very nice one; Danny would be very happy there. ("Of course it's 'nice,' " Alice remembered saying when Maureen was giving her the line. "What are you going to do, put him in a crap one?") Alice had visited Danny there twice, once with Maureen and once on her own, in a fit of atonement after the prolonged, crushing end of a relationship. He seemed to have a lot of friends and was particularly fond of a young woman named Kay. The second time she went, her timing was off; Danny couldn't talk. The residents were heading out in their van to go to the movies and Danny was anxious about getting to share a seat with Kay.

"She'll save it for you, Danny. Don't worry," said a slack, overweight woman who was helping to load the adults into the van. To Alice she said she should have called first.

"Danny certainly seems very happy here," Alice said, ignoring the rebuke. She had used the remark on the previous visit, to good effect.

"Mm-hmm," the woman had answered neutrally. "Danny's a happy guy."

TOWARD THE END of the following week, Alice came out of the hospital into the cutting wind of a bright November afternoon—alone, as she had insisted, which was in keeping with the rest of the pregnancy. Unlike the preponderance of women waiting in the vari-

ous holding rooms of the hospital, for checkups, sonograms, consul-
tations, counseling, Alice had never had her husband beside her. It
had not occurred to her that Mark would come—the same as it had
not occurred to her to go around saying, "We're pregnant"—until
she was surrounded by women to whom it had. And then of course it
had become a point of pride. (Cynical; tomboys.) Who *were* these
other women at the hospital who always had Hubby in tow? Or
rather, who were the men? "What the hell do they do for a living?"
Alice liked to ask glibly, as if she were making a comment on the
men's industriousness, when of course it was really a class boast.
Mark, of all people, with his academic schedule, might easily have
been at these appointments with her, had she but asked him to come.

They'd told her to take it easy, so rather than walk to the subway, Alice put her hand up for a taxi and gave her home address.
She wasn't going back to work today.

And yet, curiously, it seemed like any other procedure—like
getting a cavity filled or, more accurately, having a Pap smear, and
she couldn't help but feel she was pulling the wool over their eyes.
It was like when you stayed home for a second sick day because
you really did think you needed it, but by early afternoon it was
clear that you could have made it through the day at the office—
could have run a mile if you had to, or driven through the night
on some altruistic exploit—except that you never had to.

On the floor of the taxi there was, of all things, a condom
wrapper. Alice looked away at once but it was too late. She had already thought of the hour of conception. Could most couples pin-
point their children's like that? She didn't know. Perhaps it was
something you mused on once and then never again, telling yourself the one had nothing, really, to do with the other—trying, for
the children's sake, not to be tacky about it. (A toddler in their
building called "Venice" came to mind as a counterexample.) In
their case, it had been obvious because Mark had, atypically—he
rarely traveled for work—been in London for a rational choice

conference at the LSE the week before. Fourth of July weekend. They had walked to the Healys' from the station. (Kevin found the habit wacky and would greet them with an expression of disbelief—"What, you walked again? I told you to call!")

An oversized kiddie pool that had been filled up in the backyard was proving more popular with the grown-ups than the kids. Alice went upstairs to change into her suit. "Use the boys' room," Brenda told her. "Bathroom's a pit." She was thinking how ugly these boys' things were, the endless shoddy plastic electronica in place of books, the flanks of armed action figures and the guns, when there was a light rap on the door—almost a greeting. It opened, over her protest. "A-ha!" Mark murmured. "The return of the red suit."

"Please," Alice said haughtily, pulling the straps of the tank suit up over her shoulders. She turned her back to him but she couldn't keep a straight face. The door clicked shut. He was beside her, behind her. His two hands slid in underneath the suit and ran the length of her body. One wide-open hand for her nipples, two fingers for her pussy—that it was all happening underneath the suit was like a hot little secret she wanted to hoard. Then he was looking around sheepishly for a place to sit—settling, with a little grin, on the edge of the bottom bunk; the boys' wheeled desk chair deemed too flimsy. "Just hurry, okay?" she begged as she stepped out of her suit and straddled him, some childish notion of fair play preventing her from telling him he'd just have to wait till tonight to get his. "Please, please hurry." Her whole body was sickeningly tensed for the footstep in the hall, the creak of a floorboard or turn of a knob.

"Don't come in!"

For the split second before she heard the reply she thought maybe she was talking to the air, paranoid.

"What?" The confusion—no, the irritation, in Brenda's voice, of being told what to do in one's own house.

"Don't come in, Brenda!" Alice cried, begging, and somehow she said it in time. Such was her cousin's surprise—her hand stayed perhaps on the very knob—that Brenda obeyed Alice's plea. The door was shut—more firmly now. The hallway, even to Alice's straining ears, was quiet. So that Alice, instead of springing off him and ducking behind the door (poking her head around and laughing, maybe, as if she weren't "decent"), stayed where she was. She stayed where she was, and, in that strange, intransitive use of the verb that always struck her as so vulgar, she let Mark finish.

At the turn onto Alice's block, a police barrier had been erected, preventing access to the street. The taxi had to go the long way around, so it took her an extra ten minutes and, she reckoned, $2.50 to get home. When they finally stopped around the corner from her building, Alice noticed a line of people waiting in front of the elementary school across the street. She paid the driver and got out. "Is it some kind of protest?" she asked a woman walking a tiny black-and-tan dog.

The woman stared at her and said, "It's election day!" sounding appalled yet at the same time thrilled to have found someone ignorant to rage against.

The woman's tone would have irked Alice except that she was glad to have been reminded. She would have forgotten to vote, and now she could accomplish some little thing today.

She stood in line inside the school's gymnasium. Folding tables had been set up along the walls opposite a row of New York's shower-stall-like voting booths. Famously ignorant, among her and Mark's friends, about the local races, Alice hadn't voted since the last presidential election; she wondered pessimistically whether her registration was up to date. Presently she was directed to a corner table, where she gave her name and address to two women of about her age. A left-wing-looking guy emerged, in cargo shorts, with a bike chain looped around his chest; Alice was ushered in, the curtains drawn.

The truth was, it didn't matter that she didn't recognize the candidates for city council or comptroller, or even really know what the offices were. She had never pretended to be sufficiently informed about the issues, as Mark was, to make up her own mind. She voted the way her grandparents had—one blessed given in a life that had been nursed on the late-twentieth-century ambivalence of the dispossessed. Mark could debunk it all he wanted, could go into lecture mode trying to convince her: "By today's standards, Nixon was a Democrat!" She didn't care. She voted the way she did because it made her feel connected with something. She would imagine her forebears, Maureen's parents, Margaret and William, looking down on her from above, chuckling with approbation, could even hear William repeating, ghostlike, from the grave, "Always vote the straight Democratic ticket, Alice!" She was working herself down the slate when suddenly her hand slowed. She couldn't go on—she couldn't see. She was crying, nakedly crying, her eyes awash, nose running.

"You okay in there? You all right?"

A few minutes might have passed while she was doubled over, hugging her arms around her middle, trembling and whimpering, her teeth clamped shut to keep a cry from escaping. What finally allowed her to get control of herself was the realization that nothing was final; nothing was set in stone. It was all reversible. It was one of the things she'd always liked about voting, in fact: the mechanical satisfaction of it, the weighty pull of the lever from right to left that cast your vote.

Until then, she could change her mind.

SHE EMERGED FROM the booth sniffing, swallowing, even—Maureen's old trick—putting on her sunglasses, as if that had ever fooled anyone. The two women at the registration table looked frightened, and to reassure them, Alice made up an excuse: "I just kept thinking of all the people out there who are probably canceling my vote."

"It's tough, isn't it?" The ladies were quick to empathize. "It's really tough. But you know, we're looking good. The papers, they're all saying we're looking good."

There had been a time, Alice recalled, as she pushed through the school's double doors and stood blinking on the steps, overwhelmed by the crowd, grown massive now at lunch hour, when Brenda O'Halleran, newly engaged, had joked at family get-togethers about her and Kevin's votes canceling each other's out. Then abruptly, Alice recalled, the jokes had stopped. It was just like someone discovering religion: Brenda had joined something bigger now—the vows, scarily pronounced in public; the house with the mortgage; the getting dinner on the table night after night; the kids right away, one almost obscenely on top of the other. It was the boys, finally, that had changed Brenda unrecognizably from the party girl who used to sneak cigarettes and drive around Great Neck in her mother's Buick—scary she had been, back in the eighties, to Alice; Maureen a bit surprised, perhaps, without saying so, when after deciding to stay in the city for law school, Alice had started to make pilgrimages out to the Healys' on the weekends.

The line had doubled back on itself and Alice had to push her way through two rows of lusty New York voters. It came to her, as she emerged on the other side and looked around, with nowhere in particular she had to go, what it was about Brenda's expression the other day that had gotten to her, when her cousin was sitting there on the deck, listening to Tyler cry but not moving—not moving just yet. Take another handful of nuts. Another sip of wine. *Never on his watch. I'm coming already! I swear to God he plans it.*

It was the resignation. That was why she had wanted to get pregnant—Alice knew that now, too, she thought, starting up the block to her building, though at the time it had seemed just the natural progression for a couple in their mid-thirties who had been married a couple of years. She, too, had wanted to look used up and resigned. She, too, had wanted to look like she no longer had to justify her presence on earth.

It was like a populist rally or a riot. People seemed to be running from all directions to line up and vote. Alice sidestepped a baby carriage; a businessman with his nose in a PDA. In his distraction the man jostled her and she froze—the banker. The gay banker from the IPO dinner—"We're going out to meet our surrogate." Is that how he had put it? But it wasn't him—it wasn't him, after all. Some superficial resemblance she saw, with a darting glance behind her—the blond forelock, the pleased, wry smile on his face as he pecked out words on the device. Her heart was pounding, though, and with the flash of indignation that follows a scare or a humiliation, Alice reminded herself angrily that it wasn't as if the man would know. It wasn't as if anyone would know, or would have to know. People had secrets—well, now she would have one.

Her cell phone rang and she stopped to fish it out of her bag. Mark. She stared at the caller ID then dropped the phone, still ringing, back into her bag. She couldn't speak to him just now. Not yet. It wasn't that Mark hadn't supported her decision. He had been all support, of course. And that was the problem. If it had been up to Mark, no "procedure" would have been necessary. He simply would have rationalized it out of existence.

"Excuse me? Excuse me?"

Observing her hesitation, perhaps, a jolly pollster had thrust herself forward, the lapels of her wide-wale corduroy jacket dorkily resplendent with buttons for the senator; an environmental group; various obscurely numbered propositions. "I have nothing to say," Alice said bitterly. Undeterred, in that tediously impervious manner of the political functionary—no slight too great—the woman poked her clipboard in front of her all the same.

She gave Alice a canned smile of complicity. "I'm just wondering," she said. "Did you do the right thing?"

Annabel's Mother

ANNABEL CAME TO the park every day at three with her nanny, Marva. She was a reserved child, with a long, sober face, and the color hair I was taught in French class to call *chatain clair*. She did not seem sad, exactly, and even "forlorn" was putting it strongly, but her eyes were devoid of the usual spark of entitlement one found in well-off New York City children who had been stimulated with educational toys, and taken to music and swimming classes, and shown how important they were in every way from three months of age. Annabel looked rather as if she had been told to be quiet and behave. Though not, one assumed, by Marva, who had the kind of upbeat tranquility one looked for in the best of nannies. When she was in nursery school, Annabel had always been beautifully dressed, and now that she went to girls' school uptown, the shoes and headbands and coats she wore with her uniform were always of the highest quality. You could tell that her mother, unlike some of us, did not shop for her daughter by running into Old Navy at odd hours and grabbing quasi-presentable things off the rack. You couldn't picture Annabel's mother—though in fact none of us had ever met her—saying triumphantly, "Can you believe I got it for twelve bucks?"

The park in the afternoons when school got out was a lively, robust mix of mothers and children, and nannies, and the picture it painted, under the tall, graceful gingko and chestnut trees, the squares of manicured lawn bounded by long gravel walks, was an idyllic one, although a wistfulness was likely to cross the face of a certain type of passerby who stopped to peer through the iron pickets of the park's fence for the kind of prewar ideals that had been possible in a simpler, more class-based society. It was, in what was a rarity for New York, a private park, open only to keyholders who lived in the buildings on the square around it. Some, often those who had done time across the pond on corporate packages, said they loved it because it reminded them of London; detractors said we looked like animals in a zoo. The latter were mainly folks who did not live on the park, and I'll admit, slamming the heavy ornamental gate in some benighted nonkeyholder's face (as the bylaws of the park required one to do) when he or she tried to follow one inside, I could certainly understand the bitterness. I always tried to soften my personal gate-slam with a grimace and a mumble of "So sorry," though this could sometimes backfire, as on the occasion when a glowering mother, dragging a small child in each hand, thrust herself between me and the gate to stop it from closing and demanded, "What do you mean, 'Sorry'? Can't I come in?"

Yes, those face-to-face moments were awkward. Vegetarians will tell you of the time they visited the slaughterhouse and, having discovered firsthand where the Sunday bacon comes from, enjoy it no more.

Inside, though, the park was a true haven because frankly, since it was locked, it afforded all of us a break from the constant vigilance that constituted child care in New York. Everyone had her spot. The nannies with newborns in Bugaboos would walk the gravel perimeter; the toddlers would step out and wobble in the center of the park (in springtime fatally attracted to the beds of tulips), where their mothers or babysitters could sit on one of two facing semicircles of benches and talk to one another while keeping an eye on their unsteady progress. The older children would play freeze tag and capture-the-flag along the southern end, where there was an exposed patch of dirt that the trustees of the park had finally given up trying to cultivate.

Everyone who came to the park regularly recognized everyone else. We all called one another by name, and it was not at all unusual for mothers to socialize with and know intimate details about nannies (and vice versa) or to speak with children who were not their own, especially in cases like Annabel's, whose mother never came to the park because she had, evidently, a high-level job at one of the big midtown banks. That was why Annabel was always with Marva. They were a nanny and charge who seemed to genuinely like each other's company. They seemed suited to each other temperamentally, and had evidently arrived at a point where they didn't need to talk much, for they often sat together silently but apparently perfectly happily, taking in the scene. That was the other reason the two were so linked in everyone's mind: Annabel was an only child, and when she came to the park she was not particularly gregarious with the other children, contentedly eating her snack and watching the park activity without participating in it, even when one of Marva's nanny friends would join them and the two middle-aged women would make their desultory conversation.

She—Annabel—was always polite, particularly for a six-year-old. Occasionally I had a conversation with her, because she always asked about Sally when she saw her—how old she was now, whether she had said anything yet, whether she could eat real food or still drank only milk from a bottle. This was pleasant for me because it had the effect, like someone's asking one for directions, of conveying authority on me, which as a new mother I didn't often feel I possessed. Marva told me one day when Annabel was playing with my Sally, "This child have a warm heart for little babies. Her mommy buy her a hundred dolls but she like the real ones better."

She chuckled. "Does her mother buy her lots of dolls?" I said. "Oh, yes," Marva said. "She have a huge collection of expensive dolls—Madame Alexander, you know the brand? Her mommy feel guilty she work so hard." "Is that right?" I said. "Oh, yes. Since the day she born. She buy her all kinds of sweets, too, but I tell her, chocolate and gummi bears are not the same as *time,* you know?"

Now, if Annabel's mother had been the one confessing all this to me, I probably would have said something noncommittal or even gone so far as to imply a measure of opprobrium toward these highly questionable parenting decisions—"Hey, everyone needs a sweet now and then, right?" or "If you're happier working, you should work! A happy mother makes a happy child!"—but since I was talking to Marva, I said, "Gosh, we try to *avoid* sugar in our house," and Marva nodded approvingly. Then I said, "I personally just can't imagine missing the baby years." "Is better that way," Annabel's nanny said. "That's what I tell her mommy."

After that exchange it was as if she and I had really bonded. Win and I were new to the neighborhood at this time—we had bought on the park just before I got pregnant—and I didn't know many people, and I was always relieved to catch sight of Annabel and Marva from the sidewalk when I brought Sally out after her nap. That day I remember I said to Marva, "Annabel can play with Sally any time she likes." Marva conveyed the offer to Annabel, who looked up, shy and pleased, from where she was squatting down in front of my daughter. That day Sally, as all of the park babies did, had started picking up gravel and trying to put it into her mouth. Embarrassed I'd been distracted, I knelt down and opened up her palms and brushed the little stones out of them. "Sally! *That's* not your food!" I said and I must have said it a little too severely, because Sally burst into tears. "I'll make sure she doesn't choke on them, Mrs. Kimball," Annabel promised solemnly.

"Oh, I'm not worried about it, Annabel!" I said, picking up Sally and jiggling her in my arms. "Just have fun with her! Enjoy your-

selves! Please!" I'm afraid I sounded rather hysterical in those confused days of inchoate motherhood. Marva helped me a lot. She
would have a look at Sally when I was worried that she hadn't
reached some developmental milestone ("She's five months, Marva,
and she hasn't rolled over!") or when I was convinced she had con-
tracted Coxsackie disease or was becoming strangely bowlegged, or
when I thought she hadn't gained enough weight, or was crawling
in a funny way, and Marva would say, her hand on Sally's forehead,
or playing peekaboo to make her laugh, or holding Sally under the
armpits so my daughter could stretch her legs and pretend to stand,
"Ain't nothing wrong with this child, Liz—you got to stop worrying," and even though I usually kept up the protest for show, quoting one or another of my parenting books, I was secretly solaced by
this woman of experience, who clearly took such good care of
Annabel, who—despite having a mother who never saw her—
seemed remarkably—really astonishingly well-adjusted. Of course
Marva called me Liz, the same as I called her Marva. Asking your
own nanny, much less someone else's, to call you "Mrs." would have
been like putting her in a maid's uniform or having her come into
your apartment through the servants' entrance—so unheard of, that
when women posted such cases on the mommies' website I spent far
too much time perusing, you assumed they were apocryphal.

The next few times I saw the pair of them, Annabel asked politely if she could play with Sally, looking up at me with her grave
brown eyes. "Annabel, you don't even have to ask," I said. "If you
see our stroller, you can just come over and join us, okay? You're
always welcome." The suggestion seemed to make her uneasy,
however, so I said, "It's okay. If you feel more comfortable asking,
just ask, okay?" This is how the women of my generation, in my
circle of friends, talked to our children. If one of the toddlers mis-
behaved we never scolded her, "You naughty, naughty girl!" but
rather, we knelt down on the child's level and looked her in the eye
and said calmly but emphatically, "I don't like the way you're act-

ing, Hudson." Or we'd say, calmly albeit a-grammatically: "Do we hurt people's bodies in this family? Look at my face, Miles—is that something we do?" Our children had for the most part creative names like Miles or Milo or Bronwen, or they had classic names like Grace or Henry, or they had nineteenth-century servants' names like Ruby or Stella. In fact there was a lot of variety, but the one thing you never heard were the big hits from public school in the seventies. You never heard Jennifer or Kristen or Kim. You never heard Angie, and even Michael was rare. Surnames were used for first names, such as Bennett and Crawford and Grady, whereas the firms our husbands worked for were, increasingly, called "Fresh Powder Capital" and "Dude, Gnarly Wave, LLC," so you would hear grown men at cocktail parties saying with straight faces that they had left Morgan for Gnarly—but I digress.

There was a lot of gossip in the park. Like all village life, ours fed on news of its denizens. The chase for information was spearheaded by Victoria and Marnie, best friends who lived at 48 West, and whose children—each had a pair of twins—were always being paraded into the park and then handed summarily off to the pair of specially trained twin nannies who attended them. They, and through them the rest of us, knew where everyone lived, whether the apartment was A-line (meaning park-view) or D-line (shaftway), WEIK (windowed eat-in-kitchen), or just EIK; how many bedrooms and how many maids'. (The first time I heard this shorthand I thought the question was, "How many maids does she have?" and was titillated by the proximity to real privilege until someone added, "One of the 'maids' [rooms, that is] has been sacrificed to make an open kitchen.") In any case, even if you had had a maid, you wouldn't have called her a maid but rather, a cleaning woman, or, at the limit, a housekeeper. The same was true if you had a decorator: You referred to her as "this friend of mine who's great with color," for somewhere along the line, hiring a decorator had eclipsed couples therapy as the last taboo. There were seasonal topics, such as the size of the husbands' bonuses or where people summered, not that you used that verb. And there was year-round fodder, such as which park mother coming back from postpartum lockup had found her six-month-old calling the nanny "Mama" and fired the woman on the spot sans severance; or who had a shit fit and threatened the big D when she found her husband had supported her mother-in-law's feeding Carleton a banana (he was allowed only indigenous fruit). In short: the usual. Of course, the gossip often had an element of adjudication, and it wasn't unusual for a story to end with the verdict of "Bitch" handed down. Or "Asshole." Or "What a fucking shithead." The exchange of information was freer about the families who didn't show up at the park the day their news hit and freer still about the children whose mother and father, like Annabel's, were never represented. In fact a bit of mystique developed about these children, whose parents clearly had better things to do than stand around exchanging specs on people's apartments and discussing whether it was okay to allow juice at lunch.

ONE DAY IN early spring—I remember it was April, because Sally's first birthday was coming up and I was fretting about "spaces" and saying to Victoria and Marnie that over-my-dead-body would I hire an *entertainer* for a bunch of *one*-year-olds, why couldn't we do it like our mothers had, with a bunch of balloons tied to the mailbox and a lopsided cake—Annabel came over to say hi, and Victoria, who was the more officious of Marnoria, as they were sometimes collectively known, called out to her, "Hello, Annabel! Is your mommy in town this week?"

Annabel said no, and Victoria said, "Oh, she had to go to Chicago again?" Victoria was a tall, uncomfortably skinny woman made taller by the high heels she wore. There was literally not an ounce of fat on her. Her hip bones reminded me of the photo of a ski resort, where they show you the peaks overhanging the bowl. Her face was severely lined and she wore her hair in a ponytail.

Now Marnie interjected, "Mommy's a managing *director* at JPMorgan." This was for my benefit, apparently. She was in similarly irreproachable shape—they both put me to shame with my half-hearted Level One yoga and the occasional self-hating jog—but Marnie's body looked as if it had been relentlessly aerobicized into submission and might rebel at any minute with a twenty-pound gain. She had a big chest that made her look heavier than she was and she was touchingly open about the fact that she was always on a diet. "She has to work mighty hard, doesn't she, Annabel—your mommy?"

Annabel didn't say anything, just looked curiously at them, as Victoria cried, "But then she can earn money and buy you all those beautiful clothes! You have beautiful clothes, Annabel, did you know that?"

I was beginning to be embarrassed on behalf of my fellow park mothers, so I pretended not to listen, cooing to Sally, who was standing, holding on to the bench, having learned how to pull herself up.

"Look at her coat," Victoria went on. She leaned forward on the bench and took the tail of Annabel's coat in her hand and rubbed the blue herringbone and silk lining between her fingers. "Isn't this gorgeous?"

"My dad bought me this," Annabel said.

"Oh, did he? Oh, that's nice," said Victoria. Her legs were crossed and the top foot, from which her stiletto heel was dangling, pumped vigorously. Marnie usually came to the park in a jacket over indie-label jeans, but Victoria's outfits, which she must have spent a fortune on, were aggressively upmarket-nonconformist—slashed T-shirts and lace-up breeches; thigh-high boots. They seemed to scream, "If you have to ask, you'll never know!" as if the moment she put on her clothes in the morning was the closest she came to the life in New York she'd imagined for herself. "Too bad your mom has to be away, huh? She travels an awful lot, doesn't she?"

"But Annabel gets to stay and have fun with Marva!" Marnie crowed. She usually played good cop in the bloodletting. "I bet you guys have a ball, huh? Girls' slumber party, right? Hey," she said, when Annabel remained silent, "can I come? Can I be invited next time Mom's away? You and me and Marva? Wouldn't that be fun, Annabel?"

Annabel gave a frown as if this had been said in a foreign language. "May I take Sally over to the fountain?" she asked me. "I want to show it to her now that it's fixed."

"Of course, Annabel," I said. I got up and helped Sally turn away from the bench, putting her little hands in Annabel's. I can't tell you how happy this made me—those truncated little walks Sally took with Annabel, the latter leaning solicitously over my golden-haired baby, carefully helping her to step along. They were the first times I really saw Sally as a person in her own right, who would one day have friends of her own. I glanced around for Marva and when I saw her on her usual bench, talking with her friend Sophie, I gave her a little wave and called, "She's *so* sweet!"

"That poor, poor kid," Victoria said, when Annabel and Sally were a little distance away.

Marnie folded her arms across her chest and shook her head in disgust. "I'm sorry, but she's seriously out of control. It used to be—what?—once a month or so. Now she's with the guy like every *week*. It's just not right."

"It's disgusting."

"What's disgusting?" I said.

"Uh—someone having an *affair* for like a *year*."

Marnie stared at me. "I can't believe you didn't know," she said, and there was real ire in her voice. She elbowed Victoria. "She's too good for the gossip, right?"

"She met him through work," Victoria informed me. "She flies to Chicago all the time for work—"

"Her two big clients are out there—"

"She brought him to New York last year—"

"She only tried *that* once."

"Marva has seen the guy," Victoria said in a stage whisper. "She called Annabel's mother on it. Told her it made her uncomfortable."

"They were, like, fucking when Marva was in the apartment."

Victoria looked at Marnie with the happy satisfaction of having stumbled on an enormity to trump her lifetime of petty sins.

"Can I say—I *love* Marva. I seriously love her."

"How many nannies would have the balls?" Victoria said and then she dropped into the peeved undertone she reserved for talking about her own nanny, "Certainly not 'doormat Drianna' . . ."

The whole time I had been only half listening, watching Annabel's and Sally's progress across the gravel. Now I spoke up doubtfully, "You heard all this from Marva? She told you?" It was hard for me to imagine—not the situation itself, or that Marva might have felt compelled to confide in someone about it, but that she would have chosen Victoria and Marnie as her confessors. Frankly, I was a little surprised she hadn't chosen me.

The two of them looked uncomfortable. They always got defensive if someone tried to pin them down on their sources.

"We can neither confirm nor deny," said Victoria, and they both laughed like crazy.

"Anyway, I thought Annabel's mother was at Morgan Stanley," I said after a minute.

They shook their heads. "JPMorgan."

"Although she did actually get headhunted by Morgan Stanley," Marnie said.

"Oh, okay," I said, and a black wave of depression seemed to cover my eyes. Here it was a beautiful afternoon in spring and the sun was shining down on my firstborn child, who was going to start walking by herself any day now, and I was sitting here talking with these two fools about which firm employed another

child's mother, a woman I had never met. I could just see us segue-
ing into how Annabel's mother liked her coffee, and which kind of
hanger she preferred in her closets: dry cleaner's metal, wood, or
those satin-covered ones that never fill out the shoulders. To turn
the conversation back on ourselves, I said assertively, "So, what are
you guys doing this summer?"

We talked about their various plans—they were both Hamp-
tons people and I drew them out about the different towns.
Annabel had reached the fountain with Sally. I craned my neck,
but not to make sure they were all right. She was so loving with
her, talking to Sally, explaining things, never losing her patience—it was a pleasure to watch.

"So you and Win going to Nantucket again this year?" Marnie
asked me.

"Yes, we are," I said, perking up, pleased, in spite of myself,
that the Kimballs had proven worthy of gossip in the park.

"Where's your house?" said Marnie.

For just a second I hesitated. It was tempting to let them believe the wrong thing, but it was just too pathetic, so I said as
cheerfully and dismissively as I could, as if I really didn't care,
"Oh, it's not our house."

"Oh, you're just renting?" said Victoria, and when I said yes,
there went the stiletto again, pumping like mad.

"Uh-huh," said Marnie. She sat forward and brushed a star mag-
nolia petal off of her jeans. "That's fine. That's fine, obviously."

THAT NIGHT WHEN Win got home from work, despite Sally's
having gone straight to sleep after *Pat the Bunny,* and the Sancerre
having been open three-quarters of an hour, I was itching for a
fight. I started musing aloud over supper about going back to
work—never a good sign. (Before Sally I had worked in fund-
raising for a program that brought theater into the public schools.)
This was a nonargument, as Win would have been all for it, but the

truth of course was that I had turned out to be one of those overinvolved first-time mothers who have to have everything so perfect for Baby that any delegation is impossible, so a job was no more under serious consideration than a second child—I could barely cope with the exigencies of one. Nonetheless, I liked to suggest that the biggest obstacle to my returning to work was not my own maternal anxiety but the chaotic nature of our life in New York, due in part to the long hours of Win's job, which, because it was by far the more lucrative, had taken precedence first in the short term and now clearly in the long over mine. During supper I got myself into a corner and was too proud to back down, so instead of being able to watch some cozy television afterward, I had to keep up the performance. I went haughtily into our bedroom and tried to read. But I had trouble concentrating and it came to me that I was spitting mad about the exchange in the park. It was the "just." "Oh, you're just renting?" was ever so different from being asked "Oh, you're renting?" And then that bizarre reassurance from Marnie that it was "fine"? I slammed my book shut with the not very useful conclusion that Marnoria could go fuck themselves.

THE NEXT DAY I kept Sally inside practicing baby sign language and the day after that, because it was so beautiful that staying in the apartment felt antisocial, I did bring her out, but a little later than usual. I took a real estate flyer with me, and I wore a straw hat and sunglasses, and I didn't sit on the benches but pushed the stroller all the way down to the southwestern corner of the park, and camped out on a patch of grass in the shade of the plane tree. When I sensed someone approaching me I turned pointedly away from the footsteps, thinking it was Marnie or Victoria, and I held out Sally's sippy cup to her, saying, "Here's your water, Sally. Here's your wa-wa!"

"Excuse me," said a small, polite voice with little expectation in it, and I turned with a rush of shame because it was Annabel.

Embarrassed, I made a big effort with her, asking her to sit down on the grass with us and drawing her out about school and her family in a way I fancied both benign and disinterested. Of course I was trying very hard to avoid mentioning Annabel's mother at all, and I wasn't doing too badly when finally, holding Sally on her lap and playing with her hair, Annabel volunteered, "My mom's away again this week."

"Is she?" I said.

"She has to go to Chicago a lot."

"I'm sure you miss her." I turned away to dig in my bag for a wipe. I was appalled at having come face-to-face with the sordid fact of her mother's affair and the even further sordidness of my knowing this fact.

Thank God Marva strolled over to join us then. She never let Annabel play by herself too long, unlike some of the nannies you'd see, who practically had to be pried off the nanny bench and dragged over to their screaming charges when one of them fell or hit someone or had a temper tantrum over a shiny new all-terrain toddler vehicle having to be returned to its rightful owner.

"I'm going to show Sally the crocuses," Annabel announced, "if that's all right. Come, Sally. Come Sally, come Sally, come little girl," she said, coaxing her along. Once in a while when she spoke to Sally, Annabel had a Caribbean lilt in her voice, and hearing it, Marva and I looked at each other and laughed.

"Well, that feel good," said Marva, as I got up to talk to her. "I haven't laugh all day."

"Yeah?" I said. "I'm sorry. Is everything all right?" I thought she might want to unburden herself—however obliquely—about the situation at home.

"To tell you the truth, Liz, it not great."

I asked her if there was anything I could do to help.

"It's just"—she sighed—"I ask for a raise and my boss don't want to raise me."

"Really?" I said. I was very surprised. "That's terrible! You *so* deserve a raise."

Marva laughed. "Well . . . I think so!" She added, "I need to get two thousand saved."

"No, but seriously," I said. "You're such a good nanny. You're head and shoulders above everyone else. You do everything for Annabel—everything. I should know—I mean I see you here all the time."

Marva smiled tolerantly, as I went on: "If you were my nanny, Marva, I'd give you a raise."

"Well, now, thank you," said Marva. She seemed genuinely pleased by my hypothetical support, but it suddenly struck me as a foolish—nay, a total bullshit—thing to have said, the kind of crap we privileged white mothers were probably spewing all the time, because talk was so very cheap. I cast about for a way to show I was better than that and finally I said, "If it doesn't work out with Annabel's mother, you come work for me, okay? Seriously, Marva, Win and I have been thinking we could use some help and we'd love to hire you."

The injustice ate at me. I kept thinking back to my own salad days in the city, as a starving actress with nothing but a set of head shots and a useless Yale degree, and the vast, incalculably vast difference two grand would have made at different times in my life.

It ate at me even more when I heard from Marnoria that Marva needed the cash not for any loan or mortgage or purchase of her own—or, as I would have, to buy some new clothes because I simply *could not go* to one more party in my vintage black crêpe dress—but to bring her sixteen-year-old son, who was in Saint Lucia with his grandparents, to America.

"But that's just ridiculous that she won't give it to her. I mean, forget the raise—flat out! She should just gift it to her." I found myself reintroducing the topic every couple of days and I was on the brink of suggesting we take up some kind of park collection for Marva except that I was afraid it would embarrass her.

"Well, it is a lot," said Marnie one afternoon—mildly, for she didn't really care either way. I stopped juggling Sally on my knee and looked at her.

"Hey, maybe she's worried she'll blow it all in one chunk," said Victoria. "It does happen, you know. Or maybe Marva's making the whole thing up about the kid. Who knows? When we gave Drianna a bonus so she could get some decent clothes and stop wearing, like, a thong to work, the check was in Peru before you could say 'H&M.' "

I had one of those moments then of which there have been mercifully few in my life: I realized that my moral fiber was being put to the test. I could sit there blabbing with these two or I could fucking stand up and be counted. I think it was Sally that got me to my feet—it was repulsive to me to let this kind of talk pass with my daughter sitting on my lap. "You live in a two-million-dollar apartment and you think two thousand dollars is 'a lot'?" I said as I stood up. "That disgusts me." I could feel them watching me as I snapped Sally, openly complaining, into her stroller and pushed it jerkily across the gravel to where Marva and Sophie were sitting. "Two-*five*," I could hear Victoria saying behind me. "Jesus, hasn't she heard of appreciation?" Normally I didn't join Marva when she wasn't by herself, but for solidarity's sake I did now, though I got the feeling I had interrupted a conversation about Sophie's man troubles, so I didn't stay long, making some excuse about Sally's being tired.

The next day I found Marva in the park and I told her I would lend her the two thousand. I'd been thinking about it all day. I'd had an overwrought discussion—overwrought on my part—with Win the night before, who had okayed the loan without being particularly interested in the story behind it. "It's fine with me," he'd said, "as long as you don't expect to get a penny of it back." This was so irritating to me I wished I'd never discussed it with him—it seemed like he was always having the last word.

Marva was certainly happy when I asked her to sit down with me and informed her of our decision, though my announcement didn't seem to surprise her, particularly, and that took some of the thrill out of it for me, I have to admit. I guess I'd started thinking of myself as some kind of fairy godmother, and I thought she might leap up and hug me and say her problems were solved. Foolishly, I had forgotten to bring a checkbook with me to the park. I couldn't exactly give her an IOU so I invited her and Annabel to come back to the apartment with us.

The four of us squeezed into the elevator with an older woman from the building, one of those dowagers who think they own the place. "Mrs. Gregory? This is Marva—" I turned to her. "I'm sorry, Marva. I don't know your last name."

"Phillips."

"Marva Phillips, Mrs. Gregory." Marva said hello, and my neighbor nodded—rather wanly, which was annoying but couldn't be helped.

Win and I were totally disorganized about the business end of our personal lives. We'd had our phone turned off twice for non-payment; we were always sending credit cards to the dry cleaners in pants pockets or finding cash stashes that we'd forgotten about—one time we lost eighteen hundred bucks for an entire summer. Our checks never went in sequence because after writing a few we'd lose the book we were using and have to start a new one. This is what I did now, after a brief, fruitless search through the secretary in the foyer, digging a fresh book out of the top drawer of Win's bureau—it stuck a bit, because it was some Georgian thing he'd inherited from his grandfather—and writing a check out to Marva Phillips. The introduction to Mrs. Gregory was now proving fortuitous, as I've always had a squeamishness about making a check out in front of the payee, and because I'd learned her last name I didn't have to. When I came back to the living room, it smelled awful. "Sally needs a change," Annabel said nervously as if it were her fault. Marva stood up from the floor where she'd been playing with her. "I'll go and change her, Liz. Where you keep everything?"

"Oh, God, Marva. You don't have to do that."

I took Sally back into my arms and handed Marva the check. Somewhat surprisingly, she stood there studying it, which made me uncomfortable because it was as if she were questioning the amount and I had a sudden fear that she was going to ask me for more. Plus, as even a mother will admit, the smell of a dirty diaper is really intolerable for more than about thirty seconds, and Sally was struggling in my arms and demanding, "Doda! Doda!"—her talking Dora doll.

"I was afraid this would happen," Marva said.

I think I must have looked alarmed and she mistook this as concern because she laughed and said, "Don't worry, Liz, everything's fine"—which didn't seem to me quite the right tone to strike, but anyway—and she explained that although she went by "Phillips," it was actually her maiden name and since technically she wasn't divorced, I was to use "Martindale," her legal last name.

"Oh, I'm sorry," I said. "I didn't realize." As I headed to our bedroom with Sally in my arms to get another check, she called after me, again volunteering to change her.

"Don't be ridiculous!" I called back, and now my voice was hoarse in my throat. I had that feverish feeling of exhaustion coming on, which I have ever since associated with new motherhood in New York; that tragic feeling, when one realizes that instead of gossiping in the park or frantically Googling acquaintances or trying on hot outfits during tummy time, one ought to have been playing in a quiet yard with one's baby, the way one imagines one's mother used to do thirty years ago. But now it's too late, the day is spent, the baby needs a change and is overtired, supper will be organic chicken nuggets again, for both of you, and lying down in the dark is hours away. The whole gesture suddenly seemed pathetic and pointless and I wondered—in the morally melodramatic way that seemed to encapsulate my thinking in those days—why I was yet again putting someone else ahead of my child. "This'll take two seconds!"

I couldn't put Sally down while I wrote the check because Win had left a wineglass and open bottle of wine on the floor the night before, which my cleaning woman—I swear to God she was blind in one eye—had evidently missed this morning, so I had to clamp her squirming body to my side and she started to wail as I rewrote the check and I was so fed up I wanted to scream.

When I came back, Annabel had arranged the toys artfully against the wall like the well-brought-up child she was.

"I cannot thank you enough for this, Liz," Marva said steadily, so at least that was something.

WELL, I NEVER did get any of the money back, but not for the reason you might have expected. About six months later we ended up hiring Marva and for her first Christmas bonus, we forgave the loan. I gave her a little extra on the side as well, but out of some small embarrassment, for being such a bleeding heart, I guess, I didn't mention the extra amount to Win. That Christmas Marva and I were in the throes of our honeymoon. It lasted nearly a year—those blissful months when you get through the stickiness of hiring someone; the strange small shocks of their presence in your life (the half-eaten YoBabies you find in the fridge with the spoon still in them); when even the first little reproaches about the few, very few, minor disappointments about the person's MO only serve to bring you closer ("I'm so sorry, but could you not hang the bath towels to dry on the rocking chair? It's an antique, you see"). I eased myself back into work, volunteering with a downtown theater company that a friend of Win's from Andover had started. The first play got some good notices and we got a grant and I was taken on as the first paid employee, and before long I was the one showing up at the park at three to pick up Sally. I used to thrill to see Marva before she could see me. She wouldn't be sitting down—hardly ever, anyway—but walking with Sally, or showing her the squirrels, or rolling a ball to her or feeding her edamame or Cheerios or whatever we had agreed upon that morning. I felt she made my job possible, and that made our life possible, and Win and I got along well and enjoyed Sally more, and it was all, all thanks to Marva.

I never asked Marva for details about why her old job had ended. The park had told that story: of Annabel's father discovering the affair, the middle-of-the-night reckoning, the futile weekend away to try to patch things up, and, finally, the post-divorce decision to move uptown, evidenced by the appearance on the *Times'* multiple listings website of "EXCLUSIVE KEY TO PARK! Triple-mint, classic six, WBFP . . ." shortly after which, according to the residents of 48 North, a bright-eyed young couple submitted their plans for a gut renovation of 12B. I never asked if Annabel's mother had fired Marva or if Marva had quit, but from the way Marva sometimes shook her head in despair at the denouement, I figured she'd simply decided she'd had enough of her old boss.

I must say, I certainly had! When I dictated the snacks to Marva in the morning I'd think, She probably thinks I'm really tediously micromanagey compared to Annabel's mother. Or if Win and I went out to dinner and I instructed Marva to go right into the bedroom if Sally cried, I'd think, She probably thinks I'm not enough of a disciplinarian, compared to Annabel's mother. When I got really paranoid about it, though, I would console myself with the fact that at least I hadn't had an affair and gotten divorced right under my nanny's nose; at least I had raised her to a living wage.

When Marva had a crisis in her personal life I was only too glad that Win and I were there to help. In the new year, her son, Jerome, got into some trouble. He crashed a friend's car—totaled it, while driving drunk—and shortly after that it came out that he had fathered a child back home whose mother—it just kept getting more and more baroque—was the same age as Marva and was, in fact, a friend of hers. That was the first time I saw Marva break down. One morning she came into the apartment, and instead of going right to Sally in her high chair as she usually did, she sat down at the kitchen table without taking off her coat or hat or scarf and she started to cry. "My boss warn me," she kept saying. "My boss warn me many time." Marva had kept the habit of referring to Annabel's mother as her boss, which in other circumstances might have rankled but obviously today I ignored. "What did she warn you about, Marva?" I asked in what I hoped sounded like a concerned tone, though to be honest, once I found out that no one had died, I didn't really feel like commiserating with her and being late for work. When she answered she sounded as if she were giving the advice all over again, rather than recounting something someone had told her in the past. "Not to bring that child to the States. I can't tell you how many times she try to talk me out of it." Sally was banging her plastic dish on the tray of the high chair and yelling, "Want my cereal, Mommy! Want my cereal!" Marva still hadn't hung up her coat, despite how hot it was in the apartment, and I found myself wondering if she was planning to work at all that day. She started to shake her head and she said, "That's one of the things she and I quarrel over!" and when I said, "Let me just call in and say I'll be late," half hoping she would stop me, she didn't.

Other than that I guess it was just the little things that chipped away at the romance over the next couple of years. The way she was so condescending to Maria, the new cleaning woman, which meant constant negotiating between the two. The discovery that behind my back, she did all sorts of things I wouldn't necessarily have sanctioned—bringing Sally all the way uptown on the subway to see Sophie, now that Sophie was working up there; taking her to Dunkin' Donuts, and not to the park as I had thought, when she had time to kill in between music and Tumble Bunnies. I remember the day I discovered that one. I had come home to make some calls and was then going to go out to the park to fetch the two of them. Looking for my credit card, which I sometimes gave to Marva to buy groceries, or books for Sally, I found the orange and pink paper bag crumpled up in the diaper bag that hung from Sally's stroller. It was the second time I'd found a bag—the second Tuesday—which meant it was a pattern, and it annoyed me enough that I decided to go out right away without making my calls. I suppose it had also occurred to me that it wasn't a bad idea, even with a Marva, to surprise her in the job every once in a while. People found out some crazy shit on their nanny-cams. As I walked the half block from our apartment to the park gate, though, I thought twice about saying something—maybe that was really being too hysterical. After all, a donut once a week . . . ? Then again: trans fats. I spotted the two of them right away through the grille of the gate. Marva looked so remarkably happy, sitting there on the bench, with Sally playing with a baby doll at her feet, that I crumpled the donut bag in my hand. I forgave her instantly. I owed the woman for my child's well-being—for her education, inasmuch as a three-year-old could be educated. Marva had done more of the disciplining than Win or I, and as a result there was a sympathy between her and Sally that, judging from the blissful expression on Marva's face, even I didn't fully understand.

I was fishing for my key when I thought I heard a familiar voice and I peered intently into the park. Two years had gone by, but of course she looked right at home. It was Annabel, sitting, swinging her legs, on the bench next to Marva. Sally picked up her baby and held it up to them, saying something. I turned away. I walked quickly back toward my building, praying they hadn't seen me. I just couldn't bear to see them right then—Sally most of all. Victoria happened to brush by me going the other way. "God, are you okay?" she said, seeing me stricken. "Yeah—yeah," I said, clearing my throat. "Rough day at work." And I was grateful that she was the kind of person who would accept an explanation like that to my face, no matter what she would say afterward in the park. I never found out if Marva had invited Annabel down or if the reunion was serendipitous. There didn't seem to be another nanny around but I hadn't stayed to find out. Curiously, Marva never mentioned seeing Annabel to me, though for several days afterward I expected her to.

I didn't have the guts to fire her. You couldn't fire someone for that, could you? For loving another woman's child more than she loved yours? The consensus on the mothers' website was overwhelmingly for performance-based dismissal and against weaseling out with half-assed excuses. In time, the situation took care of itself. At three-and-a-half Sally started nursery school, and all of a sudden, with the pressure of the infant years gone, the thing we all started to discuss was replacing the third-world-nanny model with a younger, more energetic babysitter type, someone who would think up things for them to do. "Someone," as Marnie, who had boys, put it to me, "who can play ball with them." I dithered and fretted, and one day Marva came to me and told me that she wanted to go back to cleaning houses so she would have more time for Reggie, Jerome's child, whom she was raising. It was dispiriting to me, the idea: It seemed such a step backward from nannying, but she seemed determined, resigned, anyway, and of course I didn't stand in her way. It suited my needs, of course. We gave her a good severance; I told her if she ever needed a recommendation . . .

Another year passed and unbelievably, Win and I were looking at kindergartens for Sally. She was still our only child, and she was a handful—bright, yes, but she could barely sit still long enough to look at a book. She was physically bold and so sure of herself that for a long time now, my role had been relegated to standing on the side—of the playground, we hardly ever went to the park anymore—gawking at her latest feat. One afternoon we were uptown touring one of the more established girls' schools. The parent tour guide took us into a fourth-grade classroom where the teacher was reading aloud. Sitting there in the semicircle of girls, listening attentively, her hair grown long down her back now, was Annabel. I caught her eye and gave her an excited little wave. "Oh my God!" she mouthed. Win and I followed the tour guide out and were standing at the end of the hall, waiting for the elevator, when the classroom door opened and she came hurrying up to us. "Mrs. Kimball! Mrs. Kimball!" I was flattered she remembered—touched that a nine-year-old was inclined to make such an effort. She had never met Win, so I introduced him. "The famous Annabel," he said, for she'd never entirely left our conversation but would come up from time to time, when I thought about buying something nice for Sally—"Didn't Annabel have a coat like that?"—or when I made a comparison to one of Sally's little peers—"She's a little like Annabel except . . ." It was a happy moment of reunion, but poignant, too, because it reminded me so powerfully of the joy and intensity of Sally's babyhood, when I had been at home with her and spent my days tending to her needs. I felt I ought to say something to Annabel about Marva, but the truth was that my information wasn't up to date. "You know Marva was thinking about going home," I said gently. It was all I had and it was at least a year old.

"Oh, yeah," said Annabel. "I know."

"Oh, good." I was relieved that I wasn't breaking sad news.

"Yeah, we visited her down there last Christmas."

"Did you? Wow." I searched for something more to say. "Gosh. So, you guys actually went—I mean, you went to"—for just a second I blanked on the island.

"Saint Lucia," Annabel supplied. "We were on Anguilla, but we went to Saint Lucia for the day—my mom's new boyfriend has a plane."

"Oh, he does? Oh, wow, that must be fun—wow," I stammered,

trying to get a grasp on the various implications of what she was saying. "So, you've stayed in touch with her all these years?"

"She and my mom have stayed close," Annabel said. "She was my first nanny, you know."

The elevator arrived with a ding.

"But how's Sally?" Annabel wanted to know. "She must be so big!"

I told her hurriedly that Sally was thriving, that she loved her nursery school, that she was very energetic, very active, that Win and I couldn't keep up with her. We joked that it must have been all the gravel she ate in the park. "She's older now, obviously, so we've sort of graduated from the nanny model," I said, again feeling I owed Annabel some kind of explanation. "I've got a college girl who comes—an NYU student."

The elevator doors had opened and Win and the tour guide had gotten in and the latter was holding her arm across the door to stop it from closing and looking at me expectantly, not wanting to be rude. "It works out really well," I said. I wasn't sure Annabel had gotten the right impression—she was such a quiet, self-possessed child, she might have been thinking anything. I suddenly had a paranoid thought that all those years Marva was working for us she had been feeding every last incident to Annabel's mother. Like the time Win got so fed up with me he checked into the Roger Williams for a week; or the time, screaming "You will fucking eat this!" I had chased Sally through the apartment with a stalk of broccoli.

But then a lucky phrase came to mind that a mother at Sally's nursery school had used to describe her new-and-improved help situation. "Everybody's happy!" I called, as the doors closed.

Win explained to the tour-guide woman as we rode down, "Annabel's nanny used to work for us."

The woman quoted amicably that oft-repeated epigram about nannies in New York, that the good ones always got passed along.

Spoiled

FROM THE BARN Leigh could hear them honking for her, followed by Mrs. Murray's bark of "Morning!" and the door to the cab of the truck slamming. She wound a few more strands of the horse's mane around her fingers and yanked them out, wincing. "I'm sorry, I'm sorry, I'm sorry," she murmured, hating the moment when the hairs tightened around her fingers and she heard the tearing sound. It didn't hurt the horse to have its mane pulled, Leigh knew that: There were no nerve endings along the crest. But the gelding was finicky about it, dipping his head and sidling away from her, and Leigh had become squeamish about doing it. So even though she had been up since quarter to six, the real task of the morning—the braiding—was barely begun. She would have to bribe Kim Murray into doing it for her.

"Just one more, Rye, just one more—I'm sorry!" The gray tossed his head, rattling the cross ties. "All done! All done, I promise!"

She looked anxiously out toward the driveway, where the Murrays were honking for her again, and stepped off the bucket she was using as a stool. She took the gray hastily off the cross ties and, carrying her grooming kit with the braiding supplies, led the horse out past her father's dry, dog-day rhododendrons to the waiting trailer. There had been two weeks of a heat spell and today, too, was supposed to be in the high nineties; they would be suffocating under their coats and hats.

It was the last show of the summer. The Murrays had driven over the night before so Leigh could load her tack trunk and garment bag into the back of the pickup, along with the bale of hay for Rye. "Summer flew, didn't it, Dan," Mrs. Murray had said to Leigh's father, who had come out to help. She was a hard, unforgiving woman who took pleasure in reminding others of life's harsh inevitabilities: "You can't have everything, can you?" "You're dead a long time." She had confirmed her own remark with a satisfied nod: "It always does." Then Leigh's father had given Mrs. Murray the thirty dollars they paid her to bring Leigh and Rye to the shows, and Mrs. Murray had tucked it into her back pocket, the way she always did, without looking down at the bills. Mrs. Murray had once been Leigh's riding instructor, and not just her transportation. After she upgraded from her old pony, Butterscotch, to Rye against Mrs. Murray's advice, Leigh's father had found her a fancier trainer who came out from Hamilton. The new trainer, Meg, was usually busy on the weekends, though, taking her top students—older girls—to the "A" shows. So the Houghtons had arranged with Mrs. Murray that Rye could have the extra spot in the trailer, next to Kim Murray's pony.

Most of Mrs. Murray's students were little kids, beginners, as Leigh had been, who quit down the road to chase boys, or if they stuck with riding, moved on, as Leigh had done, something not quite correct about the woman's operation—the barbed-wire fencing, the school horses that went both western and English, the proliferating black and tan barn cats that Donny Murray would joke about drowning in Ponkawog Pond.

"Your boots, Lees! You forgot your boots!" It was Leigh's mother, coming out of the house in a panic, eyes agog with the enormity of the near omission. She was wearing her old terrycloth bathrobe over her nightgown and her face looked drained and numb. She'd stayed up half the night with Leigh while Leigh polished all of her tack—all except for the boots, which Leigh's father did for her at dawn, before he left to go run drills on base. Leigh's mother cradled the boot bag in her arms awkwardly, as a childless woman might carry a baby.

"Don't give them to *me*," wailed Leigh, turning up her hands, the horse's lead in one, grooming kit in the other. "What am *I* supposed to do with them? Just put them in the trailer."

"Oh, I'm sorry."

"Well, don't *apologize*—Jesus."

"You guys coming or what?" Mrs. Murray yelled from the bottom of the driveway, where she had parked the rig. She would turn in the road and back up so as not to jackknife it on the way out, and if a car trying to pass honked at her she would yell, "Hold your goddamn horses!" Once Leigh had pointed out the irony of her using this particular expression. Mrs. Murray, perhaps suspicious that she was being insulted, told her, "You know what, Leigh? You think too much."

"Oh, just forget it. I'll take them—it's fine, it's *fine*."

"Good luck, Lees," her mother said. "Good luck, Rye," she added, and she gave the horse a cautious pat on the neck. "Hello, Kath!" she called to Mrs. Murray, but she didn't approach the trailer. Leigh's mother didn't come to the shows anymore. She was scared of horses—scared Leigh might fall. She didn't like to watch Leigh jump and would stand cringing at the rail, sometimes putting her hands over her eyes. That was until last year, when she had gotten so frightened that she'd gone and hid in the horse trailer. Leigh had found her there when the class was over and had ordered her never to come to another show as long as she lived.

BY THE TIME they got Rye loaded, it was a quarter past seven, and Mrs. Murray's face was red. "You oughta get after him, you know," she told Leigh. "You can't let him play you up like that. That horse is spoiled. You think you're going to sell him like that?

You think anybody's gonna buy a pain-in-the-ass horse like that? Excuse my French, but Jesus, somebody oughta get after that horse."

She lit a cigarette and drove too fast down the Houghtons' driveway. The horses had to jostle to keep their footing.

Leigh pulled the collar of her ratcatcher shirt up over her nose and mouth to steal a breath of air.

"You hear me?" Mrs. Murray said. The woman's mahogany hair was limp against her temples—had lost its fight from so many dye jobs. She turned sharply to Leigh to make sure Leigh was listening.

"Yes. I hear you," Leigh said weakly. Mrs. Murray had caught her breathing.

"Kim, roll your window down for God's sake. Get some air in here. Leigh can't breathe."

Leigh always sat between Mrs. Murray and her daughter in the front of the pickup. "Your turn for the middle," Kim would say, and she'd make Leigh sit on the hump.

Mrs. Murray coughed and could not speak. Then she managed to get out, "You find a buyer yet?"

Leigh shook her head.

"Where're you advertising?"

"We're not advertising. We're doing it by word of mouth," Leigh said, briefly enjoying the sound of authority that the phrase seemed to convey.

"You'll never sell him that way," Mrs. Murray said scornfully. "Why aren't you putting an ad in the want ads?"

"Well, we don't want to sell him to just *any*body."

"Excuse me? What about us? We got Piper through the want ads!"

Mortified, Leigh was stumped for a response, but to her relief Mrs. Murray didn't seem to notice. "And Kim cleans up on him. Hah, Kim? Hah, honey?"

"Yes, Mom," Kim droned, her nose in a comic book.

"Course Kim would do real well on any horse." Mrs. Murray put a hand out the window to stop the oncoming traffic as she eased the rig out onto Route Two. "She'd teach that boy to behave all right."

"Oh, I know." Leigh was quick to agree, quick to show she didn't take offense at the implied insult to her own ability.

"Kim wouldn't put up with any of his stuff."

Leigh nodded and smiled, as if Mrs. Murray had just given her a compliment. "I know—I know she wouldn't."

"You're going to miss that horse, though, aren't you?" Mrs. Murray glanced at Leigh. "I'll bet you miss him a lot when you're away at your prep school." Before Leigh could answer, Mrs. Murray said, "Could be for the best, honey. He's too much for you. Way too much. I can't believe your mother let you buy him in the first place. It's called looking for an accident."

"My mother lets me do whatever I want," Leigh said with disdain, as if she would have expected Mrs. Murray to know better.

Mrs. Murray flicked twice on her lighter before she got her next cigarette going, lighting it with one hand, steering with the other. "Feet off the dash, Kim—I'm not blind. How about your father? I'll bet he doesn't let you do everything you want, does he?"

"No," Leigh reflected.

"I wouldn't think so. I wouldn't think Dan would let you get away with much. You toe the line for him, hah?"

Leigh shrugged as Mrs. Murray mock-saluted, cracking herself up.

Kim looked up from her comic book. She was a skinny girl, with a long brown braid down her back and a myopic squint. At nine, she already wore glasses. "How come you're not allowed to ride in private school?"

"Why do you think, Kimmo?" Mrs. Murray jumped on her but waited to hear Leigh's answer, as if she, too, had not necessarily understood the connection between the Houghtons' putting the gelding up for sale and Leigh's going away to boarding school.

"Everybody has to play a team sport," Leigh said, quoting the woman in admissions at the campus where she'd taken a tour last fall—a Georgian quadrangle bordered by a river.

"A team sport? A *team* sport?" Mrs. Murray was incensed. "What the heck's that supposed to mean? Your Pony Club rallies—that's a team, isn't it? That's teamwork if I ever saw it!"

"No—like soccer," Leigh said wearily: They had been over this before. "Field hockey. You have to do something like that." Leigh would be behind her classmates; she had never picked up a stick or a racket or a ball. She had done nothing but ride for eight years. She would be behind the kids at boarding school, and next summer, when she might have gone for her C-3, she would be behind all the Pony Club kids who had ridden all year—Kim, for instance. Already now, even though Kim was four years younger than Leigh, she was only one rating behind her. She might even have been ahead of Leigh, except it took her two or three tries to pass the written parts of the tests, where you had to state the difference between a bone spavin and a bog spavin, or answer questions such as "What is roughage in a pony's diet?"—the part that Leigh could do in her sleep.

"Well, that doesn't sound fair, does it?" Mrs. Murray turned plaintively to Leigh. "That sounds mighty *un*fair, if you ask me. If you ask me—"

"Anyway, I might keep him, you know." Leigh flushed, because she had interrupted Mrs. Murray, but she pressed on. "I might be able to get home on the weekends. I can ride him Sundays and vacations—"

"Not this horse you can't."

"—there are a lot of vacations. It's only a two-hour drive." The desperation in her voice disgusted her. "We could find someone to ride him during the week. We've been looking into it."

"Have a horse you never ride? Now, that's smart! Come on, Leigh. I thought you were supposed to be brilliant—straight A's, your mother's always telling me. Even Kim's got more sense than that." Leigh looked away as a sudden garish expression of glee crossed Mrs. Murray's face. "And she can barely read!"

MRS. MURRAY DROVE fast to make up for the late start and they got to the fairgrounds on time. Leigh and Kim got the horses unloaded while Mrs. Murray went to pick up their numbers.

"What do you have after the warm-up?" Leigh asked Kim. She felt obliged to make conversation while Kim finished Rye's mane.

"I don't know. Mom'll tell me," Kim said. "Hold him still. Don't let him move around, Leigh."

"Sorry."

"I can't do it right if he moves."

"Sorry."

"Shit, Leigh!"

Kim had a horrible mouth. She swore all the time, making swears play different parts of speech ("You're fucking shitting me") or making up new swear phrases ("Jesus Christ of Fuck"). Leigh knew things about Kim, things that Mrs. Murray had confided to Leigh's mother and Leigh's mother had passed on to Leigh, the way she did pretty much everything—Leigh's father's "issues with spending"; her friend Jo-Ann's husband's affair—concluding the confession with "I'm sorry, I probably shouldn't have told you all this." Kim had dyslexia, and Mrs. Murray wished they could afford private school but they couldn't, so Kim had to stay in the special needs classes at the elementary school. She was Mrs. Murray's youngest by a good five years. There was Linda, who was fat and sluttish and helped Mrs. Murray with the horses but didn't really ride; and Donny, the older boy, who rode dirt

bikes instead of ponies. "You have to stimulate children," Leigh's
mother would say, after bringing up the subject of Kim's intellectual deprivation to Leigh. "You have to read to them the way I
read to you. We used to sit there for *hours* in the library. Kim's
probably never been read to in her *life*."

"Everybody looks so fucking good," Leigh said. The people
next to them had a blue and white gooseneck rig; a matching blue
and white felt banner with the name of the farm emblazoned on it
had been strung up on the side of the trailer.

"What do you expect for Round Hill?" Kim said, talking with
the pull-through in her mouth. "It's not some shit show."

The elastic waistband of Leigh's breeches was cutting into the
flesh of her stomach. She yanked them up, then inched them
down, trying to alleviate the tightness.

"You want me to do his forelock, too?"

"Could you?" Leigh said quickly. "Do you mind, Kim?"

"Why the fuck should I care?"

When they were pulling on their boots, Leigh had a fleeting
sense of superiority for hers shone with a high military gloss. She
said, trying to sound casual, "Is it me, or do the jumps look insanely big?"

Kim put a hand over her eyes and squinted across the fairgrounds toward the closest ring, where the course for the first
class, the warm-up, was being set up. She made a face. "You're always scared, Leigh."

"I am, aren't I?" Leigh gave a laugh to show that her comment
had been lighthearted. A couple of years ago she had been packed
around the courses on her old pony. But then she had seen Rye in
an ad in the *Horseman's Exchange* and she had wanted him so badly
she had cried every night when her mother put her to bed. Her
father got wind of this and said they would buy the horse. From
the minute the gelding's former owners had dropped him off—
Butterscotch already sold, to a student of Mrs. Murray's—Leigh

had known it was a huge mistake; the horse was too much for her, way too much. It was called looking for an accident.

She walked over to the far side of the trailer, where Rye was tied, saddled up and ready to go. She ran a hand down his neck and chest and under his girth, ran her stirrups down the leathers, reflexively checking their length under her armpits.

"You going to be good today?" The horse's ears went forward, as she walked around to the other side, then his eyes rolled forward so that the whites showed. He was flea-bitten gray in front, dappled behind—"mixed up as they come," Mrs. Murray said. His expression seemed to answer her, "Who, me?" Leigh was just quoting Mrs. Murray. The horse was never good. Or bad. He was just out of control. He was four years old, he was totally green, and Leigh couldn't handle him. When she got into the ring her thoughts went blank as she tried not to get run away with.

Leigh's stomach turned and she leaned against the wheel hub of the trailer for a minute, closing her eyes.

"You all right, Leigh?" Mrs. Murray was back.

"Oh, sure. We're almost ready. We're about to get going." The light, when Leigh opened her eyes, seemed artificial. In the distance, Barbie riders rode model horses.

"Take a sip of this. It's not too strong."

Leigh mouthed the Styrofoam cup of black coffee without drinking. "That's better."

"Sure. You just got jitters."

While Leigh fixed her hat over her hairnet, Mrs. Murray untied Rye from the trailer, tightened his girth a hole, making the horse lay his ears back and fling up his head. "Always playing, aren't you?" She chuckled and cinched up the other billet tight. "Come on, Leigh, show-on-the-road time."

"God, my boots feel tight."

"Better get out there." Mrs. Murray unwrapped Leigh's coat from the dry cleaner's plastic and unbuttoned the top button. She held out the coat and helped Leigh into it; Kim took care of herself, got herself ready—that was the routine. "Here now, all set, hah?"

"I guess so."

"Sure you are." Mrs. Murray crumpled up the plastic to throw it away. "Better step on it, Leigh. You want to make sure you give him a good look around. Lotta funny-looking stuff here. Gotta work out the kinks, honey."

She untied the gray and led him out from the trailer.

"Here, honey, ten fingers."

Leigh put her left foot in Mrs. Murray's hands but Rye danced away, playing her up. "Hold still, Rye!"

"I can't reach from here!" Leigh cried.

Mrs. Murray dropped Leigh's foot and brought Rye up sharply. "Hold still, Rye!"

"He doesn't respond well to being bullied, Mrs. Murray! He's a sensitive horse!"

"You gettin' on, Leigh, or you wanna make a production of this?" Mrs. Murray said, exasperated.

"I'll lead him over to the fence and get on there."

"Come *awun*!" She threw Leigh up into the saddle.

"It's *o*kay, it's *o*kay, Rye," Leigh said theatrically, steadying the horse, fishing for her other stirrup.

"Boo!" said Mrs. Murray.

Leigh's face went scared, then angry, as Rye shied. Before she could say anything, Mrs. Murray barked, "G'head! G'head! Ya late, Leigh!" and turned away in disgust toward the trailer. Leigh shortened her reins and called up to Kim to wait. The younger girl was ten yards ahead, rising in her stirrups above the bay's fat rump and sausage tail. Classy, Mrs. Murray's daughter looked, on a horse, with her short torso and long legs.

THEY HAD EQUITATION in the morning and children's hunter in the afternoon. Between classes, Mrs. Murray spit on a rag and rubbed their boots. "Judge is a real bastard," she said when Kim came away empty-handed after a couple of decent rounds. Kim shrugged, putting her head down on the bay's neck, pretending to go to sleep.

"Ay, sit up, there!"

"But Mom, what's the problem in *between*—"

"You heard me. Get your hair out of your face! Keep him walking! Don't let him stand there steaming."

On the far side of the warm-up ring, Leigh was circling Rye to calm him down—jog, walk, jog, walk—but she couldn't keep him at a walk. Above her choker her face was turning pink.

"He's working up a lather, Leigh," Mrs. Murray rebuked her. "That's no good. You're leaning on his mouth."

Leigh nodded, saying nothing. She waited until she was on the far side of the ring again. After making sure Mrs. Murray wasn't looking, she pressed her left hand into the crest and with her right hand she wrenched Rye's head around viciously. The horse stopped dead, his jaw flexed open against the bit, his nose twisted almost to her knee. "Just stop it!" she pleaded. "Give it a fucking rest!" When she loosened the reins and let him walk again, a girl riding by on a chestnut pony gave her a curious look. Leigh could have cried for shame. She leaned over Rye's neck and gave him an ostentatious pat, as if she had been teaching him a lesson. "Good boy!" she exclaimed. "Good boy—you're *such* a good boy, Rye! Sometimes you act up a little, but that's okay, we all do." On the short side of the ring, straining to sound natural, she said, "I think I'm going to skip the flat class, Mrs. Murray. He's too wound up."

"There's the spirit that won the West!" Mrs. Murray got after Kim some more. "Keep his head up, Kim—you know better than that. Shouldn't have to tell you."

"Yes, Mom."

"Well, maybe I'll just take a little break!"

"That's pointless, Leigh," Mrs. Murray said as Leigh came into the center of the ring and slid off. Rye pranced at the end of the reins. "That horse is high as a kite. He needs to be worked, he needs exercise—calm him down."

"You see, that's actually the funny thing, Mrs. Murray," Leigh said, aware of how red her face was, how close to tears she was. "It's not really exercise when he's like this. It's really more like expending manic energy, you know what I mean? It's not really a workout—it's not exercise per se—"

"You're not making sense, Leigh!" Mrs. Murray said, not looking at her. "You're talking too much! And nobody knows what the hell you're talking about."

"No, but Mrs. Murray, listen to what I'm actually saying." Leigh was cut off by the loudspeaker's crackling to life to announce the ribbons for their last class, open equitation over fences. Kim had gotten second. Mrs. Murray's face went tight, trying not to look pleased. "Guy finally came to his goddamn senses!" she called across the ring to another woman instructor, a friend of hers. Then Leigh's name came ripping across the warm-up ring: She had gotten sixth.

"Oh, my *God*," Leigh blurted out.

Mrs. Murray whooped and hugged her, Leigh grinning madly into the woman's collarbone, letting herself be half crushed—delirious with joy. "What did I tell you, honey? What did I tell you?" Leigh stuck her foot in the stirrup and hopped around grabbing at the cantle, trying to get the purchase she needed to mount.

"I'll give you a leg up, Leigh, Jesus Christ!" Mrs. Murray was coughing and laughing and coughing. Kim watched them curiously from where she had halted Piper along the rail, waiting for Leigh so they could go and collect their ribbons together. Mrs. Murray wiped the foam from Rye's mouth. "Wait, *wait*!" She was giving Leigh's boots a final flourish with the rag. "Don't forget to thank the judge, now!"

Afterward, when they had reconvened at the trailer for lunch, Mrs. Murray said, "Kim, don't you have something you want to say to Leigh?"

"Congratulations, Leigh," Kim droned, her face already back in her comic book.

"Leigh?"

"Congratulations, Kim." If there was one thing Mrs. Murray wouldn't tolerate, it was a bad sport.

They sat on the Houghtons' plaid wool blanket and ate their lunches. Leigh had peanut butter and orange marmalade on whole wheat and Kim had peanut butter and Fluff on Wonder Bread. "We're not into health food," Mrs. Murray would say. Leigh also had carrot sticks, for herself and Rye, and a bag of mint Milanos her mother had put in the cooler for her to share with the Murrays. Mrs. Murray didn't eat much; she smoked. It was pleasant, sitting in the shade of the trailer, the horses munching hay, the red and green ribbons fluttering from the open window of the truck, the three of them united in the camaraderie of winning.

"Bastard finally came to his senses," Mrs. Murray said, shaking her head. "They get these judges up from New York, they think they're gonna come in, shake things up . . . It's bullshit."

"What's this say," Kim said, her finger on the page. "Ann-tag. Tag-GOAN—"

"Antagonist," Leigh said automatically, her mouth full. Kim looked up at her mother.

"That's right, Kim," Mrs. Murray said sharply. "Listen to Leigh! She knows what she's talking about."

Embarrassed, Leigh reached for another cookie, but Mrs. Murray said, "You sure you want to keep eating those, Leigh? They're pretty fattening."

Leigh smiled wanly. "Maybe I won't."

"Probably a good idea."

Leigh watched her wrap up the bag of Milanos. Mrs. Murray stretched out on her side, lighting a new cigarette. "I just had an idea, Leigh, since you're going to skip the flat class. You want Kim to ride Rye this afternoon? You guys want to swap?"

Leigh hesitated. "Swap—horses, you mean?"

"No—dogs. Come on, Leigh. Use that noggin!" Mrs. Murray exhaled loudly. "Kim could take him in the junior jumpers."

Leigh began to pick at a scab on her arm.

"Kim rides Rye in the jumpers and you take Piper in the children's hunter—could be fun, Leigh. You might win." She cleared her throat. "I was even thinking we might buy him off your dad. Kim's gotta graduate from Piper sometime. Think your dad would cut me a deal?" Mrs. Murray cackled at the idea of this.

Leigh pulled on her gloves, flexed her hands, and peeled them off. "But, I mean—Rye's never done jumpers before. Wouldn't it be kind of . . . I don't know, sudden, you know?"

"He'd make a great jumper, Leigh, and you know it. The stuff you've got him in now? It's a waste of his talent." Abruptly Mrs. Murray stopped. Kim flipped a page of her comic book. She was sitting Indian-style, her back curved in a C, her elbows on her knees, chin in her hands. It looked uncomfortable to Leigh—she didn't understand how Kim could hold the position. "Tell you what," Mrs. Murray said, consulting the printed yellow show program. "You ride him in the children's hunter and then Kim takes him in the jumpers—they don't conflict. He could do both." She studied the show program for another second. "The jumpers go first. Perfect, it'll take the edge off. Calm him down."

Leigh nodded, as if she were in agreement. She got abruptly to her feet. Rye, tied to the trailer, turned his head inquisitively. *Who, me?*

Leigh ran a hand down the horse's neck to between his legs, checking him for sweat. "But, I mean, wouldn't that be too much? He'd get really tired, wouldn't he? I mean, you're talking about ten classes or something."

"Tired?" Mrs. Murray cried. "You were telling me a minute ago he's too crazy to ride!"

"No, but I mean, I don't know—it just seems like a lot for one day." She went and got her brush box out of the back of the truck.

"What do you have today," Mrs. Murray said, looking intently up at Leigh. "Six classes?"

"Seven, actually."

"Six! Seven! You're a bleeding heart, Leigh!" Mrs. Murray dashed out her cigarette, half smoked. She closed up the cooler and stood up and stretched. "A bleeding heart." Shaking her head and looking deep into Leigh's eyes, she pinched her on the cheek. "Just like your mother, aren't you?"

Leigh smiled uncertainly.

Laughing, Mrs. Murray brushed crumbs from her jeans and hoisted them up from the belt. "Oh, God—remember? Hiding in that trailer when you jumped. And what were you jumping? Two-six? Two-nine? I'll never forget that." She shook her head, as she went around to the far side of the rig, where Piper was tied. "Hiding in the trailer like you were doing grand prix."

Her heart pounding, Leigh squatted down with a can of hoof polish to paint Rye's feet.

"Kim, get over here. You gotta fix his tail."

"In a minute."

"Now, Kimmo!"

The cooler with the remains of their lunch was sitting on the ground against the back wheel of the truck. Leigh set the polish brush down crosswise on the can and reached over, fumbling slightly with the latch. Her hand seized the crumpled bag of cookies. She took out two of them. She didn't have pockets in her breeches so she placed the cookies carefully into the brush box. Her lips puckered up to whistle as she took up the brush again.

"Caught ya!" Mrs. Murray was pointing gleefully. "Couldn't wait, hah?"

"Oh, fuck you!" Leigh straightened up all at once, her face aflame.
Kim's face shot up from the comic book.

"What did you say to me?" Mrs. Murray blinked at Leigh.

"Nothing."

"No, Leigh: What did you say to me?"

"Nothing."

"What the *hell* did you say to me?" There was something comic
in Mrs. Murray's outrage now that she was getting warmed up.
Leigh bit her cheek so as not to laugh. *"What did you say to me?"*

"You're scaring him!" Rye backed up to the end of his lead as
Mrs. Murray muscled up into Leigh's face.

Backed into the trailer, Leigh sat down on the wheel hub. She
turned her head to the side. Unable to move farther away from
Mrs. Murray, she tensed for the smack.

"You know, you're a goddamned spoiled brat!" Mrs. Murray
yelled.

"Well, you know what?" Leigh cried wildly. "You're an abusive
mother!"

"Ex*cuse* me?"

"Did you ever consider that it might be your fault Kim has
dyslexia? You have to read to children, you know! You have to
stimulate them, for Christ's sake! I'll bet Kim's never been read to
in her life!"

"Mom. *Mom.*"

The quick-release knot had slipped and Rye was loose.

"Where do you think you're going, Leigh?" Mrs. Murray called.
Seizing the opportunity to escape, Leigh had gone after the horse.

Up ahead, Rye had broken into a floating, uncertain trot, un-
sure what to do with his freedom.

"Want me to get some grain, Mom?"

"Leigh Houghton!"

"I'll rattle it in the bucket!" Kim called.

Rye stopped to tear at a patch of grass and Leigh lunged for the lead line but the horse played her up, picking up his head and trotting off another few paces.

"Leigh, you get back here!"

With a dash and another lunge that wrenched her arms from their sockets, Leigh reached out and caught the end of the line. "Leigh, goddamnit!" As she was choking up on the lead, the loudspeaker crackled and Rye shied violently away from her, yanking the cotton through her hands. "Fuck!" Leigh screamed in pain, tripping and stumbling after him, her eyes smarting. People were watching them from the bank of trailers as she lunged again for the trailing lead. "Hold still!"

Mrs. Murray was coming up after her. "Hold it right there, Leigh!"

"Hold still!" Leigh yanked the horse to a standstill again. He kept fussing, dancing away from her as if he didn't know that he ought to be on her side, as if he were enjoying making a fool of her. She took the end of the line and snapped it at the horse's barrel as hard as she could. She'd teach him a lesson. Rye's head was thrown up, his ears flat back as she raised the line again and brought it down across his flank. "Hold still! Hold still! Hold still!" she sobbed. "Hold still, you fucking piece of shit horse!"

A sickening awareness came to Leigh, like the long second in the air after you'd been thrown but before you hit the ground. Mrs. Murray had tackled her. She lay crumpled in a fetal position, her mouth open against the dirt, the wind knocked out of her. "I want my mother," she whimpered. "I want my mother!" She struggled to prop herself up on her elbows, to look around.

Rye had trotted off a few yards and put his head down to graze. Kim was walking up behind him, shaking a bucket of grain.

Then Leigh's view was blocked as Mrs. Murray straddled her. "You touch that horse again," she said, panting—she shoved

Leigh to the ground with a hand on her collarbone. The other, Leigh saw, brandished a jumping bat. "And I'll take this crop and beat the crap out of you."

IN THE PORTA-JOHN, where Leigh had fled, the toilet paper was gone and the air was hot and fetid. Leigh repeated the words, laughing to herself. "Beat the crap out of you! Beat the fucking crap out of you!"

She looked wryly at the lucky underwear—hearts—she had put on that morning. The fleshy white thighs spread out beneath her did not seem to be her own but those of a forty-year-old woman.

When she emerged, Leigh saw a girl waiting whom she recognized from the circuit of shows. She made a point of going over to the younger girl, who was standing with her mother, and saying hello. "I hope I don't mess up the children's hunter too badly," she said self-deprecatingly. "Rye's been going *fairly* well but you never know, do you? That in-and-out has been a *bear* for us today. Well, good luck, Katie! I hope you win! Nice to see you, Mrs. Ferris. See you again sometime."

She lingered at the edge of the field where the vans and trailers were parked, excited, but unable to make herself return, wondering with a shiver what she would say. She took a meandering approach, imagining them watching her—watching her all the way, imagining the punishment Mrs. Murray would have in store for her, how severe it would be. She might tell Leigh she had to clean out the trailer and muck stalls for her for a week if she wanted to ride at all this afternoon. Or she might tell her she was going to tell her father everything that had happened—or threaten her with having to find her own ride home. She had threatened her before.

No one stirred from the Murrays' trailer, however. At first Leigh thought it was deserted but then she heard Rye munching hay. Leigh hadn't seen him at first because he was tied on the far side of the trailer. They had moved him there because it was the shady side now. The horse turned indifferently when she appeared. "There you are, boy!" She came up to him, masking her surprise, even in front of the horse, that no one was waiting for her. "We'd better hurry," Leigh said. "They're going to start calling numbers soon." But instead of hurrying she sat dawdling against the wheel hub of the trailer, taking her own sweet time, thinking of unrelated things—the letter she had received from her roommate-to-be in September, who said she lived on "Park Avenue in Manhattan" and was "ranked in tennis."

Leigh let several minutes go by before she stood up and said brightly, "You know what, boy? I think we're done for today. We wouldn't want you to get too tired, would we?" She took her grooming kit from the pickup truck, dug out the seam ripper, and began to rip out the horse's braids, tearing through each thread with a sharp jerk. When the announcement for her next class, the first in the children's hunter division, came over the loudspeaker, Leigh paused for a second, listening with an ironic yet understanding smile, like that of someone who, through her good grace and maturity, has learned to swallow disappointment. Then she went back to taking out Rye's braids, humming a little tune as she worked. She ripped through the remaining threads and loosened the braids themselves until the steel-colored mane was crimped and fluffy, like a woman's after a permanent.

In the distance the man on the loudspeaker congratulated someone on a clear round in the children's hunter over fences.

Leigh got a bucket of water and sponged Rye off. She walked him dry, letting him stop here and there to graze. She rubbed his legs and carefully bandaged them for the ride home. She sprayed him and put on his fly sheet so he could be comfortable. She refilled his water bucket and made sure he had enough hay. At one point she thought she heard Mrs. Murray coming back and she immediately struck an insouciant pose, banging the curry comb against her boot, just waiting, waiting, for Mrs. Murray to confront her. But it was another mother looking for her daughter—she laughed and apologized for getting the wrong trailer. "Oh, please!" said Leigh, ever courteous. "Please don't worry about it!"

When there was nothing left to do for the horse, she sat in the cab of the truck, her ankles resting through the open window. She flipped through Kim's comic book. It was violent and stupid—the kind of thing a boy would read. Leigh cast it aside. She pulled down the driver's side sunshade to block the late afternoon sun. Clipped to it were some photographs of horses. They were old and dirty to touch, in the rusty, overly bright colors of the seventies. No Pony Clubber, Mrs. Murray, riding bareback, with feathered hair and cutoffs. What was it her father called the woman? A real battle-ax. Leigh gave a laugh, aloud, and laughed again; she felt very droll, seeing the humor in the situation.

For a long time, it seemed, she watched the particles of dust in the path the sun made. Eventually she remembered the cooler in the back of the truck, and one by one, she ate all of the cookies out of the bag.

AT LAST THE Murrays returned, leading the bay gelding between them, the reserve-champion ribbon fluttering from his headstall. That was the extra delay—they had been waiting for the awards to be given. Leigh rolled down the window and stared at Mrs. Murray, daring the woman to meet her eyes, but Mrs. Murray did not look at her. When they got close, Mrs. Murray said, "We'll make him a bran mash tonight, ay, Kimmo?" and she put her arm around her daughter's shoulders. "He deserves it, hah?"

"Yeah, Mom." Kim seemed glad of the embrace; she was smiling faintly and looking at the ground.

Leigh banged out of the cab of the truck and stood against the door, her arms folded across her chest. Mixing a wash bucket for Piper, Kim glanced furtively at her. The sharp smell of the liniment made Leigh feel it was intolerable to be excluded and when Kim began to wash the bay, Leigh said, "I'll scrape him."

"I'll scrape him, Kimmo," Mrs. Murray said.

But Leigh had the scraper in her hand.

"G'head, then," Mrs. Murray said gruffly, turning away.

Leigh began to follow Kim's hasty sponge, scraping water from the bay's coat.

"What happened?" Kim mumbled. "You just didn't want to ride?"

"It was silly, I know," Leigh said, raising her voice so that Mrs. Murray would hear her. "I guess I just felt like it wasn't our day, you know?"

NO ONE TALKED on the way home. This time Leigh got shotgun and Kim took the middle. She fidgeted the whole way, reading her comic, sniffing, to show how she suffered. Neither Mrs. Murray nor Leigh paid her any attention. Mrs. Murray kept her eyes on the road; Leigh looked out the window, keeping up her air of pleasant resignation. She looked once at Mrs. Murray's profile, when Mrs. Murray was looking in the rearview mirror to check on the horses. It came to her then that, more than anything, more than angry or shocked or disappointed, Mrs. Murray was simply baffled by her behavior. Leigh had introduced some sickness, or perversion, into Mrs. Murray's life, she saw, which heretofore it had never known.

"I think I'll make Rye a bran mash, too," Leigh said when they were nearly at her house.

At first she thought Mrs. Murray wasn't going to answer, but a minute or two later the woman told Leigh to make sure it wasn't too hot. "Put some molasses in so he likes it," Mrs. Murray said.

"I will," Leigh said. "I'll sweeten it up."

The Murrays dropped Leigh off. Kim and Mrs. Murray lowered the ramp, and Leigh backed the gray carefully off the trailer, thanking them many times for the help, for the ride. When they had closed up the ramp and Leigh was leading Rye away, Kim's horse whinnied from inside the trailer. Rye raised his head, pricking up his ears to listen, and he seemed to be considering what he had heard. But he didn't say anything back. It was as if the horse were above all that, above bothering with any kind of a qualifying comment. Holding him at the top of the driveway, Leigh watched the rig get under way. Kim's face appeared out the passenger window, looking back at Leigh, sardonic. She waved something— Leigh's green ribbon, the sixth place from the equitation class. Leigh had forgotten to take it with her. Kim waved it—"Bye-bye. Bye-bye. Bye-bye"—as the trailer went down, down to the end of the driveway. Then they took a left turn and were gone around the corner, and the chirping of the crickets began to fill in around the noiseless hole the Murrays had made.

Leigh turned Rye out in the field. She stood beside the house and watched the horse roll in a favorite grassless spot, then wander to the trough to get a drink. He raised his fine head, water dripping from the slack lower lip. *Who, me?*

Leigh could hear noises from inside the house, and then "Lees? Is that you?"

She reached up to brush the grime off her cheek with the back of her wrist. It was the end of August and it was still hot out, even so late in the day. Even her face was hot. Her head felt as if it were buzzing on the inside, just behind her eyes. Angrily she told herself that it was nothing different—it was always like this at the end of a show: This time of day just broke you down.

"Lees?" Leigh's mother called again. "Honey, are you there? I must have fallen asleep."

For a second Leigh couldn't speak she was so enraged, but then, in the background, she heard her father's voice. "Is that Lee-lee?" he said. "How'd we do?" and when her parents came to the door together, Leigh said, "Great! Great! Kim did really well, of course, and *I'm* just so glad I'm going out on a good note, you know?" She followed them inside the house.

Eden's Gate

"THESE ARE THE specials for tonight," sighs the waitress, and she props a chalkboard against a ladderback chair with a long-suffering air, as if Jessica and Josh have requested some onerous exertion on her part. Famished after the laughably long drive over from the B&B on Route Twenty-five, Josh notes the attitude, as well as the young woman's ridiculously large breasts, dismisses the former as a local intolerance for outsiders—that is, for rich people—and tries to concentrate on the food. It's the kind of place, so Jessica told him on the way over, where you get a choice of fries, rice pilaf, or a baked potato with your main; where the French onion soup will come in a "crock"; where the waitresses, in "colonial" gray shirtdresses and white pinafores, lifers all of them, will mother them and call them—both of them—"sweet-hat." She offered up these proofs of authenticity in a tone of such triumph that Josh sensed that L.A.—and by extension himself—was being indicted. But now this martyr girl who can't be any older than they has appeared (albeit wearing the costume), and the entrées have been tarted up with Thai dipping sauces and herb-infused oils and—here it comes—a reference to "how our chef prefers to do it." So now it's Jessica's turn to take it personally. Hands clasped in her lap, she listens much too intently, the look on her face so ominously pleasant that Josh loses track of the choices as he tries to remember where, in his girlfriend's elaborate hierarchy of grievances, slights from service people fit in: More egregious than men at dinner parties failing to draw her out about her career? Less, perhaps, than insufficient groveling from Sandy, her agent? He'd *like* to think that her irritation has something to do with what's at stake tonight. Despite the many conditional advances and retreats from both sides, she can't be completely sure (can she?) that he's bought the ring. For the tenth time since they left the B&B, his right hand feels inside his blazer pocket and closes around the velvet box from Tiffany's. He'd like to go on holding it, if it didn't look weird.

". . . seared sea scallops with a celery-root remoulade." The young woman mispronounces the last syllable, giving it a long *a,* and Josh, embarrassed for her, gives her an encouraging smile, which he then has to hold, idiotically. When finally she comes to the end of her list, the girl does something unexpected: Instead of bustling off, she boldly meets his eye. It's one of those direct looks that are so wildly presumptive Josh doesn't have the presence of mind to repudiate it before she's gone, walking across the room with a tarty, self-satisfied smugness.

"Oh, my God, I know her."

"Yeah?" says Josh eagerly, leaping at this unexpected conversational salvation.

"Susan O'Hare—how crazy," Jessica says, somewhat disingenuously, Josh thinks. After all it was she who chose the inn for tonight's dinner—"the only gig in town, trust me," she'd assured him, when he told her he wanted to go somewhere nice on Sunday night of the long weekend, when the wedding they flew out here for, of his writing partner, Rich, would finally be over. The town, in the southwest corner of Massachusetts, is called Maidenhead. And though she hasn't been back in a decade, Jessica spent four years in its eponymous—blissfully eponymous—girls' boarding school.

"Susan fucking O'Hare. I really can't believe it." Seeing that she's determined to milk it, Josh steels himself for another boarding school anecdote—the weekend has been rife with them—in which he'll have not only to show interest but also to hit upon the appropriate reaction (laughter? pity? consternation?).

"They used to call her 'Hairspray,'" Jessica says and, as Josh takes a sip of his water so as not to fidget more obviously, she adds absently, with just the same vacant inconclusiveness, "because when she was giving a blow job to the drama teacher he supposedly came all over her hair."

Josh spits violently into the glass. "Jesus. Now, that's refreshing."

Their eyes meet and they both turn, merrily, in their chairs to have another look at the girl. Their waitress is standing before the hearth at the end of the room, gloomily uncorking a bottle of wine. Despite her finesse at the task—the cork pops neatly out after an expert twist—she admits no pleasure in it, her eyes fixed on the wallpaper on the opposite wall (chipper-looking red and yellow roosters) as if to say *this, too, shall pass.*

She's too severe to be pretty, but, Josh acknowledges, taking another glance, that squeezed-into-her-dress voluptuousness isn't exactly a turn-off. Her heavy red hair, coiled now into a bun, is the dark chestnut variety, not the strawberry; Josh suspects she's vain about it—and about her tits—despite the attitude.

"I always think of her when I hear that Lou Reed song, isn't that funny—now, here she is."

"Was she in that singing group, too?" Josh asks, opening the menu, thumbing the pages to find the booze. "What was it called? Twelve Little Girls with Surprisingly Big Tits?"

"Twelve Little *Maids,*" Jessica says huffily, "and no, she wasn't." With a dismissive look at the list of wines, Josh shuts the menu again. "Let's just get the most expensive bottle they've got."

"She couldn't sing—she couldn't sing a note. But we used to

act together. We both did the plays." Jessica looks quickly at Josh then, appraising him perhaps, and when she speaks it seems it's the first time that night that her voice hasn't been pitched to solicit a particular reaction from him.

(The fact is, he often gets the reaction wrong, responding, for instance, "God, that sucks," as he did absently at the conclusion of one such good-old-days anecdote in the car tonight, his attention monopolized by the dead-black, snow-banked February roads, the crap steering of the rental car, when he was meant to say, in admiration, "Wow, did it *really?*" [The story in question concerned her dorm room window in her sophomore year. It had apparently been left open during Christmas break and then stayed frozen that way till the March thaw. When she said "frozen," Jessica punched the word a little, as if in meteorological reproach to L.A., whose weather, nine years out, she still maintains—aloud, anyway—a moral uneasiness with.])

But now, without any inflection at all, she says to him, "She was much better than me."

Josh nods, seeming to absorb this. Then he says gravely, "Was she much better than you at giving head, too?"

"Seriously, Josh!" Jessica cries. "I wept the night I saw her in *Macbeth.* I ran behind the schoolhouse and I leaned up against this tree and I literally bawled my eyes out because I knew I would never be as good as Susan O'Hare. It was, like, *the* moment I knew."

"And now she's a waitress and you're famous," Josh supplies, yawning, deciding on the flank steak, which comes with the best-sounding sides—fried onions, sautéed mushrooms.

Jessica fixes him with implacable brown eyes. "A, I'm not famous, you've got to stop saying that—"

"And B, she's not really a waitress?" he says glibly, and inside his pocket he runs his index finger along the gold indent that separates the two halves of the ring box. It's nothing dramatic or cheesy he's got planned. No bended-knee prostration or diamond to be spooned up in the chocolate parfait. Instead he imagines some version of the walk under the cold night sky of her beloved evergreens, snow crunching obligingly underfoot (the result, as they've been told to repeated, comic effect this weekend, of a major storm the week before), and her hard blond dissatisfaction clinging to him for life. He glances impatiently around the room, takes in the low-beamed ceilings and wide-board floors, the pewter tankards lined up in graduated sizes along the hearth mantel—the unwitting local diners, modest, in their dress khakis and fleece vests, and he has the sense of anticipation that he imagines might precede a bold crime; he has the notion that the place itself will be marked and changed for good. After 250 years, the Colonial Inn of Maidenhead, Massachusetts, will never be the same.

"Forget it," Jessica is saying airily. She examines her menu with consternation. She would like to play at giving him the silent treatment, but fortunately, Josh knows, she doesn't have the willpower. "Go ahead: mock the waitress. You wouldn't understand."

"Oh, come on—"

"You wouldn't understand," she interrupts—and he can hear the triumphant note in her voice as she chances on a specious shortcut to the moral high ground—"because *you* never had to work."

"Right," says Josh. "That's right." A not insignificant element of his desirability she seems to find the particular fact—on the days that it doesn't strike her as fatally damning.

"Anyway, that's not true," Josh says suddenly. "I taught sailing two summers."

"*Had* to work, I said," Jessica says a little too quickly, and the rage in the remark seems to surprise even her. She takes a gulp of her water, and her eyes dart around the room in a detached avian manner, as if to distance herself from it. Barbs like this continue to spring from her lips, despite her success, despite everything. They seem to pick fights on their own when she, as she has frequently averred these last couple of months—her career finally on the trajectory she's wanted and worked for her whole life—has no complaints about her life. (She makes the remark, Josh has noticed, in the tone of someone marveling at her capacity for goodwill: Do you know I gave five thousand dollars to charity this year? Do you know I have *zero* complaints about my life, Josh?)

Thinking it's about time to regroup—start setting the tone for later—Josh reaches across the table, palm open. "I'm sorry I didn't have to work," he says solemnly. "I'm sorry I had dollar signs monogrammed on my bathrobe pockets. Underneath it all I was really just a poor little rich kid crying out for love and affection."

Jessica notes the hand, raises her eyes, and impassively scrutinizes his face. "Susan?" she says abruptly. "Susan O'*Hare?*"

USUALLY SHE HAS good timing—it's something the casting directors cite when she reads for a part. But tonight she's off. The girl was heading back to the kitchen it seems; Jessica has to haul her back, calling shrilly now, "Susan? Susan O'Hare?! It's Jessica—Jessica Lacombe!"

There's a ripple through the dining room. A middle-aged couple look askance at them in the opaque way of older, country people—not ready to excoriate her personally, the way a peer would in L.A. or New York, but startled, simply, by the unpleasantly loud noise of her shout, as if a heavy truck had rattled by.

"You recognize me, right?" Jessica says, with an anxious little laugh, when Susan stands above them once again. She means, of course: Do you recognize me as a former acquaintance? But Josh hears as well the innocuous display of someone new to fame gauging her public: Do you recognize me as someone who has a growing presence in film and television? The new pilot won't shoot till March, but there was *The Sticks,* last year's canceled show that the critics loved, the scene in *Eden's Gate* with Tobey Maguire at Sundance—it won't be long, he thinks, not for the first time . . .

"*Jess*-ica," the young woman says. She draws the name out in the patronizing tone a bad shrink might affect, her voice so blasé that Josh thinks she must have recognized Jess earlier and planned this reaction. "Jessica Lacombe. How are you?"

Jess falters, agonizingly. "I thought it was you!" She clears her throat. "I told Josh, we'd probably run into some people I knew. We came in Thursday on the—the overnight flight," she says, apparently rejecting *red-eye* at the last minute. "Josh's writing partner—his—his colleague from work, got married in Salisbury. Of course, we had to drive over here for dinner, say hi."

Josh lets her fumble on keeping up the pretense of camaraderie—he's damned either way, experience tells him: If to refrain from intervening is not to care about her, to come to her rescue is to condescend.

"I was just telling Josh, oh, my God, Susan O'Hare was the most amazing actress." Jessica slaps her palms on the table in a gesture that's evidently meant to be a cheerful punctuation to this remark but instead looks awkward and odd. Josh is surprised she'd go there; she can be so guileless sometimes, so naïvely self-deprecating it backfires—redoubling the envy.

Susan lets the compliment pass with a magisterial silence, as if she's awaiting permission to speak, as of course she would, Josh thinks, considering that they're the paying customers and she is but a lowly service person. A knife slides excruciatingly to the edge of the table, clatters to the wood floor as Jessica grabs ineffectually at it. "But, gosh, it's been forever," she says, stopping herself—just—from bending to the floor to retrieve it when Susan makes no motion to do so herself. "How are you?"

At this, Susan raises her eyebrows sardonically at Josh and

though this is outrageous, Josh is no longer surprised. He's identified her, by now, as the type of waitress who tries to make a private pact with the man, letting the female half of the couple immolate and go to hell. It's a phenomenon they know well, from early in their relationship, when nobody in L.A. knew who she was but everyone recognized Al Stein's—the studio head's—son. Once in a Thai restaurant a cocktail waitress actually said to her, "And you are . . . ?" "Jessica Lacombe?" Josh said rudely, as if the girl was a complete fuckwit for not having heard of her. Josh shifts in his chair remembering—he got a blow job that night, yes, indeed; she loved him for that.

"I'm just . . ." Susan turns her palms up—looking for a word that will adequately express her joy. "I'm just great, Jessica. Things are truly great."

"And you're—you're living here? In Maidenhead? Well, I mean, obviously, you're *living* here . . . Wait, that's right! You grew up here—you were a day student!" she remembers, as Susan waits, patient as a vulture, for Jessica to dig herself in deeper and deeper.

It's funny, Josh thinks, watching her writhe and squirm, because usually poise is what attracts people, and Jessica is not poised. And it's early to attribute the quick looks as they came in tonight to fame, though she will of course be famous. (He finds her dogmatic maintaining of uncertainty on this front an amusing, puerile superstition. She knocks a lot of wood, as well; touches the medal of some Catholic saint that's clipped to the sun shade of her Miata when she runs a red light.) Nor is it her looks alone that you'd notice. If anything, the requisite blondness and thinness, the sad eyes countered by a mouth that smiles too easily, as if to preempt envy, undersell her. (Before he knew her, at the Oscar party where they met in fact, he'd heard her described, with telling condescension, as a "very pretty girl." That had been his pickup line: "Those people over there are describing you as a very pretty girl." It had been a thrill to him that she had gotten it— had known it wasn't a compliment. He wanted to lead her off to a dark room and get his hands on her, yet at the same time, he kept up the pretense of non-goal-oriented conversation. Interrupted here and there by an acquaintance of his, or hers, but mostly his, he felt a gnawing pit in his stomach, not dissimilar to the days leading up to his parents' divorce, as if he had sensed that some self-defining possession of his was profoundly at risk.)

"Wow, still putting up with the Maidenhead winters. I was telling Josh"—Jessica gestures rather wildly to him—"how when we walked to breakfast in the mornings, our hair used to freeze— oh, but that was just the boarders, I guess. He grew up in L.A., so the idea of ice that doesn't come in a rink with heated locker rooms—" But before she can finish her umpteenth dig at Josh's spoiled half-sisters, who skate competitively at such a facility, Susan squats down beside their table and says in a bizarrely inflected stage whisper, "I am *so* sorry to interrupt because this is *fascinating,* but it would be sooooo helpful if you guys could decide what you want to order." With a grimace for Josh alone, as if the two of them might yet be in this together, she jerks her head toward the kitchen to indicate some presumed demand.

"Sure, let's order," Josh says, and he can see Susan sucking out his eagerness to be rid of her and twisting it into a compliment— a desire on his part to personally help her out. "Do you want to just leave now and go fuck in my car?" he'd love to say to her, just to call her on it, except he's too busy cringing as she whispers, "That is so nice, thank you," and winces gratefully at him.

"What a fucking freak," Josh says when she's gone. He gives a loud shudder at the thought of her bizarre, implicating assumptions. "Bluuhhhh!"

Jessica is watching him pensively. She takes a deep calming breath, exhaling through her nose. "It's actually really sad."

No, not tonight! thinks Josh. He might have predicted she would go this way, but had assumed the ad hominem attack would quell the pity.

"She was genuinely talented, Josh."

"Uh-huh."

"She *was*," Jessica says huffily. She's taking herself seriously now—flirting with it, at least—trying out the righteous stance. "And now, yes, okay, I'll say it: She's a waitress. And you know it could be me—it could be the other way around."

"Talk to Sandy," Josh says dismissively, sitting back in his creaky chair, authoritative. "Talk to my *dad*. I know the type. Those girls who go to auditions with their high school plays still listed on their résumé?" He shakes his head. "No way, no how. Not everybody has the killer instinct, Jess. Besides"—he looks around for Susan—"isn't she kind of fat?"

"That's *so* obnoxious. That is so sexist and obnoxious."

He shrugs.

"Especially considering you know that my sister is obese. *And* that I've had eating issues as well, Josh."

Josh makes a gesture like a traffic cop—"bring it on"—as a goateed waiter in a butcher's apron appears to introduce himself and to tell them, "My personal favorite on the whites is the California chardonnay." Over Josh's audible groan, Jessica gives the young man a brilliant smile and says: "Great! That sounds really great." She removes the menu from Josh's place setting and hands it to the man. "Thank you so much . . . Kurt. We'd love to try it."

"God," Jess says, when it's been brought and, over her objection—"I'm sure it's fine"—tasted and poured, "it's really awful." Cautiously, she takes another sip. "No, I mean, obviously it wasn't going to be good but this is—wow, seriously bad. Almost undrinkable."

Josh just shakes his head, looks at her: What am I supposed to say?

"Never mind," she says, and her voice catches.

"Oh, my God. You're actually upset."

"I'm fine." Unaccountably, though, there are tears in her eyes.

"Jess! Come on! Who cares?" He looks at her across the table, gulping and pressing her lips together. "No use crying over oaky chardonnay," he tries. The bad wine should be funny—something they laugh about and forget. But all day he's picked up on this sense of desperation from her, more acute than the usual anxiousness. It's as if she designed this nostalgia day trip to Maidenhead in order to pitch her adolescence to him but has only just realized that she should have presented it to him in an entirely different genre: instead of the edgy, depressing, premium-cable miniseries that aired most nights the first several weeks of their courtship—all anorexia and best friends' backstabbing, near date-rape and walks of shame—a, well, if not a sitcom, then something pretty close—an upbeat hour-long drama, perhaps; *Gilmore Girls* meets *Facts of Life,* filled with learned compromise and character-building challenges. She had gone through school with serious financial aid, after all. Boarding school had been by no means a given, not that she dwelled on it, or seemed to resent in any way the sense of outsiderness it might have created; she only brought it up when it gave her an edge in an argument—when she could play, as she had been playing a minute ago, the poor card.

In the early afternoon, skipping out on the wedding brunch, they had been to see the school itself, though it meant an extra round trip from the remote B&B. "I will say this about these New England boarding schools: They're very picturesque, aren't they?" she'd said, watching his profile carefully, as they drove up the long driveway, past the trim Greek Revival colonials that constituted the original campus, and turned down the river road (the jigsaw-puzzle chunks of ice floating in the running water as if she had cued them to underline the hardship—or at least the inclement weather—she'd overcome), at the end of which the modern buildings lay, the auditorium among them, which housed the theater. "I mean, this is the image of a picturesque New England boarding school, isn't it?"

"It's . . . nice," Josh had said uncomfortably, avoiding looking at her. It was clear she wanted the school's archetypal attraction to confirm something for him, to satisfy some outstanding question she presumed he had. But while he enjoyed rounding out the picture with a quick visual to go with her story line, he was baffled by the urgency in her voice. He found himself tempted, as the tour dragged on (dormitories, sports fields, though she had never played sports), to say boldly, "I don't give a shit about all this," and would have, if her sudden eagerness to expose this part of her life to him hadn't made him think that would be just a tad harsh.

THIS MUCH HE knows: When Jessica was thirteen, she and her mother, Nancy, conspired for her to leave the Warwick (bumfuck central Massachusetts) public schools and go to Maidenhead. Up till then, boarding school was beyond the family's ken, let alone their means. Vicky, Jessica's older sister by three years, was plowing through Warwick-Dunham High School, head down, blinders on. But plump, embarrassed Vicky, her diffident father's daughter, had never been into theater—that was Jessica's thing; it had been from the age of four, when she used to memorize and perform commercials for the family. By eight she was doing TV commercials out of Worcester: a family-owned Italian restaurant; a furniture warehouse—"Make Yourself a Home!"

With Nancy backing her up (or, Josh suspected, having grown up among the more extreme examples of stage mothers, lying awake nights to strategize), Jessica told Jim that she didn't want to go to Warwick-Dunham because the academics were "pathetic. And only like one person every year goes to a four-year college." This was close to the truth, but unlike her sister, Vicky, a worker bee and teacher's favorite, Jessica was a haphazard student. The real reason she wanted to go to Maidenhead was that she had read an interview in *Seventeen* with the school's one famous graduate— a TV actress from a preppie background, who now played the mother in a prime-time sitcom. The woman had cited the Maidenhead drama program as having nurtured her ambitions—and Jessica wanted to be a movie star. Another thing she considered pathetic was when people were asked what they wanted to be when they grew up and they said, "A teacher, maybe?" as Vicky did, "or a vet?" or "I'm not sure yet, I'll have to see" because she felt they just weren't being honest with themselves and admitting that they of course wanted to be movie stars. Until that career ceased to exist, what else would anyone conceivably want to be?

"SO, JESSICA . . ."

With an unhurried, leisurely air, Susan serves Jessica her butternut squash soup. She sets down Josh's walnut–cranberry– goat-cheese salad in front of him—gives the plate a maternal quarter turn. ". . . You've really done it, haven't you?"

Jessica averts her eyes—preparing to be complimented, Josh realizes, amazed that she can continue to miss the antagonism in her old friend's voice.

"We all saw your spread in *Maxim.*"

"Oh—right." Jessica's burned her mouth on the first spoonful of soup; she has to reach for her water. "God, that was a while ago."

"Jason, the chef, gets it." Susan giggles, hand to mouth, at the lasciviousness of this.

"You don't say," Josh says rudely, starting to get fed up.

"He brought it in one day and there you were on the cover." She turns to Josh.

"There she was! I couldn't be*lieve* it."

"Really?" Jessica frowns. "Well, you have to do it, you know. You've got to get yourself out there. Mine was actually very tasteful—"

"I almost didn't recognize you! I mean, it's not as if you're actually naked, but . . ." She looks again to Josh, as if for confirmation.

"It's pretty close!" he says. Now Jessica looks at him slowly, mistrusting what she's heard.

Susan laughs aloud, again putting her hand to her mouth, a look of worried pleasure in her eyes, as if to say, "Oh, gosh, we shouldn't gang up on her like this, you and I!" "So, are you an actor, too?"

"I'm a writer?" Josh says, the question in his voice a trick he finds useful to keep these interactions brief.

"Oh, wow. What do you write?"

"Television, mostly?"

"Like, scripts? Pilots? They're called 'pilots' aren't they?" Susan says, and giggles at her bold segue into shoptalk. "Oh, did you write that show that Jessica was in—"

"For Christ's sake!" Jessica says. "No, he didn't write that!"

"—that only lasted six episodes?"

"She's so jealous of you!" Josh makes his preemptive bid, lunging for her arm, before Susan's even out of earshot. "She's so jealous of you she can't stand it. You just *know* it was her copy of *Maxim.* I'm sure she ran right out and bought it." He swallows some wine though he keeps telling himself not to drink it, it's that bad, and cracks up at his own picture: "I bet she owns the boxed set of your Clearasil commercials."

Jessica puts her spoon down and looks out into the dining room, visibly trying to control herself, her mouth working, her eyes flashing. "It's not funny."

"It *is,* though—here she's this fucking waitress . . . !"

" 'Fucking waitress.' You just can't stop, can you?"

"Oh, come on!"

"Where the hell do you get off, Josh?"

"Bullshit, Jess—you can't have it both ways!" Knowing he's

risking a blow-up, Josh sticks with his stance: "What'd you want me to do? Make a long speech about how you're a *serious actor*? You want me to defend your career to some fucking waitress?" Defiantly, nervously, he picks up his fork and knife and starts on the salad.

"It's not my fucking fault that your dad gave me my first job," Jessica says after a moment.

"My God, Jess!"

She begins to spoon her soup, her face tense with misgivings. Josh wishes he could reassure her—none of that matters now: Dad was just a conduit. Like God, Al Stein helps only those who help themselves. But with the marriage proposal in the air, it's become a taboo subject. And right now, as when he Googled her before their first real date (they'd slept together a few times but had yet to have dinner) and what he found left him omnisciently speechless in her presence, he's afraid he'll expose himself once again as knowing too much if he says anything now. A few months ago, just after she got the final payments for *The Sticks,* Josh found a crumpled Starbucks napkin in a Windbreaker of his that Jessica likes to borrow. On it was a budget of sorts, a list of income set against large itemized expenses—rent, food, clothing, car; a fifth category she called "personal maintenance." He couldn't fathom it, but it was definitely her handwriting. It took him a day or two before he understood it. She had tallied up an alternative life, one in which his parents don't own the house they live in, in which she pays her own way and always had. On the napkin she had added up the money she would owe him now, as if she was contemplating paying him back. Uneasily, he had recalled a plan then, a short-lived plan, which he himself had never taken seriously: that when she moved in with him, she would pay him rent. He hadn't cashed the first check she pressed on him (and there had been just the one). He thought he'd squirrel it away and drag it out in a couple years, give it to her framed—remind her of her salad days. As for now, he'd told her, pocketing the check, he would be demanding sexual favors instead.

"So was he at least hot?" he says, polishing off the salad.

"Who?" Jessica frowns suspiciously.

"The drama teacher whose dick she——" He pumps his fist to his mouth.

It's a gamble, but she relents, the tiniest bit amused, and gives a long sigh, like a teacher dealing with a remedial student. "No. Mr. Tooker was not hot. Mr. Tooker looked like . . . Al Delvecchio."

"God, no wonder he was molesting all the girls," Josh says broadly, but finds himself fighting a wave of uncertainty now. In his pocket, he grasps the ring again. This bonding over TV references: It reminds him of the kind of thing you talk about after a one-night stand with a girl, as they indeed—he doesn't see fit to remind her—talked about the morning after what he assumed would be theirs (somewhat predictably, ABC's *Love Boat/Fantasy Island* lineup of the early eighties). But then he reminds himself, exhaling, that it's a sign of maturity that he doesn't need them to have everything in common. He doesn't need to be able to discuss the political situation in the Middle East with his fiancée. This was how he put it to his shrink, as he described what he called a "breakthrough": "I don't need to be able to discuss the political situation in the Middle East with her, you know?"

AT LAST JOSH has coaxed her back with him, on the cozy track toward bliss. Generic cozy restaurant glow, which tonight is replicated by the fire in the hearth and enhanced by the black New England cold beyond the mullioned windows, has begun to infuse not only their faces and their fellow diners' faces, but their thoughts as well. She makes herself vulnerable; he is generous. He tones down the glibness. They touch frequently across their entrées—the acceptably indigenous flank steak and halibut. A big wedding, he thinks, in Santa Monica—the beach, maybe, or wine country. He's already assured his mom that she won't want to be married at home.

When Jessica goes to the bathroom, he dares to upgrade the wine.

"Sorry," says Josh, coming clean as she returns and tries the new stuff—an Oregon pinot noir he had missed earlier. "It had to be done."

"Whatever," she says, but he knows she can't keep up the censure because she's greedy about her wine and clearly likes this one. "It's probably the high point of his night recommending the chardonnay—but whatever, Josh."

"He'll survive," Josh says, topping off their glasses.

"So, anyway, you see her in *Macbeth* with the boys' school— Whiplash Soldiers or whatever—"

"*Whipple*, Josh—it's not that hard—"

"Whiplash Johnnies or whatever, and it's the worst night of your life." While she was in the bathroom Josh decided he would be the good boyfriend and hear this one out. How she almost ended up a waitress, how but for a few chance strokes of Fate.

"Yeah, and after I have my half-hour crying fit I go back there to congratulate her."

"God, that is so you." He shakes his head at the realization that she was already following some arcane, self-flagellating code by the age of fourteen.

"And I'm really embarrassed because she's such a loser, and I'm talking to her, trying to get it over with and get out of there, and instead of thanking me for the compliment, she's like, 'I think I saw you at auditions.' I had tried out, but when I didn't get the lead I said screw that. She's like, 'I'm sorry it didn't work out, but maybe next time. I'll bet we'll be in something together soon. It's *great* you're interested in drama. And he-ey'"—Josh laughs, she does a good dorky ingenue—"'didn't I see you in the financial aid office at the beginning of the year, Jessica? I'm on financial aid, too. But I suppose it's easier for my parents because, you know, I'm a day student, and it doesn't cost as much.' " Jessica shudders. "She was so—desperate, you know, to draw the line around us both."

"Good luck!" Josh mutters.

"Exactly. I never even noticed I was on financial aid. It was like, who gives a shit? So, then at some point she tells me she'll put in a word for me with Mr. Tooker, for *Our Town,* which they were supposed to be doing next. And I just can't believe she thinks she can condescend to me like that, so I interrupt and I start asking her all about her special relationship with the guy because of course I'd heard the blow job rumors. I say, all sort of impressed and envious, 'So, how far have you and Mr. Tooker gone?' The latest was that she'd fucked him on this drama club outing to Hartford—"

"Hartford!" Josh interrupts, spearing a last bite of steak. "Of course."

"And she's not embarrassed at all! She's like, 'Mostly—' " But Jessica can't continue because she has started to giggle uncontrollably. When she can manage to breathe, she locks eyes with Josh and murmurs, "Is she here? Is she in the room? Because this is really bad. It's like . . . talking about your hosts or something, when you're staying in their house. Anyway, she's like—she's like—" Jessica cracks up again. After two more false starts, she chokes out, " 'Mostly blow jobs—you know. I did let him 'put it in' once or twice, if you count All-State, but that was just for relief.' "

As she dissolves into paroxysms of giggles, one of the older waitresses gives her a darting glance as she passes, hysterics unusual in this quiet, creaky eighteenth-century room, where indulgence is typically moderate—dessert, rather than another cocktail. Josh laughs, too, but his laughter is detached, like his shrink's when the guy is legitimizing his worry, as if to say, *Dude, you were right to be concerned.*

"I'll never forget her saying that: 'That was just for—relief.' God, I told everyone . . . I must've done that line twenty times that night alone: 'That was just for relief.'" Jessica shakes her head.

"What?" he says, catching her in a half smile.

"No, I just—I just thought of this funny line from a horoscope I used to get: 'The stars impel, they do not compel.' So," Jessica concludes happily, as if this were the foregone conclusion the story had been heading for, "I blackmailed him."

Josh, who'd thought the punch line had come and gone, sits up in his chair. "You blackmailed the drama teacher."

She nods. "Oh, yeah."

"I can't believe you."

"I see him in the dining hall the next morning and I'm like, 'Susan O'Hare was so great last night. I talked to her for a *while* after the play.' And he's getting all nervous and he's trying to wrap up the conversation, but he's *scared* to wrap up the conversation, because he doesn't know exactly what I'm implying. So, I'm like, 'Oh, Mr. Tooker? There's just one thing—I'd love to talk to you about the auditions for *Our Town*. I think I'd make a great Emily,' I say."

Josh gives a bark of a laugh at the shamelessness of it. It's like listening to his father tell war stories from his early days in Hollywood—the shit he and Paul Furman used to get up to, the fake business cards they printed up—"Score One Productions" . . . He swallows, as a funny wave of unhappiness washes over him. He busies himself with pouring more wine, does the old everything's-cool outward glance toward the other diners. In a moment the feeling subsides, and the two of them drink silently, not uncompanionably, but with a certain tension in the air of something unresolved. Josh has the feeling of having skipped a sentence a page or two back. "So, after that—what?" he says. "You got all the leads?"

"What? Oh, yes, I mean—sure, of course, I did," Jessica says deprecatingly. "But see, that was the pointless part of it. I would've gotten them anyway." She sounds a little irritated at the waste of ingenuity, as if she'd been cheated of a victory. "She didn't come back. After all that, Susan O'Hare didn't come back. She dropped out at the end of the term. I never even had the chance to beat her."

"Oh, right," says Josh. He nods to himself with an air of finality. "Of course."

It's not until they've ordered dessert and are waiting for their pie that Jessica narrows her eyes, as if studying the color of the wine in her glass, and says lightly, "I'm just curious—what do you mean 'of course'?"

"I mean"—Josh turns his hands up, bored now—"of course she left."

"Ri-ight . . ." Jessica says slowly, as if following a complicated argument. "But, I mean—why would *you* assume that she left school?"

Heedless—perhaps purposefully so—of the warning note in her voice, Josh says flatly, "Come on, your daughter gets raped by some pervert teacher, you're not gonna pull her out of the school?" He smiles and says, "Now—on to something else? *Un peu de champagne,* perchance?"

Jessica regards Josh curiously. "Tooker wasn't why she left. It was a tuition thing. They couldn't afford it anymore. I heard—I mean, she told me herself."

"Right," Josh says. "I'm sure."

"Yeah, I think her father lost his job. He was . . . laid off or something. I forget what he did."

They are tucking into their mud pies when she says pleasantly, "Yeah, I mean, 'rape' is actually a bit strong. I heard—there was this rumor, I mean it was totally assumed—the whole point, Josh, is that she came on to him."

"Oh, so it was her fault, was it?" Josh says with a laugh. Jessica's argument is so absurd it's as if she's baiting him, as if she's daring him to disabuse her of her foolishness. And his girlfriend does depend on him from time to time to sort through questions of morality lite, though more often his role is to release her from the agonies of guilt that attend her every success—to tell her she should be happy, she deserved what she got. "Look, legally, it was rape," he says idly. "Legally speaking, it was statutory rape."

"Well—*statutory* rape," Jessica interrupts. "Date rape! Come on. The point is it wasn't rape rape, it was—the—she had such a big chest, I can't even tell you." She laughs now, too. Part of her shtick with him has always been to be pointedly, provocatively un-PC. "You think she's chesty now? I swear to God, she's had a breast reduction." She eats her ice cream blithely, gesticulates with her spoon. "I mean, if that was rape, we were all raped."

"You all had sex with teachers?" Josh says pedantically, enjoying his prosecutorial moment. "You all let him 'put it in'?"

"Well, that part—she got herself into that. She didn't have to screw the guy."

"That's a bit harsh!"

"I've often wondered," Jessica says reflectively, "what the hell was she thinking—"

"Isn't that pretty obvious—"

"—going all the way with some skanky teacher."

"Isn't that, uh, blaming the victim just a tad?"

"He came on to me, too, you know," Jessica says, so venomously that for a second Josh thinks it's some kind of joke. He sits there swallowing, sweating in his shirt and flinching, wondering where this can possibly end. "My sophomore year, he started dancing me around the room—there was this cast party at his house. He's saying, 'I *made* you'—and all this sick Pygmalion shit. He's got his hands all over my ass and then he's trying to grab my tits. He *suggests*—get this—that I may want to stay late after everyone else leaves!" She leans forward across the table, and all at once her tone drops to gentle, coaxing—he's the remedial student again. "You know what I did, Josh? *I* laughed it off! I went along with the guy for a little while so he didn't freak out and then I went and hid in the bathroom all night. Big fucking deal." Jessica drains a last drop from her empty wineglass, tipping it all the way upside down, her mouth gaping unattractively. "People were all saying, 'Oh, my God, Jess, weren't you traumatized?' You know what? No, I wasn't! It was one of the least traumatic things that ever happened to me. I still did the play—I did every single play, I got all the leads, why wouldn't I? For three fucking years! And every year he was all over me. It was like, okay, cast party, here we go again, let's just let Mr. Tooker grab my tits so we can get it over with." She draws a dramatic breath. "You know what, Josh? He was a great fucking director. Tooker may have had his problems but fuck, he did sort of make me!"

There comes now the sheepish, fraught silence that follows an outburst; neither of them refers to any television show now. "So . . . now do you want to rethink your comment about blaming the victim?"

"Of course *you* laughed it off," says Josh after a moment.

"What the fuck is that supposed to mean?"

"It's just"—he weighs whether to be frank—"it's totally different. You were never not going to make it."

"How dare you say that?"

He shrugs—no other response left, accused as he is of stating a fact.

She nods briefly, looking blindly into the room. "I'll remember that the next time I fuck the boss's son."

Oblivious, Wine Guy brings the check. Josh tosses down his platinum card without bothering to look at it. "How'd you like the second bottle?"

"Well, *I* liked yours better," Jessica starts to say, giving the waiter a brittle smile.

"So, I guess that was really onerous, huh? Fucking the boss's son?"

"O*kay,*" says the young man, looking fearfully from one to the other of them and retreating a step. "A little disagreement here, I guess, ha, ha. Let me just go run this through."

"You have no idea what it takes," Jess says into the room, her voice trembling. "You don't have the slightest fucking clue."

Josh gives a strangled, frustrated sigh. "Why do you act like I'm accusing you? I just feel bad for her!"

"I'll say it again, Josh," she says, more evenly now. "You don't know what it's like."

"You take your time with this now," says Wine Guy, returning and retreating hastily, with a frightened mug for the peanut gallery as he goes.

Josh signs; sighs. "So—what?" he says wearily. He's lost track of the argument—can't remember what he's not allowed to say. "You're actually trying to claim with her it was . . . ?" He hesitates, looking down at the twenty in his hand, weighing whether to add it to the twenty he's already put down as a tip. It's a habit he got from his father, who always tips in cash.

"That's too much," Jessica says quickly. She's much faster at simple math than he is. "That would be thirty percent. That's ridiculous."

"You're actually trying to claim it was consensual? That this fourteen-year-old—"

"*Sixteen*-year-old!"

"—really wanted to be having sex with Al Delvecchio?"

"She was really passionate about theater," Jessica says, as Josh takes his wallet from his back pocket to look for a smaller bill. There's the barest hint of deadpan in her voice now, the first indication, perhaps, that she knows she's being absurd, that this will shortly end in laughter. It's not the first time that it's happened: She delivers the heated, accusatory manifesto, only to turn to him a few minutes later and say, "So . . . should we watch *Idol?*" "As you said, you know the type."

"You're so fucking naïve," Josh says kindly.

"Excuse me?"

"How can someone be so fucking naïve and so fucking cynical at the same time? I honestly don't get how the two strains can coexist in one mind. You, you blackmail a teacher to get what you want, you shake off his attempts at—*molesting* you—and yet, it never even crosses your mind to think that this other poor girl maybe didn't have the resources you had, or maybe was actually pretty desperate . . ." Josh's voice trails off as he sees the futility of trying to get her to acknowledge his point.

There's a pause and then Jessica says coldly, "She didn't have to go along with it." The humor in her voice is gone and her face sets impenetrably. "She could have hidden in the bathroom, too."

She sits stiffly in her seat, and after a moment, perhaps remembering that they're in a restaurant, the ominously pleasant look from the beginning of the meal steals slowly over her face.

"This is so fucked!" Josh cries. Jessica doesn't flinch, doesn't react—the picture of composure. "I'm supposed to be the one who was so protected—who grew up with money, who's been an insider my whole life. You'd think *I'd* be callous—and it's like, it's like—" He stops and looks at her caustically. "Didn't poverty teach you anything?"

"We weren't fucking *poor*," she says, aghast.

"Of course it didn't," he says. "Because it had nothing to do with you."

"You know what, Josh? *I* didn't fuck the guy, okay?"

"*You* could have! And you still wouldn't have ended up a waitress in the Colonial Fucking Inn!"

Susan has overheard. She stands a little away from the table, hands clasped behind her back, her eyes brimming, her chin trembling with mortification. "Are you guys all set?" she whimpers.

Looking down at his wallet, which has failed to turn up a smaller bill, Josh says, "You know what? Fuck it. Yes, we are," and throws down the twenty.

Jessica slides the American Express bill protector toward her old acquaintance. "Susan, we're going to need some change."

When she withdraws her hand, Josh slams his down, on the leather case. "Actually, that's not necessary. It's all set, Susan." He looks at Jessica, still pressing his palm down on the case. "Let's go."

Jessica faces him tranquilly. "This night is over if you leave that twenty."

"I can come back later," mumbles Susan.

"That's all right—you're not bothering us." Josh gets to his feet. Not realizing that he still has his eye on her, Jessica makes a grab for the bill protector. He physically stops her hand against the table and she shrieks.

"Why don't you leave the ring, too, Josh?" she screams, rising to her feet. "Just leave the goddamn ring, too, while you're at it!"

ABOUT EIGHTEEN MONTHS later he sees her up on a bill-board. He's driving down Sunset and there she is. It's goofy Jessica, smiling/grimacing Jessica, arms around Movie Hubby's neck, knee right-angling for a fifties-style toe lift. It's some heaven-sent reincarnation thing—there's a gold halo painted on over her head. He nearly rear-ends the convertible in front of him, craning to see the expression on her face—whether the eyes are smiling as well as the mouth.

He always told her she'd end up in a comedy. She was better in motion than still, something fundamentally elusive—you could even say evasive—about her charm, as if to pin it down would be to kill it. Ironic, that when buddies of his, Rich included, used to give him the old good-riddance pep talk, they'd always remind him of what they saw as her fatal flaw—that she was incapable of having fun. That she just had to ruin everything. And that, Rich used to conclude, that would have gotten really, really old. "'Member that time we drive up to Ojai and we're sitting there having champagne and it's gorgeous and she's just gotten *Eden's Gate* and she's dating my buddy Josh Stein and it's totally sick how nice it is and she can't fucking stop talking about those orphans in Romania? That was not fun. That was the opposite of fun." And aloud Josh would always acknowledge the point. He raises a hand from the steering wheel to signal "Sorry" to the driver of the convertible; starts forward slowly, chastened, leaving an exaggerated distance between himself and the other cars. But while the criticism, unlike most of the others (she wasn't really a bitch, and she definitely wasn't dumb), was valid, it never mitigated anything for him. The particular point of her being incapable of enjoying herself has never made him feel any better about being free of her. Lately, he's kind of gotten over the idea that one day you get there, you stand alone as the fully realized humanoid, needing no one. It just started to bore him, all the self-actualization. Silently he would answer, *But that's where I came in.*

The Red Coat

I N JANUARY, TRISH returned to the restaurant she'd been frequenting before the holidays. It was a contemporary Italian café, dark inside, with bare wood tables and narrow metal chairs that seemed to have been designed to give people the impression that they needed to lose weight. Trish had eaten dinner there only once, to celebrate Tim's promotion. But a cappuccino could set you back only so far, even on Madison Avenue. Trish fancied the idea of becoming a regular, and it worried her a little to think that the progress she had made in December had been wiped out by her recent two-week Christmas vacation. She hurried a little as she walked the crosstown blocks from her apartment, leaning forward into the wind, sacrificing her normally excellent posture.

Despite its being an off hour, there was a noisy party at the bar this afternoon. Two long-haired, angular women—models, Trish guessed—were getting messily drunk and pouring themselves all over the bartender. The man did not detach himself to wait on Trish, as he should have, and after being neglected for a few minutes, she looked around with annoyance, a peremptory hand raised in the air. One of the women had a cigarette between her teeth and was leaning across the bar to solicit a light from the bartender. Oldest trick in the book, Trish thought disgustedly. "Excuse me!" she fairly shouted. Then she put her hand to her temple and hunched down in her chair, hiding herself, just shaking with loathing and the injustice of finding her here. For it was Evgenia.

IT WAS FOUR months since she'd met the girl—four months since Beth and John had been transferred to London. "London calling!" the invitations had said, and the apartment on East Ninety-third had been mostly packed into boxes. People stood around drinking Dom Perignon out of plastic cups amid garbage bags of clothes and other things to give away, making bids on the Upshaws' IKEA couch and console. Early on in the evening, Beth came out of the kitchen with a tray of bacon-wrapped scallops and said, "Hey, does anyone need a great cleaning lady?" but there were no takers.

Everyone seemed to have someone already. Perched on the chunky arm of the sofa, Trish had listened, smiling from time to time, as Karen and Kelly and Meg and Christine—some colleagues of John's, some, like her, wives of colleagues—griped on insufferably about their inadequate help: Lupe, who shrank a $250 cashmere sweater and refused to clean the oven; Sancha, who called from São Paulo the night before a dinner party to say she'd be back in six months; Liubov, who eschewed the organic products purchased online by her employer and instead cleaned the whole apartment with industrial-strength bleach that made even the cat's eyes water. Trish laughed with the others and clutched her champagne, seething. Perching there on the arm of the sofa, pretending to commiserate with Meg Tedeschi for her inability to get rid of a particularly careless cleaner on account of the exigencies of the woman's personal life (single mom, dangerous ex), Trish became more and more incensed. It was as if she had been duped, as if she had played the stooge. Perhaps there was a whole host of things she was ignorant of, that she would discover by accident, in some unsympathetic public forum. "Why don't you just fire the bitch?" she said finally, relieved when she got a laugh.

TRISH MEEHAN, NÉE Moore, had come to New York in the late eighties with a degree in business affairs. The once-industrial town she'd grown up in, in southern New Hampshire, was a former mill city, with all that the phrase implies: the rows of abandoned factory buildings lining a polluted river; the deserted downtown with the barely subsisting, family-owned department store displaying corsets and fedoras and other dusty anachronistic goods in its windows. For several years after moving to New York, Trish's emotional sustenance had derived almost entirely from that: the achievement of the move itself.

There were days, well into the mid-nineties even, when she could hardly believe she had done it. She had squeezed some money out of her mother, but by the end of that first summer of endless résumé-photocopying and Thai takeout, she had found a real job crunching numbers at a midtown consulting firm. She had rented herself a studio apartment on York Avenue; later on she put up a wall and advertised for a roommate so she could afford the rent hike. When she took the Greyhound bus to Lowell and then on up to New Hampshire at the holidays, she would tell people she lived in "Manhattan" and she vowed never to leave, no matter how poor she was, for an outer borough. Though her own apartment building was a former tenement, a site of bare bulbs in porcelain sockets, archeological layers of peeling kitchen linoleum, and knotted plastic grocery bags of trash left on landings, at least her phone number had the 212 area code—that was very important, Trish knew.

The city had been different when she arrived. The gaunt, unshaven men who wore undershirts in the middle of the day had not been driven out of the East Village, there were no national-chain coffee franchises to kill time in without arousing suspicion, and in certain neighborhoods, where trash cans were chained outside of buildings, the door frames and stoops of which had been splashed over in mud-brown paint, you could still catch the grotty scent of the 1970s as it fought its way up from the subway grates—a stimulating aroma for some, suggestive of funkier, more authentic times; alarming, merely, for someone like Trish.

She had, from those first few years in the city, a half-dozen unsavory memories. One involved answering a roommate ad in the *Voice* and realizing, when the man offered her a glass of sweet wine before showing her around the apartment, that she had been complicit in something sleazy. Another time she had taken a cab home from a bar downtown when she knew she didn't have the fare. She had the driver stop at a cash machine, and went through the motions of trying to extract money; she knew her card would be rejected, but she figured that as a pretty girl she could charm her way out of it this once. She emerged from the bank with a goofy smile, saying, "I just can't believe this . . ." and was about to launch into a highly nuanced apology for why she could not, at that particular moment, access her checking account, when the cabbie demanded, "How much you got?" And when Trish said, "A dollar-fifty?" he said, "Ah, fuck you!" The tone of the man's voice just gutted Trish—the disgust, yes, but what was even more painful was his utter lack of surprise. It was as if, the cabbie seemed to imply, she did this kind of thing all the time.

Trish had been raised Catholic, and for years, when she woke up hungover and full of recriminations, she would revisit a laundry list of these moments of mortal shame in an attempt to marshal the sins stacking up against her. Once in a while, when she was at her lowest, Trish would go to church on Sunday and pray, the way she had as a girl, with her eyes squeezed tight, picturing a bearded man in long white robes. But most Sundays she lay in bed till noon and then rose and cleaned the apartment from top to bottom, scouring the bathtub, scrubbing the patch of kitchen floor on her hands and knees, washing all of her lingerie by hand and hanging it to dry, and finally taking a shower and combing out her hair to let it dry naturally.

All those first years, too, Trish feared that until she changed her ways and stopped waking up hungover she would be punished. She figured the punishment would manifest itself in the thwarting of her most obvious goal: marriage.

But life did not seem to play the retributive role Trish had cast it in. Life was altogether more charitable—it was almost Christian in its forgiveness. At the midtown firm where she'd worked her way up to managing a research team, she met Tim, fresh from business school in the Midwest following a stint in the Army. Trish got drunk and slept with him on the first date—he was not deterred. She floated the subject of matrimony two weeks into their relationship—he married her anyway. She had not changed her ways, yet she had been rewarded.

AS SOON AS she got the ring, Trish quarreled recklessly with her boss. Trish gave the woman an ultimatum, which meant that when she lost, she had to give up the job; she had already given up her apartment and moved into Tim's studio. It was an upgrade for Trish, in that, though the studio was small, it was in a luxury building, with a health club and parking in the basement. It was a given between the two of them (Trish had waited vainly for an opening at Beth and John's party to make this clear) that because she was not working, she would of course do the cooking and cleaning. And Trish honestly didn't mind housework. Mopping the floors and feeling her muscles begin to tire from running the German vacuum over the carpet were among the times that Trish felt most robustly connected to the promise of her and Tim's union.

"It's not like we were rolling in dough," Tim liked to say, of his childhood outside of Detroit, "and yet my mother never worked."

"Of course not!" There would be a scornful edge to Trish's voice when she agreed. "It's so much better for the family," she would say, as if she, too, could remember family dinners of chicken and mashed potatoes rather than the broiler fish sticks or macaroni and cheese out-of-a-box that she and her older sister, Jan, had made the nights neither her mother—an ICU nurse in the town hospital— nor her father—a tax advisor, who faced yearly crunches—could make it home to prepare a meal. In public and in private, too, Trish and Tim would agree on this one issue with that avid, defensive posturing that had lately become characteristic of all kinds of tra- ditionalists in Manhattan. Tim's theretofore unarticulated hope for a stay-at-home wife, teased out by Trish on their second date, had become their sustaining vanity as a couple.

Just two months after their wedding had come Beth and John's going-away party. Trish waited until the end of the night, when only the stragglers remained. Then she caught Beth alone in the kitchen tying up the garbage and asked for the cleaning woman's number.

"You're gonna love her," Beth had said. "Real self-starter. I've had her over a year and I don't have a single complaint."

"Just 'Evgenia,' huh?" Trish asked, eyeing the Post-it.

"I don't know her last name, can you believe it?" Beth said. She gave a pleased self-indulgent laugh. "Here she scrubs the crotch of my underwear by hand, and I just put 'Cash' on the check."

THE WEEK BEFORE the cleaner was to start, a funny thing hap- pened. When Trish collected the dirty dishes from the bedroom and living room and stacked them in the sink, she couldn't just leave them there soaking for a night as she usually did—she rinsed them right away and loaded them into the dishwasher. When she put two weeks of old newspapers into the recycling box, she thought, I'm being really nice not to leave these for the cleaning lady, and yet she wondered whether, in the future, Evgenia would take over that task. On the morning itself, Trish stripped the sheets from the bed and organized the things on Tim's bureau, and, before she could stop herself, she had wet a sponge with

Comet and run it over the bathroom sink. Polishing the mirror she caught sight of her face, red from exertion.

The doorman buzzed and Trish said giddily, "Yes! Send her up, please!" In Trish's head a narrative had begun in which the cleaning lady (heavy and saturnine, with an air of the Old World), in addition to her cleaning duties, would set out little snacks for Trish, admonish her to eat more, not to wear such high heels; would tell her she'd freeze outside, in what she was wearing. Trish, meanwhile, would indulge the woman, with unexpected bonuses and thoughtful gestures: "Do you want this *Vogue*? I was going to throw it out." The picture was so compelling that she was disoriented for a minute—thinking someone had gotten the wrong apartment—when she opened the door on a young woman she might have hung out with, in her single days, on a Friday night. The cleaning lady—the phrase no longer worked in Trish's mind—was dramatically made up, with heavy eyeliner and long streaks of blush on both cheeks. Her white-blond hair was pulled back from black roots into a devil-may-care ponytail, and she seemed to be sucking on something—a piece of hard candy or a cough drop, which clacked against her teeth when she talked. Her outfit, when she took off her coat, made Trish look away, embarrassed: The girl was wearing a ruffled blouse and a miniskirt over tights and sling-back sandals.

"You sure you want to wear that?" Trish said doubtfully. "It's kind of a dirty job, you know."

"I have apron." The young woman removed one from the large zippered black satchel she had brought and put it on.

The Meehans' apartment was new since the honeymoon and Trish liked to show it off: the wall of plate-glass windows that faced the street; the eat-in kitchen decked out with gifts they'd been given from their registry—the standing mixer and top-of-the-line cappuccino maker, the cedar knife block filled with German steel. In the console on the shelf above the television stood a silver-framed picture of Tim and her cutting the cake at the wedding. Black-tie it had been, and she'd had five attendants to Tim's two. She half expected a compliment but the girl was silent, offering only nods, and unsmiling ones at that, with the result that Trish felt compelled to keep up the conversation.

"So, how do you spell your name, Evgenia?" she asked politely. "I hope I'm pronouncing it right."

Evgenia was squatting down to peer into the cabinet under the kitchen sink where the cleaning products were kept. "It is complicated—Russian name."

"Oh, I know," Trish cut her off. "Where are you from— Moscow?"

"No, no." Evgenia's voice was muffled. She withdrew her head from the cabinet and turned a face up to Trish that was sardonic in the extreme. "Every American say that to me! Every American think I from Russia. I am from Ukraine," she said. "Former Soviet Union."

"Oh, okay."

"Look on map! You find." Still squatting, Evgenia held up a box of Brillo pads and rattled it at Trish. "Empty."

"Not a problem," Trish said. "I'll buy more." She asked Evgenia how long she had been in America. When Evgenia said three years, Trish asked if she had come by herself, and Evgenia, straightening up, laughed aloud and said, "Oh, my God, no! I come with my mother, my father, my two brothers, and my husband."

"You're married?" said Trish.

Evgenia explained that everyone married young in Ukraine. "Not like here. I was married at seventeen," she said, and it was clear from her intonation that she expected Trish to react with surprise, that she had developed, as Trish had noticed the savvier immigrants did, a sense of what went down big here—had perhaps herself learned to be impressed with the fact of her teenaged betrothal, where once she had not been.

"Wow!" Trish said gamely. "I just got married last year and I'm thirty-one." She led Evgenia through the bedroom and into the renovated bath. "I still beat all of my friends, though," she added quickly, so that Evgenia wouldn't get the wrong idea. "A lot of them don't even have boyfriends. They'll be lucky to find someone by the time they're forty. It's different in New York. Women have careers, you know? Other priorities."

"You work?" said Evgenia.

"No. I mean, not now," Trish said, annoyed that she was flustered. "I mean—not anymore." She mumbled vaguely about trying to get pregnant, though in fact Tim was bent on their enjoying themselves for a few more years—and on their paying off their debt first. "What about you?" Trish said firmly. "Do you have any kids?"

Evgenia shook her head.

"Well, maybe you will soon." Trish felt like dropping the subject and was about to explain how the shower worked when Evgenia said, "No, not soon." Confused, Trish looked at her, and Evgenia said, "I cannot."

"You can't—not?" Trish faltered.

"No."

"Oh, my God." Trish pressed the hand-shower nozzle into her thigh as she tried to summon some appropriate words. "I'm so sorry," she said, swallowing. "God, I'm sorry I even brought it up."

Evgenia wiped a finger along the inside of the tub, holding it up to show the grime. "You have Soft Scrub?"

Trish stared at her. "I think we ran out."

"No Soft Scrub? Okay, next time," Evgenia said, shaking the finger reprovingly at Trish. "And Brillo. Don't forget."

"Look, why don't you just make a list, okay?" Trish told her. They came out into the bedroom, and then into the living/dining area. "Well, I guess I'll take off," Trish said briskly. She lingered a moment for the girl to ask her where she was going.

"See you later," Evgenia said, waving, as she donned yellow rubber gloves.

"I think I'll head over to the Met," Trish said. "There's supposed to be a good exhibit right now."

But when she got outside it was gray and threatening rain. It seemed odd to Trish to go to a museum on a weekday morning; she couldn't recall ever having heard about anyone's doing so. Sheepishly she walked two blocks to the Starbucks and sat down with a latte, noticing with distaste that a dusting of crumbs and a wad of used napkins had been left on the table by previous customers.

TRISH HERSELF HAD never cleaned for money, but all through her teens she'd held tedious after-school jobs—babysitting mainly, some office work (stuffing envelopes for a state rep; typing and filing for a father/son dental practice)—and she knew how irksome and debilitating it was to have the mother, or the boss, lurking around, checking up on you, so you couldn't even use the phone to call a friend and joke around or make the kids watch TV for five minutes just to alleviate the boredom. She considered those afternoons the most hateful, wasted hours of her life. Even now she would feel her face get hot when some acquaintance of Tim's from B-school mentioned, as if it had been onerous, having had to go to "practice" every afternoon after school. Yet at the same time it could still cheer her, fifteen years out, to remind herself that she would never have to take another babysitting or filing job again.

Having whiled away nearly two full hours with coffee and errands, and having dawdled all the way home, Trish could have screamed when she finally returned and heard the television on in her apartment. She was exasperated in the self-conscious way that only killing time can make one, and as she stood outside the door listening, she became more and more enraged by the noise. Was it that Evgenia had carelessly forgotten to turn it off when she left?

Or was she still working—could she possibly be? in a one-bedroom? and worked with the television on? In the case of the latter, Trish decided grimly, her key in the lock, she would say something right away. But when she came in, Evgenia was sitting on the couch with the remote control in her hand. Seeing her there confused Trish, and the apartment itself, which was fantastically clean and smelled of Murphy's Oil Soap, confused her also and touched her somehow as well, so she swallowed what she was planning to say and exclaimed instead, "Wow, the place looks great!" She knew at once that by gushing, she was exposing herself as gullible and lacking in authority, but she couldn't help it; she couldn't hide the grin that had stolen across her face.

"I go now," Evgenia announced. She clicked the TV off and crossed the room. She took her coat from where it was hanging in the coat closet by the door and put it on, unhurriedly buckling the belt around her waist. It was a red coat, cut long and gathered in the back, with a stand-up collar and two rows of gold buttons down the front that gave it a smart, military appearance.

A hammered silver mirror, another of Trish and Tim's wedding presents, hung to the right of the door as one went out. Evgenia paused there to redo her lipstick.

Trish said with a touch of impatience, "Were you waiting for me?"

The girl rubbed her lips together to blend the color. "No," she said, making a pout and then a dentist's lips-only grin for the mirror. "Just waiting." She turned and smiled at Trish. "It's okay. I am student. I go to class now."

"All right," Trish said uncertainly. "Well, I may see you next time, I may not. It depends on my schedule." When Evgenia merely nodded, continuing out, Trish called after her, down the hall, "So, what is it that you study?"

"Fashion design!" Evgenia called back. "I want to be next Donna Karan!"

An eventless week followed, but the week after that—Trish was vexed to find—the television incident repeated itself. Again Trish heard the noise from the hallway, and again when she entered, she found Evgenia sitting on the couch, remote control in hand.

"What are you watching?" Trish asked. She detached several plastic grocery bags from her arm where they had cut into her wrists and made red marks. She was unable to keep the irritation out of her voice.

"*Oprah,*" said Evgenia, standing up. She was not tall—Trish was taller—but her posture was erect. When she came toward Trish she seemed to lead with her collarbone, in the wake of which the rest of her body seemed to glide. "She is so great. I love how she can talk to anyone, you know? Cat or king, it doesn't matter to her.

"Your cable remote is totally screwed up," she added. "Why you don't have universal?" Before getting her coat, Evgenia passed the device to Trish, who turned it over in her hands several times, frowning. As Evgenia was doing her lipstick, Trish told her not to wait in the apartment in the future, but to leave when she had finished cleaning. "My husband and I just don't feel it's professional," she said. She shut the door and bolted it and went to the fridge to see if there was an open bottle of wine. Standing at the counter she poured herself a glass of chardonnay and gulped it down.

THERE WERE TIMES when Trish seriously didn't know why she bothered. Her sister, Jan, who had followed her to New York, and who now taught preschool in Hoboken, was still single. Trish had engineered a setup for Jan with one of the technology guys from work. When the guy never got around to calling her, having promised to, Trish tried to put a positive spin on it when she talked to her sister on the phone. "Forget this guy! You just have to get out more, Jan—get out of your neighborhood, you know? Come to Manhattan. Meet people. Maybe you should move here."

"How am I going to do that?" Jan asked, her voice trembling with hostility. "I'm not going to bleed Mom and Dad the way you did!"

"Well, maybe you'll meet someone in Hoboken," Trish said, swallowing the insult, though it made her eyes smart.

"Yes, Trish," Jan had replied bitterly, "it may surprise you, but it actually does happen."

Then there was the box of Christmas cookies that she had left for the cleaning lady, just before the holidays. They were home-made frosted sugar cookies—reindeer, bells, Christmas trees. Not only did Evgenia not thank her for them, but she called Trish on her cell phone while Trish was away to inform her that she had forgotten to leave Evgenia's check. " 'I look in drawer but you never put!' " Trish said, mocking Evgenia's syntax to Tim. "Wouldn't you think she could wait a fucking week? Does she really have to call me on my vacation?"

"I don't know," Tim said, noncommitally. "These people live pretty close to the edge."

"Oh, please!" Trish cried. "This girl wears high-fashion! She probably spends more money on her clothes than I do! You should see her." With loathing, Trish recalled the encounter she'd had with Evgenia just before she left for vacation. Trish had been heading home, on one side of the street; Evgenia was walking toward the subway on the other. Trish saw her first. She looked rather jaunty in her red coat, carrying the tin of cookies, stepping around a dog. It was not a beautiful coat, but Evgenia seemed to take a huge amount of pride in it. There was an arrogance in her carriage, Trish noticed, an unbecoming arrogance, when she was wearing it.

Trish was on the point of letting the girl pass without saying hello when she instead hailed Evgenia and darted across the street.

Trish's stopping her seemed to unsettle Evgenia; she barely managed to greet Trish, stammering out the words, as if she'd been unprepared for a sudden segue into English, and she looked worried and unhappy, as if she thought Trish was going to tell her something unpleasant—find fault with her work or even fire her. Seeing this, Trish said quickly to reassure her, "You do such a good job, Evgenia. Tim and I are always talking about it.

"It must be really tiring—cleaning," she went on when Evgenia didn't answer. "I'm sure if I were in your place—"

She was only getting started, but Evgenia, who seemed to have found her voice all of a sudden, cut Trish off with a laugh and said, "Are you kidding? Your apartment is nothing! Wednesday, I have classic six! Classic six have two bedrooms, two-and-half bath—"

"I know what a classic six is!" Trish said furiously. "You don't have to tell me!"

AND HERE SHE was, three weeks later, being made a fool of at what had very nearly become *her* café. She ought to go right up to Evgenia and say, in a blatantly condescending voice, "Oh, my God, what are *you* doing here?" as an acquaintance had once said to her at a party. Or better yet, walk up to the bar and, when Evgenia accosted her, turn to the girl, and look faintly puzzled, squint and frown. "Oh—hi. Gosh—how strange. I mean, I'm sorry—how are you?" as if the coincidence was simply too bizarre to make sense of. With a stealthy movement Trish snatched her overcoat off the spare chair and sat there motionlessly for a moment, hugging the coat tightly to her chest and holding her breath. Then she got abruptly to her feet and left the restaurant. It seemed like an act of defiance, like walking out of a meeting or a bad movie in protest—she refused to be cowed by other people's expectations.

Among the jobs Trish had held to eke out a living her very first summer in New York, one of the less disagreeable had been that of coat-check girl in a steak house. Trish had been a pro at the job.

The right, customer-pleasing mixture of professionalism combined with ingratiating touches—"Yours was the navy blue, wasn't it, sir?"—had netted her better tips than the girl who worked the other three nights of the week, the waiters always told her. It was the only one of her preprofessional jobs that Trish looked back on fondly. In recent years she had developed a habit of smiling at whoever was manning the closet, to wish the girl luck or pass on some bit of optimism about the future. At this hour the tiny room was deserted. The door was ajar, though, and Trish glanced into it automatically. Except for a few forgotten items in the overhead bins, the coatrack itself was all but empty; there was only one coat on the whole rack. The red coat. Ludicrously solitary it hung there. Or not so much hung as clung, precariously, from one of the numbered hangers, one sleeve already having slipped off, as if the coat had been carelessly tossed aside and left to its own devices. For a moment Trish actually believed she was going into the room to set something aright—hang up the coat properly by buttoning the top couple of buttons around the hanger, as everyone knew you had to do. But she slipped the coat from the hanger and tucked it over her arm.

"I'm sorry?" she was going to say, if anyone stopped her. "Oh, my God, I'm such an idiot! Of course it's not! Jeez"—she would shake her head for emphasis—"I think I'd lose my head today if it wasn't screwed on."

Two blocks from the restaurant, she stopped to replace her camel's hair coat with the coat she had stolen. She made a bundle of the former and stuffed it into a paper shopping bag—not an easy task, as it was thick and luxurious, a Christmas present from Tim. As she slipped her arms into the sleeves of the red coat, she saw its lining for the first time: It was cheap red satin, rent in several places. Galled, because the damage was so unnecessary and could have been prevented, Trish nevertheless did up the buttons. She gathered the belt around her waist, and buckled it. She felt her head rise a few inches as she set off again, throwing her shoulders back and walking briskly, with a sense of purpose. She happened to be right up the street from one of the high-end grocery stores that dotted the neighborhood, and she suddenly got an inspiration: to make Tim a five-star dinner for when he got home from work that night. She would buy candles and wine and make lots of courses—even better: She would do an entire menu out of *Gourmet,* to which, after buying it off the newsstand for years, Trish had finally subscribed.

THE NEXT WEEK, Evgenia caught Trish in the apartment before Trish could get out. Trish was so preoccupied with reconstructing the whereabouts of the red coat (she had moved it from the hall closet to a box under her bed, and finally, one evening when Tim was working late, to the storage locker in the basement of the building) that she was almost out the door before it occurred to her to have a look at its replacement. It wasn't a proper coat but a jacket that Evgenia took off—an unflattering man's football jacket in kelly green and black, with what looked to be a new zipper sewn in.

"What happened to your red coat?" Trish asked plaintively, pausing in the threshold of the door.

Evgenia made a disgusted noise in the back of her throat as she tied on her apron. "I lose it—in a bar somewhere."

"You're kidding me," Trish said. The recounting of the fact dismayed her. "You mean someone took it?"

Evgenia shrugged. "Is my fault." She made a gesture of raising a glass to her mouth. "Too much party."

"But—that's awful!"

"Yeah," Evgenia sighed. "And I really like that one, too."

It was the friendliest conversation the two young women had ever had. Trish tried to think of something to add just to prolong the camaraderie. "Oh, Evgenia? I meant to tell you, " she asked.

"I'm actually giving away a whole pile of clothes. I have so much stuff—I never wear half of it, and, I don't know if this would interest you at all, but—" Trish put her handbag down on the floor, letting the front door of the apartment close behind her, and opened the coat closet. She took her camel's hair coat out and removed it from its hanger. "I've just never liked this one. It was expensive and all that, but I don't know—it's just not really me. Course I can't tell Tim . . ."

"Yeah?" Evgenia seemed truly to look at Trish for the first time then, in all the months she'd been working for her, and though she looked at her skeptically, sizing her up with reservations, Trish could see she was not displeased. She took the coat from Trish and when she saw the label, her eyes flew up. "You mean it? Are you serious, Trish?"

"It's yours if you want it," Trish said hoarsely. Hurriedly, she picked up her handbag and left, leaving Evgenia trying the coat on over her apron. Normally Trish never took the stairs down from the apartment; she didn't like the hollow sound her shoes made on the concrete. But today she didn't feel like waiting for the elevator. She was a little embarrassed, she found, by her own good deed.

Bad Ghost

MARGERY'S MEMORIAL IS at 4:00 P.M. on a Tuesday, all the way up the West Side, in a defunct movie theater, known nowadays as a "space," that's put to various uses—staged readings of new plays, Latin dance programs, obscure offbeat awards shows. The setting seems about right for the gathering Stacey's expecting for her former boss: odd solitary fans, not professionals but backpack-carrying overgrown teenager types who have time for this kind of thing—the few people left in this city who aren't flogging their own books, who still enjoy making up the audience.

Stacey's only in New York for three days and she hasn't been this far uptown in years. At home in L.A., she'd known, as she read the clipping from the Dulwich *Herald* Anita sent the week before, that it would be an effort to show up, that it was more than likely she would decide at the last minute, indolent and probably hungover in her downtown hotel, that she couldn't be bothered. The slightest nuisance—rain for instance—might have deterred her, but the May day itself is fine, if breezy, and Stacey alights from the long, expensive cab ride with the confidence of having hit upon the right outfit for such an event—her double-breasted navy skirt suit, with the oversized buttons and Peter Pan collar, open-toed shoes, and bare legs: formalish, yes, but zippy. You wouldn't want to overstate the connection, she thinks, slamming the taxi door behind her and adjusting her sunglasses, by wearing anything too severe or gloomy. For Stacey is going not to mourn Margery's death, some six months past, but out of some light curiosity. She has the notion that her being there will bolster the turnout, in terms of both numbers and quality—she's had a feeling all morning of "lending her presence" to the event—and why not? When she's finally in a position to lend it? In the end, it was simply too much of a coincidence *not* to show up—her happening to be in town for the network upfronts, Anita's sending her the article just in time. And now that she has managed to show up, Anita will be able to say to her Dulwich friends, "Oh, yes—Stacey was at the New York memorial. I guess it was quite a scene."

These small gestures of thoughtfulness toward her mother are easy for Stacey to make nowadays. It seems perverse that when she was first in the city after graduation—then out in L.A., praying that she wouldn't have to come crawling back—she'd go weeks without calling home, taking an angry pleasure in ignoring Anita's messages on the machine; withholding any good news she got and then doling it out in terse, defensive admissions: "So . . . I guess I can tell you that I got an agent." "Well, I sold this one pitch." "I'm getting on a show, but it's for a season only, Mom—*nothing's guaranteed.* So don't get all excited."

Leaving behind trash-blown upper Broadway, Stacey steps into the gilt and marble lobby of the theater. At the entrance to the large, sloping auditorium a pert young woman hands her a program. She thanks the girl but hesitates before going in, taken aback by the voluble, good-looking crowd that fills the first several rows of the main seating section and the outer seats of both of the side rows. She wouldn't have thought Margery would draw such a crowd.

There must be three times as many women as men—a publishing crowd, Stacey realizes, walking a little way down the near aisle. Of course. She'd forgotten Scholastic was throwing the party. For a party it suddenly seems to be, the air chatty, anticipatory, punchy. All the people, Stacey thinks, slipping into an empty side row, who couldn't be bothered to return Margery's calls this last decade, turning out now to show it was nothing personal—they always loved *Margery.* It wasn't *their* fault her books didn't speak to teenagers, with their autoloading irony, their careless dips into bisexuality, their alternative online lives. What on earth would a provocative YA "problem" novel even consist of today? Stacey wonders, glancing around to see if she recognizes anyone. An anti-rebel perhaps? Instead of *Dinkie Hocker Shoots Smack,* maybe *Dinkie Hocker Is Planning to Stay a Virgin?* But no—even the super-straight movement had been mainstreamed already. Hell, Stacey herself had written a fundamentalist Christian episode for a WB show years ago; at the time, it had seemed a radical departure.

She's been away too long; she can't see a single familiar face, and although she's the one who left—quit publishing, tore up her MFA applications—Stacey keeps glancing around, as if someone at least ought to know her. Then there's a respectful murmur through the crowd as a stout, graying woman of about sixty in a brocade jacket walks up to the podium and adjusts the mike. Stacey recognizes Margery's longtime editor, Renata Townsend, as she turns her knees to the side to let two girls—office temps, perhaps, they are slouching and giggling—squeeze by her. Renata is—or would be—her peer, and seeing the woman, Stacey suddenly wonders why she hasn't made more of the fact that Margery died young. Stacey didn't really dwell on the fact at all when Anita called her with the news last fall: Margery's massive stroke in her sleep, at fifty-six, that had rendered the paramedics' quick response—and for such a small town, too—useless. It didn't help

that Margery had been alone in the house, Anita had said, and
Stacey had thought—of course, she'd thought briefly—of Helena,
though the girl was long, long gone. She'd dropped out of the
high school at sixteen or so; run off with some older, bearded
(Anita had always remembered that detail) boatbuilder from
Maine. She had left the man, one child later (a son? a daughter?
Stacey couldn't recall), downgrading, seemingly, for a short-order
cook she'd met waitressing, who was going to start an indepen-
dent brewery. After that Anita had lost track, and if she couldn't
keep it straight, then certainly Stacey could not be expected to,
long-distance.

Perhaps it was the knowledge that Margery didn't suffer that
mitigated, in Stacey's mind, the suddenness of the death. The
truth is, Stacey would rather not focus on the element of personal
relief in her old employer's sudden death, however tenuous her
and Margery's connection had become in the years since Stacey
had worked for her. Unexpected, too, you could say the woman's
death had been. But you couldn't really call it premature, at least
in terms of her career. That sense, all-around, must be contribut-
ing to the air of giddiness in the crowd: Writing-wise, anyway,
Margery was way past her prime.

At the podium Renata Townsend—Stacey has got the name
now—draws up smart black half-glasses from a chain around her
neck. A hush falls, and the giggling of the two girls next to
Stacey is grating. They both look a bit cowed and Stacey wonders
if they've turned up for the wrong thing and are too embarrassed
to get up and go. Most of the other women here today are dressed
like Stacey, in of-the-moment flats or pumps, with sharp haircuts
and pricey totes; the older ones are tweedier, that's all. But these
two girls are something else. The one sitting closer to Stacey is
tall and makeupless and would be severe-looking if she wasn't
trying not to laugh, a hand clamped, childlike, over her mouth.

Her lank dirty blond hair reaches halfway down her back, and you never see truly long hair in New York. The other girl, a brunette, is shorter, with buckteeth and freckles. But what's more noticeable are the outfits: They're both wearing sheer black dresses, and high heels. The latter has huge breasts popping out of décolletage. On second glance they're not all that much younger than Stacey—twenty-two or twenty-three to her twenty-nine—but their touristy getups (for this is how out-of-towners often seem to dress for Broadway shows; for bachelorette nights out on the town) and their drunken-seeming hilarity give them an air of much younger girls. The brunette drops her handbag and reaching down to grab it bangs her head on the seat in front of her. At this the taller girl laughs so loudly and rudely, with no consideration for the setting, or the nature of the event, that Stacey looks sharply at her, ready to say something—enforce some decent behavior, for Renata has started to introduce herself. "I was Margery McIntyre Flood's editor for thirty-three years," she says, with smooth quiet confidence.

In the moment before she recognizes the taller girl, Stacey's mind seizes on a fact she'd forgotten—excised it so thoroughly from her mind she would have denied it outright a minute before. She wrinkles up her face in distress. She never returned Margery's calls, either—so to speak. Not that she actually received any message on her answering machine, but several years ago—Stacey had been in L.A. maybe six months—Anita had written in one of her letters that Margery was having trouble selling her latest book; her agent had evidently dumped her a while back. Margery had buttonholed Anita after a town meeting and when Anita told the former about Stacey's "success" (For Christ's sake! Stacey remembered thinking, *what* success?), Margery had asked Anita to ask Stacey if she could talk to her agent out there on Margery's behalf. Stacey had been seized with rage at this presumptuous importunity. (In the hard auditorium seat she crosses her arms over her chest, remembering.) It made no sense! TV agents didn't do fiction—surely Margery realized this. And even if they did, Stacey hardly knew Ryan. She was probably the least important writer on his list. What was she going to do, call him up and say that this woman she used to babysit for who had been big maybe fifteen years ago but now found herself agentless had a new *novel*? The arrogance—no, not even the arrogance but the absurdity of the request! When she was beyond helpless! She was lucky if Ryan returned even her legitimate phone calls.

The thought that now, of course, it would have been different, mollifies Stacey a little. She would have at least been able to respond. (As it was, she never mentioned or acknowledged in any way Anita's vicarious request.) She might now have made some little introduction that, while it would surely have come to nothing, would have satisfied her mother and Margery both. But *then*? When she was a complete outsider? How could she possibly have been expected to help?

Remembering the innocence, as it were, of her guilt, Stacey shakes her head in anger. Yet when she opens her mouth to speak, her voice comes out hoarse with supplication, as if, in the five seconds before Renata really gets into her eulogy, she might eke out an absolution.

"Helena?" she says.

IT WAS HAPPENING again. They were in Bob's Market buying ice cream, Stacey had taken the box out of the freezer and was herding Helena up the aisle to pay when the little girl planted her feet and yelled, "Vagina!"

"Helena!" Stacey cried, the pretense of shock for the benefit of the boy minding the cash register.

"PEE-nis! Vagina! Penis!" At the feral flash of the girl's baby teeth Stacey's nails found her palms. She'd had no idea children could have this effect on you, before she started the job. That mere restraint from physical violence would be a quotidian victory. She dropped to her knees now in front of the girl, the better to beg her to behave.

"Penis! Vagina! Penis! Vagina!"

"Helena," she pleaded, then stopped herself and went on, more sternly: "Helena, I thought Bad Ghost wasn't going to come out in public? 'Member? I thought he was going to stay in your bedroom—"

"I want to play it," Helena said coldly.

"Okay! Okay! We can play it when we get home, but—" When Stacey hesitated, some part of her resisting total capitulation, Helena seized a chocolate bar off the candy shelf. "I'll rip this!" she threatened.

"Helena, please don't! Please put it back!"

Too late—she'd torn the wrapper right off. (And what incentive could there have been, Stacey thought disinterestedly, *not* to do it?)

"I'll play it!" Stacey cried. "I'll play it, okay?" She was close to tears. "Let me just pay—let's get out of here, okay?"

"All day!" Helena demanded. "You *have* to *play* it *all* day!"

"I'll play it all day—that's no problem, Helena," Stacey said, getting to her feet. The fatuous tone she resorted to disgusted her. She sounded like a car salesman, as if her next promise might be to throw in AC.

She and the boy at the cash register avoided each other's eyes as she withdrew Margery's money from her jeans pocket and handed it to him. She seized the plastic bag and hustled Helena out of the store.

Outside, they were laying the new bit of road in front of the post office. The men in hard hats were standing by as the heavy roller smoothed the new tar, the smell of it heavy and pungent in the airless July day. It was a day for swimming in the pond, or sitting in the cool of the house with a book, or even condescending to help her mother by folding a load or two of laundry—things, Stacey could hardly bear to think about, she had been doing just two weeks ago. At the crosswalk in front of the post office she seized Helena's hand. "Don't forget to look both ways!"

"I know that!" Helena shouted, yanking her hand away.

Whenever Stacey used one of the admonitions that she'd picked up babysitting for other children in the last year and a half, Helena seemed to sense the tentativeness that entered her voice and to become incensed by it. At night Stacey would practice saying things in front of the bathroom mirror. "Excuse me—the bowl goes in the *dishwasher,* not on the floor, Helena. You know that!" But when she saw the child the next morning, she could feel herself avoiding the girl's eyes and hear the quaver in her voice.

"Why don't you just make her behave?" Bev had asked her when Stacey hinted at the problem without, of course, admitting how bad it was. "You're right," Stacey said, picturing her friend, who shouted at the children she babysat for, shouted and wheedled and bribed with M&Ms and Rolos, bullying them into leaving her alone to make calls to friends—Stacey, or Rich, a guy she liked. The calls were an indulgence Bev wasn't in the least embarrassed about, but which she considered her right as part of the job. It was as if, early on, someone had told Beverly she was in charge and that all the children would accept her authority. But Stacey had somehow missed getting her orders and so was left alternatively dithering, pale with hatred, remorseful, and apologetic—though in general, of the two of them, she got the easy families: the Larsen girls, Andrea and Alison, and Mrs. Thibeaud, whose baby, Madeleine, was always asleep when she came, while Bev ended up with the boisterous, pig-pile-on-the-babysitter types: the Kings, and Sampsons, and Nadia Chamberlain, Dulwich's autistic girl, who had been known to go nuts and start smearing her shit on the walls.

"That's what I should do," she'd said to Beverly on the phone, as if this were just the enlightening advice she'd lacked. "I've just got to make her behave."

TWO WEEKS EARLIER Beverly had gotten the request. Mrs. Purnick had heard from Mrs. Delacroix in the post office that Margery McIntyre Flood was looking for a babysitter for the month of July.

"Oh yeah?" Stacey had said when Bev told her, as if she was really too distracted to digest the information. She was sitting dangling her feet in the Purnicks' backyard pool; Beverly had just surfaced in the shallow end after swimming her one languorous lap. "Sounds like a good job," Stacey added in the same bored tone. This past fall, she and Bev had started a babysitting "service." All it really amounted to was a referral agreement, to keep the business their way, but in that limited sense it was successful.

Bev got out of the pool and stood dripping, her long, freckly knees hyperextended at Stacey's eye level. "Yeah, too bad I can't do it," she said. She tapped the side of her head in an exaggerated fashion to get the water out of her ear.

"You can't do it?" said Stacey, and she had to cough because her voice cracked. Now Bev was doing the other ear. Stacey scowled: It was a gesture she considered pretentious because she knew Bev did it in imitation of her older sister, Eileen.

"Uh-uh—duh. We're going to the Cape in two weeks."

"Oh, that's *right*," Stacey said, turning as Bev took a gingerly seat on one of the plastic chaises longues that faced the long side of the pool. She must have laid on the gravitas a bit too thickly because Bev shielded her eyes from the sun and said, "Jesus, you sound like someone died! What's your problem?"

"No—no, I was just thinking: It's too bad, that's all." Stacey got up and reclined, still in her shorts and T-shirt, in the chair next to Beverly's. "Since you're, like, a true fan of hers I mean. You're the one who's read all of her books."

"That is true." Bev half grinned, half grimaced at Stacey. "I'd be scared, Stace! She's, like, famous."

Stacey laughed aloud, because she didn't know what to say. The idiocy of people amazed her. Or not the idiocy but the short-sightedness—the guilelessness; the fact that they didn't lead their lives looking for an opening. She said she thought she could probably take the job herself, but she'd have to look at her schedule and see.

At supper, when Stacey let slip to her parents the possibility of working for Margery McIntyre Flood, Anita stopped chewing what was in her mouth and looked at her. "Really, Stace?"

"It's not a big deal. Don't act like it's a big deal."

Beside her, Stacey's father, Chris, stuck his hand out and snatched an uneaten piece of corn bread off of her plate, but when Stacey snapped her head around, he froze and made a poker face as if he hadn't moved, and Stacey laughed.

"I could drive you over," Anita said, watching Stacey. "Why don't I drive you over, Stace? For the interview, or whatever."

"There never was a man, was there?" Chris said to Anita, who ignored him. "As I recall, She already had the kid when she showed up in town, didn't she?"

"Don't be ridiculous," said Stacey. "I can walk."

"Is Margery Flood famous?" Stacey's brother, Brian, asked, his mouth full of corn bread.

"Why would you drive me somewhere that's under a ten-minute walk?" Stacey asked impatiently when Anita didn't say anything. "That's completely stupid. It's totally idiotic."

There was a long silence in which Stacey and her dad played another round of snatch-the-corn-bread. "Mom? Did you hear my question?"

Getting up to clear, Anita said, in what was little more than a whisper, "I don't know, Stace. You tell me."

And this was the voice Stacey could not—simply would not—tolerate. "But by the time the air-conditioning got going," she said furiously, "we'd already be there!"

"How much is she going to pay you?" piped up Stacey's dad.

"She'd do it for free," Anita interrupted, pausing with the plates, scorn finally entering her voice. "Wouldn't you, Stace? I mean, she could really help you."

"Ah, *no*, I would not babysit for *free*, Mother," Stacey said, and she caught her father's twinkling blue eyes with derision. "I'm not *that* desperate."

THE OTHER PEOPLE Stacey babysat for went out when she got there—often as quickly as they could, handbags on counters seized as soon as she assured the mother she remembered where the emergency list was; that the leftover lasagna would be fine for supper. She came in the evening and they went to dinner or the movies in Watford, or she came in the afternoon, and the mother left to go food shopping or to an exercise class—Mrs. Thibeaud was always going to a modern dance class at the Unitarian Church. It seemed to pay off, for she was young and sexy. Stacey admired her and wanted to be like her, although Stacey wouldn't have used the word *sexy* then—happy, she probably would have called Mrs. Thibeaud.

Working for Margery would be different, Stacey was told, when they spoke on the phone (Stacey a little disappointed that the woman didn't insist on meeting her in person), because Margery would be in the house writing. "I'm afraid I'm still making changes to the page proofs of *Where Were You on Sunday?* when I'm supposed to have finished outlining and writing five chapters of its sequel!" Margery told her breathlessly. "Needless to say, my editor is not particularly sanguine about my meeting the Labor Day deadline!"

Stacey, who had been prepared for a test of some kind—a sussing out of her own intelligence, and interests perhaps—instead found herself trying not to interrupt with irrelevancies, to interject a few ingratiating "Oh, wows" and "Sure, no problems" into Margery's blast. At the end of the call she hung up frustrated and flopped down on the sofa, annoyed with herself—she had gotten the job after all. That was the important thing, wasn't it?

MARGERY MCINTYRE FLOOD was an author—again, this is how Stacey would have put it at the time, the more urbane *writer* eluding her for several more years. She wrote novels about troubled teenagers, aimed at a section of the population that, Stacey had picked up—perhaps from the bookstore in the Watford mall—was referred to as "Young Adults." Although Stacey had long known this and, like most people in Dulwich, could recognize Margery on the street (wide bottom, frizzy perm, drab-colored drapery-type clothes), until she started the job, Stacey had not read any of Margery's books. Beverly, however, had read all of them, and she told Stacey how good they were—amazing, Bev said. "They're so amazing." And she always made Stacey promise to read whichever one she'd most recently finished, which Stacey would readily do. But then she would leave the book unopened on her bedside table, annoyed by its sensational cover—the angry mug of the teen in distress. And with another friend of hers—Becky Greer, whom Stacey knew from her advanced math class—she wrote ongoing spoofs of Margery McIntyre Flood–type YA novels: "Jessica turned on her heel and left," she would write on a sheet of paper and pass to Becky as they reviewed quadratic equations for the millionth time. "A gamut of emotions crossed her face," Becky would write, passing the paper back. "Her overweight, alcoholic stepmother shot her a withering glance." And so on.

Over the past winter, one of Margery's books had been made into an After School Special, which Stacey and Bev had watched one afternoon on television, Bev excitedly, Stacey skeptically, but ultimately drawn in.

After the show aired, Margery had come and spoken at an assembly at Addison, the combined middle school/junior high where Stacey and Bev were in their last year. With very little prompting from Bev (who herself lagged back, unwilling to make an overture) Stacey introduced herself to Margery afterward and, in the course of explaining that she wanted to be an author too, lied and said she'd really enjoyed reading *You Can't Do Anything Right,* when of course she had only watched it on television.

THE LIE PAINED Stacey now, starting the job, for she realized what an obvious one it was, and she wished that she had chosen a more obscure title—*Mom's Coffee Smells Like Gin,* for instance, or the birth-control one—*You Would if You Loved Me.*

(Pressing the small of her back into the hard auditorium chair so as to avoid looking at Helena, Stacey recalls with wonder the rude confidence with which she glided through the first few days of the job. It reminds her, now that she thinks about it, of the two disastrous post-college relationships she's had, one in New York and one in L.A. Those, too, had seemed to start off with a grace period: those initial couple of dates on which she had blithely, ignorantly been herself—harshly critical, impatient, funny—before the transformation into the slavish, would-be-long-term girlfriend she became so automatically it seemed the happy version of herself must have been the act. In any case, it never lasted long.)

Nearly a week had passed by before Stacey noticed the books. She was coming back from the bathroom, stalling a little no doubt, having left Helena in the living room playing tea party, when she happened to catch sight of Margery's own copies of her novels. There they all were all there, sitting on the hallway bookshelves, two or three rows of them, hardcover and paperback editions beside what were evidently their foreign translations, some in languages Stacey didn't recognize. The shelves were a revelation to Stacey: It hadn't occurred to her that authors would have copies of their own books. Here, then, was the segue she'd been looking for, the perfect jumping-off point for a discussion with Margery about writing, about her own ambitions. She had eased *You Can't Do Anything Right* off the shelf and was deep into the third or fourth page when she finally registered that a smashing sound had come from the living room. It was as if she had heard it and not heard it, as if she had heard it and been so paralyzed by the idea of it that she just couldn't react. "It's pretty cool," she called nervously into the room, "that your mother wrote these, isn't it?" Then, fear in her heart, she raced down the hall.

As usual today the furniture had been rearranged to make a fort—armchair dragged into place, piano bench yanked out and overturned. Except for Margery's office upstairs, no room in the little eyebrow colonial was off-limits; no object forbidden to touch. On the first afternoon when Stacey had said, "Ooh, maybe we'd better not play with these," indicating the collector's tea cups in the corner whatnot, Helena had given her an obtuse look and replied, "Why?"

The little girl was standing behind the sofa in her tattered eyelet nightgown; Stacey hadn't managed to get her dressed this morning. "I wanted to do flying saucers," she said to Stacey, her eyes bright with the drama of what she had done. Stacey followed her gaze to the bricked bit of floor in front of the fireplace, where half a dozen of the cups lay shattered on the floor.

"Oh, dear, Helena! We'd better sweep all this up now!" Stacey started to say, trying to hide her despair in the can-do voice she'd heard Mrs. Larsen, one of the other mothers she worked for, use with her girls, when Margery appeared, treading heavily down the stairs as if she wanted to give them plenty of warning.

"Mommy, there was a big accident!" Helena cried excitedly.

"I'm so sorry," Stacey said, her voice shaking, she was appalled to find, at the confrontation—at the knowledge that while one tea cup might have been excusable, there was no explanation for this; she would certainly be fired.

A look of alarm flickered across Margery's face, which she immediately hid with a vacant, irritated smile. She avoided looking at the fireplace at all, keeping her eyes up, first on Stacey, then glancing past Stacey down the hall to the kitchen. "I've had an unbelievably trying morning."

"I'm sorry," Stacey mumbled, as Margery went on in just the bright, unflappable manner she had used when a boy asked her a rude question at Addison ("What base did Karen and Theo get to when they were making out?"). "You see, Scholastic is supposed to flow through the money for *Gin* and *Anything Right* but what they don't seem to understand is that if I don't get the money, the bank doesn't get the mortgage!" For the last several words of the sentence Margery's voice grew more and more emphatic until she came gasping up like a swimmer barely making it to the far end of a long pool.

"Silly, silly, silly bank, Mommy, right?" Helena cried, and she clapped her hands together in a manner so contrived Stacey looked away in disgust.

"Silly bank indeed!" said Margery. Her eyes darted to the brass clock on the side table by the sofa. It had Roman numerals and, as Stacey was beginning to learn, could lead to tragic misreadings of the time. "Well, it's lunchtime, isn't it?"

Stacey didn't know what to say so she nodded, flushing, though she didn't know why.

"I was thinking we'd have ice cream for lunch," Margery said.

"Yay! Ice cream for lunch!"

"I've only got *ten* minutes, Helena, then it's right back upstairs for me." She looked at Stacey. "You'll join us, won't you?"

Stacey swallowed and gave a tight smile.

Another mother, Mrs. Thibeaud, had taught her always to throw out broken glass and china in paper bags, not plastic. She got a broom and dustpan and a brown grocery bag from the closet in the kitchen and swept everything up.

THE AFTERNOON, ONCE Margery had retreated into her study, was hot and endless. (Supposedly Margery was working all day but once when Stacey had to go up to Helena's room to fetch a pair of shoes, she found Margery sitting at her bedroom vanity with her compact mirror out, making eyes at herself and pursing her lips.)

Helena wouldn't, of course, look at a book or be read to; she wouldn't play "Colonial Times," a game of Stacey's devising that was a favorite of the Larsen girls; she tired of drawing—began to scribble on her hands, marker her face. She seemed to have a nose for anything that gave Stacey the smallest modicum of pleasure, anything remotely intellectual, and to be automatically suspicious of it.

"No!" she said when, sitting up in her bedroom now, Stacey suggested crazy eights. She snatched the deck of cards from Stacey's hands and tossed it impudently into the air, scattering the cards across the floor.

"*No,*" Stacey was surprised to hear herself say. She narrowed her eyes at Helena in some unfamiliar expression, one that was not compromised, as her face usually was, by the desire to be liked; the fear of being overheard; the desperate striving to set the right— maternal yet authoritative—tone. "Bad Ghost doesn't want you to do that," she said in an ominous murmur. "Bad Ghost is very, very mad at you." At the look of surprise on Helena's face, Stacey stopped short. What the hell was she doing? She started to make light of it when Helena gave a little squeal and said, "Am I going to get in trouble?"

"Umm . . ." Stacey hesitated. Helena was nodding vigorously and whispering, "Yes! Yes! Say I'm in big trouble."

"You're in *big trouble*!" Stacey said obediently.

"No!" Helena cried savagely. She whacked at Stacey's calves in frustration. "Not like that! The other way! Do it the other way!"

"Shut up!" Stacey barked. And with her right arm, she swept a load of stuffed animals violently off the bed. "*You will do as I say. Or Bad Ghost is going to come and get you.*" Helena was watching her avidly. "*And you will be very fucking sorry.*" The *fucking* slipped out—more than she intended—but Stacey gulped and ignored it. "Now go and stand in the closet," Stacey snarled, "and count to ten!"

"No, a *hundred*!" Helena said under her breath. "Tell me to count to a hundred. Make me stay in there a really long time!"

"I don't know, Helena . . ." Stacey said weakly.

"*Tell me to count to a hundred,*" Helena demanded, her little face gone hard, irritating.

"Fi-ine!" Stacey agreed huffily, as if she were talking to a peer of hers. "What the hell do I care? A hundred. Count to a hundred if it makes you happy. Go wild."

"Yay!" Helena jumped up and ran to her closet. She closed the door on herself, then opened it, beckoning Stacey over to murmur to her again. "I'm bad, right? That's why I have to stay in here."

"Helena! Of *course* not," Stacey said, flushing.

"*No!*" Helena banged the door open so hard it slammed the bedroom wall. "Say I'm *bad,* Stacey. Say I'm really, really, really bad—like the baddest person you've ever seen."

"But, Helena—"

"*Say it, Bad Ghost!*"

OVERNIGHT, HELENA BECAME tractable and easy. She actually seemed to like Stacey now—rushed to greet her when she arrived in the morning, jealously seizing the older girl's hand to draw her away from whatever small talk Stacey was making with

Margery. Stacey always hoped that Margery would detain her for a minute or two, share something else about the book she was working on—gripe about her agent, who ought to have gotten her more money for this one, her editor, Renata, who had completely misunderstood a passage in *Where Were You on Sunday?* and whom Margery was therefore not convinced she could really trust. The bits of shoptalk were thrilling to Stacey, and she was quick to think up follow-up questions that would keep the conversations going. But the instant Helena appeared, Margery would hurry away, snatching her legal pad and mug of tea from the mess on the kitchen counter. "I'll leave you two to play!" she would sometimes say, which cut Stacey to the quick, because it was as if Margery thought of Helena and her as peers.

If Helena was suspicious of Stacey for her interest in books, what Stacey suspected in Helena was how fast she took to the new game. The girl's instant preference for it reminded Stacey of the kids at school who passed around *Flowers in the Attic,* with the lurid, half-obscured face on the cover. What sort of person, she wondered, was attracted to the trappings of evil?

BOTH GIRLS, AT least, seemed to hit upon the necessity of the game's having a narrative arc—or at least a daily trajectory of punishment—to keep it interesting. According to this never-stated but mutually agreed-on principle, in the mornings, like a felon starting with minor infractions, Helena would commit petty crimes only. She would refuse to make the bed, for instance, forcing Stacey, as Bad Ghost, to make it for her, with the understanding that the little girl would pay later. "You are going to be in *such big trouble,*" Stacey would say ominously. "Now get out of my sight!" Helena would shriek and run to hide in the closet, emerging (when Stacey pretended not to be looking—when she went to the bathroom or overcasually opened a book) to mess up her room, throwing stuffed animals against the wall, seizing books from the little painted bookshelf and chucking them to the floor.

(Stacey, raising her hands to join in the clapping that follows Renata Townsend's remarks, flinches in her seat remembering having to watch the books land sacrilegiously open, the pages getting smushed, the spines splayed. Helena's clapping, too, clapping and looking at her watch.)

If, at any point in the day, Stacey made the mistake of talking in a normal voice, say to ask Helena if she had to go to the bathroom ("Don't worry, Helena, you won't miss anything—I'll wait for you!"), the little girl would erupt in an indignant fury. "I'm going to pee all over the floor!" she had screamed in response to that particular question. And she'd squatted down in a corner of the room saying, in an alarming way, "Psss, psss, psss!" until Stacey hissed, "Stop it! You go and use the bathroom or . . . I'll whip you with chains for five hours!"

The mornings were all setups for the afternoons, which officially began after lunch—when the little girl would go on a crime spree. A Barbie, whose head, arms, and legs popped conveniently off, suffered the most. She broke her neck being thrown down the stairs; she was drowned in the bathroom sink; she was defenestrated out the back of the house. The trickiness was that Stacey had to think up punishments that were commensurate with the offense. Nothing aroused Helena's ire so much as getting away with murder. Sometimes Stacey, her imagination dulled by the monotony of the game, would distractedly throw out a tired, subpar sentence: Bad Ghost is going to put you through the spanking machine! "You already did that!" Helena would scream. If Stacey didn't think up anything better, and fast, Helena would throw a tantrum and Stacey had no choice but to raise the stakes again to keep the girl in her thrall. Throwing her in jail (the closet) would work for days and days but occasionally it went flat and that was when Stacey gave in to Helena's wishes, and improvised a new, harsher-than-the-last-time "Bad Ghost telling you how bad you are." This involved Helena's lying on the bed, or the sofa if they were downstairs, and Stacey creeping up to her to whisper in her ear that she was the naughtiest, most awfully behaved girl she'd ever met, the worst child she'd ever babysat for. And so on and so forth.

As the days went by Stacey's face felt tired, with keeping it in a threatening scowl, her throat ached from the constant, disgusted berating that now constituted her days. She felt hot and sweaty cooped up in the house all day, and she caught herself, when Helena was doing her jail time in the closet, looking wistfully out the little girl's window at the backyard, where Margery's garden went unweeded and a spotted bouncy horse rusted on its springs.

ONE MORNING TOWARD the end of July, Margery announced with a self-satisfied air that she would be working in the Dulwich library doing research all week on adolescent drunk driving, "which can start as early as sixteen if the parents are uninvolved or unaware!" she informed Stacey and Helena. This was a boon for Stacey, who felt she could give rein to the game and please Helena more, since she could worry less about Margery's wondering what they were up to—not that Margery ever had.

They were playing in Helena's bedroom, the shades drawn so it was dark. Books, toys, and clothes had been dumped and scattered willy-nilly all over the floor. Stacey was lying on her back on Helena's bed, trying to raise and lower her feet, as they'd done this year in gym, by tightening her abdominal muscles, while berating Helena for her bad behavior. Helena was "locked" in the closet, a large crate of books blocking the door so she couldn't escape. "You're a horrible, horrible girl," Stacey was shouting. "I'm never going to be able to forgive you. I'm doubling your punishment, do you hear me? I'm so mad at you I might just leave you here all by yourself and go home! You're so bad you don't *deserve* a babysitter!"

"No, tripling it!" came Helena's yell—muffled from the closet so that Stacey barely heard her. And of course, a person coming up the stairs, she realized, straightening up, as they creaked, would not have been able to discern the little voice at all. Now there was a noise, right outside the door. Stacey sprang from the bed and pulled it open, coming face-to-face with Margery.

Helena's mother took in the trashed room without a word. "We were just playing!" Stacy cried. She fumbled and tripped, scraping her forearm as she yanked the crate from in front of the closet door, so Helena could come out.

"We're playing Bad Ghost, Mommy!" Helena said. "Stacey's telling me how bad I am and punishing me—I'm in jail! I'm *really* bad today!"

Margery didn't say a thing. She walked straight across the mess on the floor, not bothering to pick her way, grinding toys and books beneath her heels, and went to the window where she gave the bottom of the shade several jerks until it snapped up around the roller, letting in the daylight. Her eyes lowered toward the bed where Stacey had been lying, she said, with extreme irritation, "You don't want to pull it down so far. It's a good way to break it."

"Margery, I'm sorry—it's this game—" Stacey blurted out in dismay, but Margery had strode from the room.

Trembling on the bed, Stacey clutched a stuffed animal to her chest as Helena called after her mother, "Mommy? Are you done with your research for today? Mom-my! Answer me!" The little girl stepped out into the hallway. "Mommy, I hate you! Mommy, do you hear me? Mommy, you're not my mother anymore!"

"Let's murder her," Stacey said. Her heart beating like crazy, she got up off the bed and drew Helena back inside the room. "Bitch!" She picked up the Barbie and kicked her across the floor, then snatched her up and started snapping off her limbs, throwing them into the "fire" (a red blanket). At some point in the midst of the mutilation she noticed Helena sitting on the floor, back up against the wall, watching her. When she saw Stacey looking at her Helena smiled and that just killed Stacey—the idea that the little girl felt she had to fake that she was having fun. "Helena?" Stacey said at once. "You know it's just for pretend, right? I mean, we're not *really* killing or hurting anyone."

"I know! I know! I'm not *stupid*!" said the old furious Helena, and Stacey felt a fool for letting her guard down.

"Well, then, come on—what's your problem? Why are you sitting there watching me? I can't do this by myself, Helena! Don't you want to do something really bad so you can get punished?"

A few days later the girl seemed to weary of the game altogether. She got into her bed, pulling the covers over her head, and made the muffled suggestion "Maybe we ought to play something else."

But the truth was it made the afternoons pass faster. Even though the monotony of the anger and crime bored and exhausted Stacey, too, there were no more scenes in Bob's Market. Nothing else got broken. They hardly ever left Helena's room.

For days after the incident, Stacey thought up explanations for what Margery had seen, from the straightforward "She likes it when I pretend I'm mad at her" to the slightly more far-fetched "Why don't you try controlling your fucking brat of a daughter, you fucking bitch?" At the end of the week, the summons finally came. Stacey was to put on the television for Helena and come up to Margery's office for a word. For the first bit of the conversation Stacey was so nervous thinking she'd be fired that she couldn't concentrate on what Margery was saying. She stared at the framed book jackets and reviews and blow-ups of Margery's author photos on the walls—something about a trip that Margery was meant to be taking with Helena in August but would have to cancel . . .

Stacey must have looked fearful, for Margery hastened to reassure her, "Of course I understand if you can't do it. . . . These edits—they're just taking longer than I'd expected. You'd think that with my *fourth novel . . .*" She went on and on and on about the book, talking faster and faster, going into more and more confusing detail, and when she finally stopped short, Stacey could only mumble, "So, I guess . . . Helena's okay with this plan, then?"

Margery rose hurriedly from her desk. "So, you'll stay then, Stacey?" She hardly ever used Stacey's name, and Stacey was distracted by the flattering effect this had on her. "Till the very end of August?" Margery had opened the door and Stacey walked through it. On the landing she could just barely hear the violent cartoon Helena was watching two floors below, the muffled bells and blasts and shrieks. She swallowed and nodded. "Sure," she said. "Anything I can do to help."

WHEN THE SPEECHES end, the crowd floods into the lobby for wine and cheese. Gulping down the syrupy white, Stacey cranes her neck around for Helena and her friend. Bizarrely, they left about two-thirds of the way through the program, standing up just as a young editor, of about Stacey's age, began to read a passage from *Where Were You on Sunday?,* the book the editor said had made her want to go into publishing. They attracted a few glances as they left, clumping awkwardly in their high heels; crashers, people must have thought, as Stacey had, though in fact the event was open to the public. Now catching sight of the two of them pushing sheepishly up to the drinks table, Stacey has an urge to play a trump card—surprise someone here by revealing Helena's identity. But this hasn't been her crowd for years and there's no one she can tell. Keeping an eye on the two young women, who retreat hastily with their cups to a corner of the lobby, Stacey gets herself another and follows them over to where they're making fun of something, snickering and sipping.

"Helena."

Stacey plants herself in front of the two of them, surprised at the undercurrent of anger in the word. She remembers herself and says awkwardly, "I'm so sorry about your mother. When my mother told me . . ." But at once there seems to be nothing more to add. Helena is looking down at her wine, her expression wan and discomfited. Stacey can't believe how much the girl has changed physically. As a child she was slight to the point of frailness, a slip of a girl. Full grown, she seems to have put on bone density as much as weight—the line of her jaw is strong, her shoulders broad. She's tall and thick around the middle, too; she has the kind of normalish body you see outside New York and L.A., the kind that always makes Stacey feel gauchely thin and toned. She glances at the other girl, wondering if she's made a mistake by seeking Helena out when Helena did not seek her but perhaps she wished to remain anonymous. "I thought you guys left!" Stacey says finally, her mind going blank and panicky at the cool reception she's being given.

"We had to buy cigarettes," says the friend, holding up a pack of Marlboros. "We got a day off." She looks past Stacey at the milling, babbling crowd. "Gotta make the most of it, right?"

Stacey gushes her agreement, asks where they both work.

"*I* don't work. I've got three kids at home."

"Oh, my God!" says Stacey. "Three?"—moving smoothly along from inane to asinine. "And where's home for you?" she asks, as if she's the kind of person who says things like that.

"Portland," Helena's friend tells her, adding her name—Patty.

"Portland, Maine, not Oregon, right, Helena?" Stacey says, but her former charge is still avoiding eye contact, standing uncomfortably, clearly, but not moving, as if she doesn't want to give up her spot.

"You guys want a refill?" Stacey asks, thinking perhaps they're too shy to go up themselves.

Patty holds out her cup. "Make mine a double!"

"I mean—don't let me corrupt you with my bad habits!" Stacey roars. "It's five o'clock, after all, though, right? I think we deserve another, don't you?"

Evidently, she thinks, as she waits for the drinks—dejected, hating her outfit now, its smugness and vanity—although she hasn't had to reach for it in a while, abject conciliation still suits her fine in a pinch. She gets three more white wines and, concentrating so as not to spill, manages to get them over to the girls. "Take mine?" Helena says to Patty, and Stacey sees that the young woman is holding something out to her—photographs. Her mouth twists ruefully, as if Stacey might reject her offering. As Stacey drains her third wine and examines the pictures, she has an epiphany. It's nothing personal—Helena's silence. Or rather, it is, as far as it has to do with Stacey's clothes, her polished palaver, her ease in the setting. Helena is shy, stubborn, defensive because of all that and not because, Stacey posits hopefully, she's been harboring some fifteen-year grudge against her old babysitter.

The older of the two boys is cocky-looking, grinning through missing teeth, posed next to the flag in front of the sky-blue backdrop of an American public school. The other, who's perhaps three, has soft, sandy hair like Helena's and a sad, sweet ingratiating smile for the camera—mama's boy, Stacey thinks, looking up, her face fixed into a strange mask in which she is trying both to simulate delight and hide how flattered she is that Helena has made this gesture. "Are they—?" she says noncommittally.

"Five. Three." Helena comes very close to Stacey as she says this—so close that Stacey can feel the warmth of her skin. It seems very un–New York to stand close to someone like this, and a childlike elation passes through Stacey as Helena points to each of the pictures as she says the boy's age.

"Wait—which one's the five-year-old?" Stacey says vacuously, just to keep the conversation going.

Helena points to the darker-haired boy again. "Jim. And Dylan's my baby."

"They look just like you! The little one—what is it, Dylan?—especially."

"*Doesn't* he—I mean, right?" agrees Patty affably. She takes a cigarette out of the pack and taps it against the box, as if she might light up right inside the theater.

"Yeah, when he was born, everybody said it must've been the milkman 'cause you can't see Harold in him at all," Helena says in a burst of conversation, and then she keeps going, as if, like other shy people Stacey has known, she's either fully off or fully on. "Although it'd be more like the doughnut drive-thru guy, wouldn't it, Patty? We're there like every day!"

Patty sneers. "You are—you like that guy."

"Ha, ha, ha, ha, ha! I can see why!" Stacey manages to curb herself as Renata Townsend appears at Helena's side. The woman's eyes rest briefly on Stacey, dismissing her. She clasps hands with Helena and murmurs, "Is it all right? How are you, dear? Are you having fun? It won't be too much longer, and then we can go to the restaurant. A small group of Margery's close friends are going to go on."

Helena shrugs. "Sure, okay."

"We're starved!" says Patty.

The editor gives Helena's arm a proprietary squeeze before moving on to another group.

"You know, your mother's practically the reason I became a writer!" Stacey interjects, hoping Renata will hear her.

A few short minutes later, she's saying, "Well, it was great to see you, Helena," viscerally longing to escape to the jumble and noise of Broadway. "Look me up if you're in L.A.!" But when she scribbles her e-mail on her program and hands it to Helena, the falseness of the gesture fills her with disgust. It's not just that she knows Helena will never look her up; that sort of pretension is a given in today's world. It's that she knows Helena will never come to L.A. She knows it and pretends that she doesn't.

OUTSIDE, THE BREEZE has died, and the sidewalk, littered with newspaper inserts and plastic bags, looks blown out and abandoned. Stacey has had the bad luck to emerge just behind a group of publishing people who are looking pessimistically up the street for cabs. She sees that she's going to have to walk to the train and sets off peeved, as if she's been cheated of something that was rightfully hers.

Fucking babysitting, she thinks, getting more upset as she walks rather than less, as if the dire awkwardness of the first few minutes of soliciting Helena are getting to her only now—now that they can, now that she doesn't have to keep up the conversation, keep up the entertainment, the clown act. Earlier this afternoon, when Ryan, her agent, caught her on her cell phone as she was leaving the hotel, Stacey had said coyly, "Guess how I knew her?" after explaining about the memorial. (That he is still her agent, five career-making years later, Stacey likes to cite as proof of all sorts of capabilities she has—loyalty mainly; on occasion, love.) Ryan, like most people of their generation, had remembered Margery McIntyre Flood with a joke, and a botched title: *Mom Puts Gin in Her Coffee!*

"*Mom's Coffee* Smells *Like Gin*," Stacey corrected him and when she told him how she met Margery, he said, "Oh, my God, *you* used to babysit? You *hate* kids!" Stacey had laughed in the moment but now, starting to wallow, she feels grievously slighted by Ryan's remark.

Beverly had quit jobs, Stacey remembers, smarting at the injustice; so why hadn't she? Mrs. Purnick had marched Bev up to the front door of one of the boys she babysat for, had rung the doorbell, and had said, "Your son is stealing and my Beverly can't be responsible for that." Of course, Mrs. Purnick knew all about the Goren kid's shoplifting from day one, whereas Stacey can't recall ever having shared any salient details with her mother, ever having given Anita any real notion of what the job for Margery was like.

What she can remember, however, she thinks, breaking into a run for a chance taxi, are the long, enjoyable conversations she and Anita had had about how spoiled Helena was. Stacey looked forward to the conversations all day—they got her through to five o'clock. She had relented on Anita's picking her up in the car and at four-thirty would start to count down the minutes until Anita's car would arrive. Sometimes she would excuse herself and go into the bathroom and sit on the toilet, staring at the peeling wallpaper and counting to one hundred—two hundred, if she dared— just to have a couple of minutes go by without having to be Bad Ghost, without having to berate or punish or be angry at anyone. At five on the dot she would look out Helena's bedroom window to see the blue Chevrolet pulling up to the house. The rush of relief, of pure love, she felt when her mother's car appeared—she had never loved Anita so well. It could send her running to Helena to pick her up and hug her and kiss her, the little girl outwardly happy, too, but in a muted way, as if she knew she was being duped.

At first Anita had come in to say hi to Margery, whom she knew slightly from town, and was eager to get to know better, but then she and Stacey would get stuck there, listening to Margery pontificate, and so the two of them agreed that Anita would wait in the car instead.

With the barrier of the car safely separating them, Stacey would wave enthusiastically at Helena, who would watch them from the stoop as they backed away, the little girl motionless, poker-faced. Most days Margery stayed in the house but once in a while she came out and stood beside her daughter, a puzzled smile on her face, as if she hadn't fully internalized the fact that Stacey left at the end of the day.

Anita would back the car carefully out of the driveway onto the road. "So, how was it today?" she'd ask once they got on the way.

Stacey would slip happily into the self-righteously beleaguered tone she'd started to use when discussing the situation with her mother. "Well, today I tried to get her to go outside and she said no. And she starts throwing a temper tantrum. And so I say, 'Fine, we'll play inside'—what do I care? I mean, what can I do?"

"Nothing, Stace." Anita's answer is knee-jerk, condoning; her eyes are on the road.

"I mean," Stacey says, looking quickly at her mother's profile, "I just don't think it's up to me to *force* her to go out. In the first place, I can't. It's not like I'm her mother, you know, Mom?"

"Stace, you're right. You can only do so much."

"I do the best I can, you know?"

"I think you're managing incredibly well."

Here Stacey might have squirmed a little in her seat. "Mom?" she might have said, thinking that today she would drop the pretense—give some small hint about what it was really like, which Anita might pick up on. And it was always on the tip of her tongue: "No, I'm not, Mom. I'm not managing at all. I'm the baddest babysitter you've ever met."

But Anita would be shaking her head—getting into it. "It's just terrible for a child when the parents can't set limits. The kids have all that control. They don't know what to do. It's really not good for their self-esteem. Not to mention what it does to their moral development." Another shake of the head. "That surprises me about Margery—she's such a smart lady. Writing all those books . . ."

"Yeah, well, smart isn't everything," Stacey would say, enjoying quoting Mrs. Purnick, though it was a sentiment that her entire upbringing belied—the report cards plastered to the refrigerator, the compliments passed on from teacher, neighbor, dentist ("Dr. Villanova thinks you're *very* bright").

She and Anita didn't have that many things they could talk enjoyably about in those days, and to make the conversation go on a little longer, Stacey would say, "I mean, you'd agree with that, wouldn't you, Mom? Smart isn't everything?"

But there was always a certain point in the conversation where Anita would fail to hold up her end. Where Stacey's mother would lose interest in the topic and be ready to move on to something else. "So, did she talk to you about your writing at all today?" Anita would want to know. "Did you tell her about the *Globe* essay? You know, I was thinking you ought to just bring it in and show her. I mean, you were runner-up of over three hundred and fifty essays. Do you know how incredible that is? Do you know what the odds are?"

Stacey wouldn't have anything much to say to that, but Anita would go on. "I know Margery would love to read it. You know what? I'll have Dad Xerox it at work, so you don't have to worry about losing the copy." At this point Anita would take her eyes off the road to give Stacey a quick darting glance. "Has she talked at all about . . . you know, helping you get started?"

And Stacey would lie.

She might say, "Well, she was *really* interested in what I thought about *You Can't Do Anything Right*—did I tell you that? She wants to know if I'll read *Where Were You on Sunday?* even though it's not published yet and tell her if I think it would make a good after-school special, too." Or maybe, "Margery asked me to bring her in a sample of my creative writing—that story I wrote last year about the two friends who have the fight—I guess she really wants to read it." And later on: "Margery actually thinks I should try my hand at a YA novel. She's going to talk to her edi-

tor because she basically thinks I'm ready. She wouldn't be surprised if I published something as a teenager."

For this story, too, it seemed to Stacey, had to have a narrative
arc to keep it interesting; or at least a daily trajectory.

Stacey gets to the cab before someone else can take it, and the
small victory mollifies her. In a moment she's relaxing against the
black leather, heading toward blissfully canned hotel luxury, putting blocks and blocks and blocks between herself and Helena and
Margery McIntyre Flood. It comes to her, thus comforted, that of
course she was kidding herself. There was no chance she would ever
have quit the job. She might have scoffed at it in the moment, but
the truth was that she and Anita agreed on something fundamen-
tal: Stacey's brilliant future. And what Stacey had reacted to so
many years ago was not the truth of the remark—"She could really
help you, couldn't she, Stace?"—but the baldness of the statement.
She shied away from the quid pro quo demarcation, holding out for
a more elegant, a more subtle interpretation of her motives—her
luxury, perhaps, as the talent, whereas her mother, agentlike, had
to stay on message.

STACEY HAD WORKED all summer for Margery, and on the last
day, as a going-away present, Margery gave her a copy of *Where
Were You on Sunday?* The book was still in its galleys, and this
seemed to Stacey wildly desirable. She really was going away,
too—she even fancied she was making a massive leap toward some
kind of success, though it had nothing to do with Margery. Alison
and Andrea Larsen's mother had sought out Anita at the firemen's
muster on the Dulwich green in August and told her that they
were moving and would be sad to lose Stacey as their sitter. They
were moving so that Mr. Larsen, who taught chemistry, could take
a job at the Downing School, a boarding school in New Hampshire, and Mrs. Larsen stammered a little and suggested that

Stacey apply—there might be a last-minute spot, even a scholarship, for a bright girl like her. When she said good-bye in September, Stacey promised Helena she—and Bad Ghost, too, of course—would keep in touch, and she even wrote a letter to the girl on one of the first slow weekends away at school. She didn't particularly expect to hear back and she did not. That would have required Margery's sitting down with Helena to help her write a reply and that never would have happened. Stacey didn't care—she had the special copy of the book, to show she knew Margery.

As for Helena—Stacey bites her lip. She looks out the window and chokes convulsively on a sob. Hunched down in the cab, she presses a hand to her eyes. After all the years of glum shame, the tears have finally come. Couldn't she, she asks herself, as her face goes wet and unseeing, couldn't she have made a success of a simple fucking babysitting job? Couldn't she have carried off this basic thing with a modicum of grace? Was that too much to ask? She's bawling when her cell phone rings. She's glad no one can see her, tear-stained, sobbing, and fumbling for it in her bag: the tragic lifelong remorse—that nevertheless permits one to check one's caller ID. It's Ryan—he called twice while she was inside the theater, wanting to finish their conversation—to hear more about the upfronts, bask a little in her enthusiasm and gratitude, as he likes to do from time to time, for all that he's done for her. Shuddering, wiping her nose with the inside of her wrist, Stacey chokes it back. She gets control of her voice and answers the call. "Ryan?" She wasn't the girl's mother, after all. She could only do so much.

Taroudant

I T WAS A mistake. She woke grinding her teeth, with the idea that it had all been a huge, shockingly expensive mistake. They should not have come to Morocco. They certainly should not have come all the way to Taroudant on an offhand recommendation from Will's old boss. Vanity had led them; the self-congratulatory notion that they could do better for themselves than Europe, as if they had seen half—one-tenth—of Paris or even London.

No doubt they shouldn't have gotten married, either, Lydia thought, turning in the bed, her back to Will, but the thought failed to compel her. Theoretical pronouncements were no help. She was of the type that cared more, cared ardently for the specifics, for the seeming superficialities: a point on a map, a brochure listing room rates she would study as if evidential.

Behind her Will stirred. The bed was comprised of two twin mattresses, separately made up, sharing a single frame. His right arm reached across the divide to wrap around her, and then, because she had removed his hand so frequently from that position, moved down to her hip bone. She detached it from there as well, rose, and put on his robe.

She went to the bathroom and washed her face vigorously with the cedar soap. It wasn't that she wanted to avoid sex, but that she wanted to avoid it at this hour. When the sun was shining into the room with the urgency of the day she could not help feeling trapped, would focus her gaze on the ceiling and her thoughts, peevishly, on what she had to get done.

The problem now, she was beginning to discover, was that there was nothing *to* get done. It was something no one had warned her about, no one had seen fit to mention. She hadn't pictured even an hour past the wedding reception. She had thought mainly being rid of her credit card debt, had pictured herself writing the check to pay them off—the surprise of the teller who managed her account, as if someone like that even existed. "Good for Lydia!" the woman would say, opening the payment envelope in Topeka or Tampa or wherever the company was based. "Darn, if she didn't come through."

Lydia stood indecisively at the foot of the bed, listening to Will's trusting, childlike breathing until the familiar panic rose in her. Then she picked up the telephone and ordered breakfast. *"Oui, oui, Madame Norris, tout de suite."* She put up her hair and went out onto the terrace.

The rooms at the hotel were detached stone bungalows built in two concentric arcs, the inner of which faced, across a vast expanse of manicured yet stubbornly scrubby lawn, the main building of the hotel. It was an old shooting lodge, turned hotel in the seventies by an enterprising Frenchman and his Moroccan wife. Will and Lydia had been given a bungalow on the outer arc of cottages—the less desirable arc, clearly, though no less expensive. Lydia had attributed the assignment to something more than chance—their being Americans, or their relative youth. Will, however, who did not think that way, had told her to relax—"It's still pretty damn nice!"

Despite the heat, the mornings had a freshness (albeit an artificial one) created by the staff's caring for the grounds—pruning, weeding, watering—the orange trees and olive trees, the banks of rose bushes. With an impatient look about, Lydia sat down on one of the iron café chairs to wait. *"Tout de suite, Madame Norris,"* the man in the kitchen said each morning, but the amusement in his voice suggested she would be a fool to believe him. It was as if he were humoring her with the response—with keeping up his part in the masquerade in which she played one "Mrs. Norris" and he the properly obsequious servant.

Her neighbors across the way, a pair of Brits, were already out on their portion of lawn, oiled and baking face-up on their chaises longues. Lydia watched them with suspicion. All they seemed to do was lie in the sun and drink. She could hear them, from ten in the morning onward—"Two shandies, two white wines, two gin and tonics"—whenever she and Will returned from swimming or tennis, from their excursions to the walled town, to the desert beyond. "They might as well have gone to Fort Lauderdale!" she had said indignantly to Will.

"Morocco's closer."

"You know what I mean," she persisted. "They clearly don't appreciate it here—you know, the way we do."

Two of the hotel's groundskeepers skirted the couple's chairs, dragging a hose and sprinkler, and crossed in front of the Norrises' terrace. "Bonjour!" They gave a friendly wave to Lydia; did not add "Madame," as Frenchmen would have.

Lydia stood and waved back, eager to make the connection. "Bonjour! Bonjour!" She was aware of the picture she made, in the hotel robe and flowered mules, but there was nothing remotely prurient about the expression in their eyes.

The glass door slid open behind her. "Bonn jour!"

Will's accent incensed her and his presence on the terrace—it put an end to her little adventure.

He put his arms around her from behind, his lips to the top of her head. The gardeners turned promptly away, kneeling down to attend to a row of flower beds. How vulgar we are, Lydia thought, yet knew the vulgarity was in her thoughts, not Will's kiss. It was she who had been vulgar, in transferring her loyalty from her husband to the gardeners, however briefly.

"I ordered breakfast," she said reluctantly.

"Good."

"I suppose that'll be my major achievement of the day."

Will took a seat on the chair she had been sitting in, pushing it back from the table so he could sit more expansively. "I'm starved." He was tall—six three in his socks, her new husband. She found the length of his legs erotic and looked away furiously.

AT THE POOL, disagreeable memories of the wedding came back to her. It seemed the party had scarcely started before the manager of the club had tracked Lydia down to tell her, "You'd better cut the cake now. It's getting late."

It wasn't, of course, their club; someone had been so kind as to lend it to them, and though Lydia had strived to gain the upper hand with the man, she had ended up meekly obeying his orders.

"Why didn't we just go down to City Hall, the two of us?" she said, putting down her magazine. "We'll never see half those people again . . . Will? Did I not tell you the way I wanted to be married was just to go down to City Hall, two witnesses? Didn't I ever say that?"

"Mmm . . ."

"I mean, since I was a little girl—that was my plan."

"You said you wanted a church wedding—that's what you said." Will turned a page of his mass-market paperback, bought two days ago—another world, another era—in the bookstore at JFK.

"A church wedding?" She took out the sunscreen and rubbed it vigorously onto her face and neck. She was scrupulous about protecting herself from the sun. "Well, even if I did say that, why should you have gone along with it? You've never even been baptized." She picked up her magazine and put it down again. "Do you have sunscreen on, Will?"

"Hnnn . . ."

"You should be careful, you know. The sun's a lot stronger here. Will?"

When he still didn't answer she yanked off her sunglasses and walked alongside the pool until, choosing a place at random, she dived into the water.

She surfaced, half expecting to find herself reprimanded for diving, but the Papillon wasn't that kind of a hotel. It almost seemed as if the guests ran the place, the service was so understated; the men in their *djellabas* would appear from time to time, unhurriedly, as if to say it was all no big deal. The pool was empty, and Lydia practiced each of her strokes, not sticking with any of them for long. Will did not put his book down and watch her, as she would have done him. He went on turning pages. When he was finished he would find a new book—a thriller or some tired Grisham; he wasn't picky—and repeat the process. Gazing at his immobile form from the shallow end of the pool, Lydia shivered. She took a great, loud inhale of breath into her shoulders, as a child might, and dived back underwater.

"HE'S REALLY VERY good, isn't he?" Lydia said.

They were having cocktails in the main building of the hotel, just outside the dining room, in a long stone-floored outer room that was anchored by a fireplace at one end, a little bar at the other.

A mustachioed man played a singularly wonderful piano bar each night; his name was Kent and he was an attraction of the hotel. His manner was remote, however; to Lydia's disappointment, he didn't mingle with the guests.

Will nodded. "I'm sure he's classically trained."

"Is he? Can you tell?" It was the kind of thing she liked him to say. "I'll never be one of the careless rich," she remarked pleasantly, watering down her Campari. "This will never not be a luxury." The drinks were served as in a club, the alcohol poured into the glass, the individual bottles of soda or tonic left for the guest to mete out himself.

Will smiled through the bottom of his drink. "We'll get them at home," he said, talking with the ice in his mouth. "I like having the little bottles on hand. I hate it when stuff goes flat."

Beside them a French couple made a graceful move to go in to dinner. The two had sat without speaking, looking out at the room, frank in their boredom. Lydia had seen them in the mornings, playing beautiful, languid tennis. As they rose, she took in the woman's face, lined and painted; the elaborately structured jacket she wore, the gold amassed on her wrists, neck, and ears, and looked down at her lap, conscious of her wispy dress, the dash of mascara and lipstick that served as her makeup. One day, perhaps, she would learn.

They drank up, noticing themselves among the last in the foyer. "But now I'll have to leave it." Lydia held up the miniature bottle of soda and drained it. She couldn't help herself; just as she knew she would pack up the hotel soaps when they left in the morning, for Marrakech—another unattractive compulsion she no longer tried to break herself of.

Perhaps following her train of thought, Will said, "I used to want to have just enough money so I could order pizza whenever I wanted," as a waiter appeared, noiseless in his *babouches,* to show them to their table.

Lydia fumbled with the clasp of her clutch, hiding her face. He had taken her out of herself, in spite of herself; she loved the humble nature of his dream. She had tried—from New York to Newport and back she had tried—but she had proved incapable of dating a man who wasn't self-made. It was like that with the acting—her laughably short career, the one abortive trip to Los

Angeles; with other aspects of her life. She was more than ready, she was poised, eager to sell out, but when the opportunities presented themselves she would dash her hopes on her own inflexibly honest core. There was nothing to do about it. It was like observing a character in a movie, wishing he would take the money and run, all the while knowing he will go to his needlessly honorable fate.

THREE NIGHTS' HABIT dictated that they adjourn to the foyer after dinner and take their coffee there. The windowed room was elevated from the dining room, the pairs of armchairs and card tables arranged with a view to the grand piano just inside. The pianist was playing Gershwin now—"An American in Paris." Lydia followed Will's gaze. "Can't we talk to him tonight, Will? Compliment him or something? It's our last night—we ought to at least thank him."

"What do you want to say?" he asked after a minute.

"I don't know. You talk to him. You say something." What she wanted was to be taken in where others had been excluded. Will got her that, pretty often.

Her husband rose and went to the bar for a pack of cigarettes. Lydia remained at the little cocktail table, sipping her coffee and brandy and humming along. She was smiling, but at nothing external. Drinking made her nostalgic for the promise of her youth. He might not have been there, and it was as if she was determined to keep it that way—as if Will had joined the list of uncomfortably problematic facts that must not directly enter her conscience. Even at the altar, her mind had been elsewhere.

Will tossed a pack onto the table, reserving two cigarettes, which he stuck in his mouth. He lit them, passed one to Lydia. She took it distractedly. "Oh, God, Reds? I'll die. So . . . shall we say something to him now?"

She could tell Will would rather leave it alone—that his code was telling him to leave it alone. "Please, Will? We've sat here three nights in a row—we leave tomorrow . . ."

Kent was closing up the piano, pushing in his chair.

"We'll thank him—come on."

But they were too late. The man slipped outside as they rose. They could see him a moment later through the window, smoking, under the moonlight, his profile half turned to them.

Walking back to their bungalow along the winding flagstone path, she said, "It's not as if he's a concert pianist—he's an employee of the hotel. Part of his job description should be to be civil to the guests. He shouldn't be able to get away with that condescending act—as if he thinks he's too good for us." Her voice rose in the night. "Do you know the gardeners were eyeing me this morning—on the terrace? If you hadn't come out when you did . . ." When Will didn't answer, she stopped dead on the path. "It was borderline harrassment, Will."

"Well, tomorrow we'll be in suck-up city." Will was referring to the hotel they had reserved in Marrakech, one of a global chain that stretched sybaritically from Bali to Beaver Creek. "You oughta like that."

"Don't talk like that—please!" Lydia began walking again. "I hate it when you talk like that. It's not really you—it's not who you are."

"Twelve hundred bucks a night."

IN THE MORNING they had their last breakfast on the terrace and called for the porter. In the driveway of the hotel they examined the rental car, a two-door hatchback, procured the day before from an agent in town.

"God, we'd be lucky to make it to Agadir in that thing."

"You're not serious, are you?" Lydia said anxiously. "It'll be fine, won't it?" Will shrugged and tossed her the keys. "You want *me* to drive?"

He nodded. "I'm beat."

She pretended to find the request onerous but couldn't hold the pose. It was a joy to drive, even in the cheap rental; Manhattanites, they did not often get to. She pushed the car on the long flat open stretches and was soon through the foothills and climbing into the High Atlas. At the sign pointing her toward Tizi-N-Test, the mountain pass, she said impulsively, "Let's have cigarettes—do you want to?" But Will, who was close to sleep, gave an incoherent murmur. She reached across him to the glove box and took out the pack of Marlboros he had bought the night before, slowing to light one.

They didn't smoke much at home, either, but these trips abroad seemed to call for the creation of certain touchstones. Since they'd met—six months previously, at a party on the Upper East Side where neither of them had known anyone; she was a temp in the office of one of the hosts—they had traveled a lot together. They had eaten many room-service breakfasts. The hotels ran happily together in her mind from Istanbul to Isola di Giglio; they had spent a long weekend in Cape Town, another in Dubai. Only secretly did Lydia take pride in their travels. It was a vanity she ridiculed in other people, after all: management consultants who counted the number of stamps on their passports; whitey's trips to Africa, his guided scaling of Kilimanjaro, in her mind only a step up from bragging about the expensive restaurants you had eaten at, the stars you had seen dining in your neighborhood—anyone could do it, and she had a fear of finding satisfaction in ordinary achievements. Yet, it must be admitted, it was she who had said months ago, of a proposed honeymoon in the south of France, "I don't know . . . I just wish we could do something a little different." She had been sitting in the window seat of Will's apartment on Eighty-fifth Street. (A cramped studio apartment: Ten years at the firm and he had never bothered to upgrade, never seeing a reason. Now, he wanted to and Lydia, superstitious, begged him to leave it.) A whine had come into her voice as she said it—that would also have to be admitted, and the "just" of the spoiled wife, ready at her lips even then when, memory would have otherwise assured her, she was still behaving well.

SHE GOT THE cigarette going and raised her head at a flicker of shadow that a split-second's forewarning deemed out of place. An enormous bus was barreling down on them—it was on top of her. Lydia screamed, and with her left hand wrenched the wheel around, her cigarette hand clutched uselessly to her body. "Oh, my God! *Fuck!*" A couple of men who were standing in the front of the bus jeered down at her as they passed. The hatchback had screeched to a halt on a narrow ledge of road and—a standard shift—stalled at once. "Oh, God, oh, God, oh, God. Oh, my God, we almost died."

Will opened his eyes briefly, startled from a dream, then resettled his head against the seat belt.

A strange and pleasant thrill went down Lydia's neck when she realized he was asleep—had stayed asleep; a new idea came into her head. She didn't look at him. She started the car and pulled carefully back out onto the road. Her heart was beating and the shifting of the gearbox seemed preposterously loud. She rolled up the window and got the air-conditioning going on low. She wanted to drive all the way to Marrakech without his waking up, to pull into the Bridge Continental and say briskly, "Well, here we are. That wasn't so bad, was it?" He mustn't wake up. If she made it, absolution would be hers: They would get a clean start.

THE ROAD WOUND up, up, up, until Lydia was switching between the first two gears and not daring to look over the precipice. Unexpectedly, it dipped through a wooded village. Two Berber women, unveiled, were prodding a cow alongside the road. A little farther on, beside a citadel of some sort—the town's well?—

a game of ball was stopped to let her pass. The gaggle of boys split smoothly in half, moving to either side of the road. They watched her, a few littler boys and then a taller, older one, the ringleader, looking more curiously when he saw the driver was a woman. Lydia gave a little wave, bold behind the glass of the moving car, and the boy raised a hand as well, his expression half derision, half some inchoate proposition.

Two more buses passed, both of them going south and nearly crowding her off the road. Emerging from a hairpin turn, she glimpsed another village across the way, the stone houses tiered into the next mountain slope. She pressed the gas pedal harder, as if she could make the car take off into the air and skip the road in between. She pushed the pedal again, annoyed; the car was sluggish. Belatedly she checked the gauge—zero. Zero, after less than two hours. The unfairness of it gave her a sick, baleful feeling. She drove around another razor-sharp turn and over a rise—and she saw a gas station. Feeling cantankerous that the problem was so easily solved, Lydia had half decided to press on past it when the car sputtered for real and, with a fearful gasp, she braked at once.

SHE HAD PULLED into a clearing across the street from a pair of pumps and a small, concrete structure, the once-yellow façade now nearly all peeled away. "A mini-mart, of course," Lydia murmured—as if they were at a rest stop on the Merritt. She looked hastily at Will and got out of the car; she would go to the bathroom, then fill up. As gingerly as she could she shut the door. Still, the noise reverberated and the truculent sickness threatened to overwhelm her. She had to lean against the car to steady herself. On the rocks above her, two men were working with pickaxes and shovels, apparently to widen the road. They seemed to be standing with their heads directly against the sky rather than beneath it. The sky itself was vast—impenetrably blue. To her left, behind the gas station, the mountain fell off, a thousand feet or more. It was absolutely still and silent, except for the sound of the men's tools chinking and scraping the rock and a hushed din from whatever village lay below them, so extremely muted that it might have been a murmur in the air itself. Lydia gazed pessimistically up the road. The ridge that lay before them gave the impression, like all mountain ridges, of being the last before the summit. Feeling the men's eyes on her, she hurried across the road trying not to clutch her stomach and went into the store.

"*Bonjour, monsieur. Il y a un w.c. ?*"

The proprietor, skeptical, indicated a door in the corner. *Yes*— Lydia understood, crossing to it, the universal expression—*if you're whore enough to use it.*

The door opened onto the outside of the building; she had to inch a few steps along an iron railing before entering the bathroom itself. It was a Turkish toilet, of course. While Lydia was doing her best to manage, Will's voice from the other room, gregarious and self-deprecating, broke through her thoughts. She buttoned up her pants and stood leaning on the railing outside for a couple of minutes, contemplating the thousand-foot drop, listening to him laughing and speaking his bad French; she had an alert yet blank expression on her face, like an expression she might have put on to pretend she didn't know him. She walked back into the store.

"You're supposed to use the subjunctive with *il faut,* don't you know that?"

Will was laughing in negotiation with a man and a young boy who, having arrived from nowhere, had spread out their things on a rug on the floor. They wanted to sell him a pipe, an ashtray, a knife, the cedar soap, a ceramic pig; rosewood to keep clothes smelling fresh; *pierre-ponce* to use as pumice stones. The proprietor was looking on, amused now.

Lydia repeated her grammatical correction and said, "Tell them we're not going to buy anything but gas," and when Will seemed

ready to object, she insisted, "Please just tell them!" False prem-
ises were intolerable to her.

"They want to know if we'll trade—if we have Levis in the car."

"No!" Lydia's hand flew to her mouth. "*No.* Didn't you bring
yours?" but Will was already shaking his head. "Too hot."

"Oh, Will!" she said reluctantly. "That would have been a good
one to tell."

"*Monsieur, monsieur—priez vous—bonnes choses,* I tell you, *bonnes
choses,*" the man said.

"But I can't pay that much," said Will, his jovial expression indicating he would pay whatever they wanted. "I already told you."

The man repeated that the things were nice.

"No, you don't understand. It will look bad in front of my
wife." The proprietor came out from behind the counter as Will,
who seemed to have decided that the situation called for primal
communication among men, pantomimed chopping off his own
balls. As the men and boy took their cue with a big laugh, Lydia
wandered to the threshold of the little building and looked out.
Across the road the two men had stopped working and were leaning against the rock eating their lunches. After a moment one of
them stood and beckoned to her. He, too, had something he
wanted to show her—metal trinkets, it looked; ornaments of some
kind. Lydia shook her head gently and averted her eyes, being
careful to smile so as not to offend.

My wife. It vexed her to think that without Will's presence to
legitimize her, she wouldn't have stood a chance.

She felt something push against her leg, and the little boy, the
peddler's son, or grandson, slipped by. The man who had beckoned to Lydia waved the child over. Darting reptilelike up the
rock, the boy conferred briefly with the man then picked up one
of the wire boxes and started toward Lydia, summoning her ani-
matedly and pointing. The thought of having to talk to them
filled her with exhaustion but she couldn't very well retreat into

the shop now, and having to look at something, she shielded her eyes and squinted to take a polite look at what they were selling. Not metal trinkets, she saw now, but tiny wire cages they were, a dozen of them, stacked one on top of the other. In each was a live lizard.

THEY REACHED THE city in the late afternoon. It was Will who drove along the wide, tree-lined avenue of Gueliz. He turned north, away from the city center until they found themselves on a high-walled road that wound through the golf courses built by the golf-crazy former king. After passing turnoffs for two or three of these, they came around a wooded bend and out into a stretch of flat open space. Directly in front of them a massive gated complex rose up. Not yet! Lydia thought. As Will sped through the gates she convulsively clutched the door handle. "Will—" she began. But she couldn't think of a thing to say that would legitimately detain them, or keep them in the car for another quarter of an hour. Already he was unbuckling his seat belt, climbing out. She was alone in the car.

"What, drove yourselves?" The concierge had come running out to greet them, a bevy of foolishly grinning baggage handlers in tow. "Mr. Norris! Mrs. Norris!" the man protested. "You ought to have called me. Next time I will arrange a car for you."

"But we didn't want a car," said Lydia, climbing out as well.

At once she was homesick, as the fawning foursome surrounded her, for the desultory service at the Papillon. There would be no use, she saw, for their high school French at the Bridge Continental.

"Or a flight. It's a very pleasant flight from the south."

"We didn't want to fly. We wanted to drive ourselves." But the man didn't hear her. She had lagged back while he had taken a proprietary hold of Will, leading him through an immense open-air, rose-pink pavilion. Emerging again, they walked along the side of a vast, shallow reservoir, the surrounding pink edifices and their green-tiled roofs reflected with eerie perfection in the pool's water.

"What hotel did you visit in Taroudant?"

"The Papillon," Will said, looking around skeptically.

"It is a nice hotel."

"Yup."

"Not, however, comparable to the Bridge Continental, of course. Here, you will find all the amenities—"

"We liked the Papillon," interrupted Lydia, dragging her heels so they would have to wait, and when Will turned, getting irritated, to check on her, she made a face at the man's back.

In their room the sucking up continued. Except you could not have called their quarters a room. The huge bedroom suite came with its own outdoor real estate—its own wading pool, tanning beds, gazebo. Despite herself she gawked and Will smiled. The concierge thought Will was smiling at the room and said, "Yes, sir, I think you will be very comfortable with us at the Bridge."

"I ought to be at the price."

The man laughed uproariously, paused for a stern aside to a hesitating porter, and finished the laugh. "Come, sir"—he took Will unctuously by the upper arm—"let me show you some of the many wonderful features of the suite, including the granite and marble bath."

This was nothing new: The global service industry was delighted with Will—salespeople, concierges, drivers. He did not disappoint them, the way so many did in this modern world in which overweight American girls with shaved heads traveled by backpack. Will looked the way they wanted an American to look—tall, large, with the long legs and developing paunch of the ex-athlete, the high color suggestive of good living. In his khakis and English shirts you could see him on a golf course or at a football tailgate, though in fact he shunned both—of late using Lydia

as an excuse. In the man's quick, assessing gaze Lydia was reminded for a moment of something her girlfriends had decided
among themselves just before the wedding, while the bitch of a
hired hairdresser yanked and tamed her curls into a respectable
twist. Martine and Jackie weren't the kind of bridesmaids one was
supposed to have. They were the odd friend here, the odd friend
there Lydia had been able to hold on to. But cracking open a bottle of champagne and sharing one of Martine's cigarettes, they'd
agreed on something: Will was wasted on her. "She would have
been happy with some short, freakish, penniless asshole—"

"She certainly *dated* a number of short, freakish, penniless—"

Foolishly Lydia took the bait; she tried to say something in her
defense—he isn't wasted on me, he's *not,* you have no idea—but
the hairdresser swore because she'd moved her head and they
laughed and told her to finish her champagne. Then Lydia's
mother came meekly to the door of the hotel room—cowed because the groom was picking up the tab—and said it was time to
go, the cars were waiting.

"My God, he loves you. He absolutely loves you." The
concierge had graduated to grand gestures of summoning and dismissing, "disciplining" the obedient porters with theatrical censure.

Will grunted. "He wants his tip."

"I feel like a third wheel."

When he left, though, they felt the man's absence; that, as well
of the motor's whir and the soothing reel of landscape that had ac-
companied them all day. Each was aware that it was the time of
day when they normally got into a fight and each of them listened,
half unconsciously, for the complaint of Lydia's that would set
them off.

After a moment Will began to undress.

Lydia watched him, not saying anything. She picked up a
leather volume from the bedside table, the word *Amenities* em-

bossed in gold script on its cover, and alit on the edge of the ridiculously large, canopied bed. Too late she realized her mistake, for Will sat down beside her and put his arms around her.

"This is a horrible place," she said. He smelled of the cedar soap, some faint residue of the spices in the food they'd been eating and his own familiar deodorant, masking sweat.

"It sucks." He spoke into her hair, pushing his nose into it.

Lydia let him remove the book from her hand, unhappily let him kiss her. But when he ran his hand up under her shirt she flinched, pushing it away. "Will—*please.*" Her tone was indignant, like a parent's, on discovering a child has broken a rule agreed upon not five minutes earlier.

He released her without a word.

"Where are you going? Will? Please don't be mad at me. It's been a long day—and a long drive—"

"It's our *wedding* trip."

"You know how it is for me," she said, despising the words as she said them but unable to stop—unable even to sit there. She watched him rummage through their bags.

"Where are you going? Are you going outside? Are you going to take a swim?"

"I thought I'd take a shower," he said coldly. "If that's all right with you."

He padded across the stone floor naked but for his striped boxer shorts. Lydia longed to follow him, to lay her cheek against his chest. Instead she listened to the door slide shut, the rush of water. She wandered around, restless. In the basket sitting on the trunk at the foot of the bed there was a bottle of wine; Lydia picked it up and studied it. "Complimentary" it was called—and she wasn't above taking it as a compliment: It made her feel better about herself.

When the shower stopped she spoke. "What do you want to do about dinner?" She went to the bathroom and peered in.

Will was shaving, a fluffy white towel wrapped around his waist. The lights on either side of the vanity lit up the tanned muscles of his upper arms.

"Oh, I didn't realize you were shaving."

He tapped the razor on the edge of the chrome sink, methodically ran the blade under the running tap, and brought it up to his face. She watched him watch himself in the mirror, the razor plowing paths of skin through the foam.

"So . . . any thoughts?" Her throat was dry and she cleared it. "I'm ravenous."

"I told the guy we'd eat here tonight."

"Oh, but—Really? Did you really do that?" She went back into the bedroom and began hurriedly to unpack her clothes, thrusting piles of shirts and fistfuls of underwear into the wardrobe drawers, as if trying to hide some contraband. (The underwear was lacy, ridiculous, bought for the honeymoon, as if she would suddenly emerge the kind of woman who wore it.) "I thought we'd go somewhere local for dinner."

"Somewhere authentico, eh? Martin mentioned a place," Will said from the bathroom, after a minute.

"Yes?" She paused in her manic organizing. "But that's perfect! He's someone who really knows the country!"

BUT THE RESTAURANT turned out to be closed on Mondays. In the back of the chauffeured car, Lydia stared out the window at reddish walls of the medina. A man driving a donkey cart who had come down out of a side street drew alongside them. The driver was perched gargoylelike on the front of the cart, knees drawn up to his chest. In one hand he held the reins, in the other a thick piece of wood, more log than stick.

"Let's just get some food," Will said wearily.

Lydia dug her nails into her arm. Every other beat, keeping time with the donkey's trot, the driver raised his fist and slammed the wood into the animal's hindquarters. The thrashing seemed to have no effect, however; the blows did not make the donkey speed up, or even so much as twitch its long ears.

"Oh, don't say that—can't you say 'eat dinner'?" Lydia said viciously. "I hate it when people say 'get some food.' It makes me think of animals at a trough."

"No car," the driver said, pointing up the way toward his suggestion. Obediently they got out and walked in the direction indicated. Lydia hurried a little, hopeful suddenly that the dung-strewn alleyway meant they were being directed to a find.

"Here it is!" She stopped briefly at a stout wooden door before pushing through it impatiently. They waited without speaking and were led presently down a short flight of stairs and under an arched colonnade into an interior courtyard. It was empty. There must have been twenty tables all elaborately set for dinner, with pleated napkins fanning out from glassware, all of them unoccupied save one, under the *logge,* where an American group was winding down a blowout dinner of some sort, a belly dancer circulating among waiters dispensing tea. Lydia looked despairingly at Will, but he was remote, beyond caring.

In the center of the room an alabaster fountain rose up. On the slow, inexorable way to their table, Lydia peered hopefully into it; but seeing that it was dry, she looked away, embarrassed for the thing.

They managed to order; their soup was served, their wineglasses filled.

Eventually the soup bowls were removed and replaced with dinner plates. Will ate his couscous hunched over his plate, shoveling a bit. Lydia began to wonder if their not talking had been noticed, by the Americans, perhaps, or by the waiters. She glanced up at the bougainvilleas spilling like paint onto the high, white walls of the courtyard. How easy it would be to mention the flowers, to point them out to Will, whose back was to them. But it was too late for that. The evening was spoiled—the thing had its grip on her; it had plunged her into its underwater orbit.

"If you really don't like the Bridge, we should move," Will said, making an effort. "We'll go to La Mamounia, like everyone does. It's my fault—I thought it would be fun to see something ridiculously luxe. Treat ourselves, you know?"

Lydia nodded. She couldn't bear to see him try hard. It was all right for smaller men, but he was too large a man to make an effort. His gears seemed to wind uncomfortably and it struck her with sadness. Her throat ached terribly. I must be coming down with something, she thought.

In the corner, the Americans were toasting "Todd—the birthday boy!"

"I can't stay here," Lydia said. "I can't. I'm sorry." She threw her napkin down and rose from the table.

Will stood up as well, looking around for a waiter. "I'll pay the check."

"I'll wait outside."

"Don't." He restrained her with a hand, which Lydia shook off angrily.

"It's not as if there's any real danger."

"Sit down for two minutes while I pay the check."

Ignoring him, Lydia crossed the patio and ducked into the arcade. Will swore and called her name. She ran lightly up the stairs, started first to the right, then, confused, went left, till finally, with a sense of hysteria, she walked back right again and found the door through which they'd come in. She could hear Will apologizing to the maitre d'—requesting the check. She pressed through it, just in time: She fancied she heard his footsteps on the stairs behind her. She found herself in the alleyway and hurried down it, away from the direction they'd come, instinctively drawn to the pulsing heart of the city.

After about ten yards the path stopped short. There, at the

edge of the immense, wide-open space teeming with human activity of every kind, Lydia hesitated. The prospect, even, of such vastness, of such essential liveliness seemed to blow her preoccupations sky-high. She laughed aloud, turned around and half cried, "Will? Hurry up, will you?" as if all along she'd been planning to wait for him. But when she heard the muffled footsteps behind her, a contrarian impulse seized her and she plunged into the square alone.

She walked rapidly among the jugglers and craftsmen, the acrobats and musicians, unsmiling, as if she had been to the carnival so many times she had begun to tire of the acts. Fixing her gaze in an annoyed, shortsighted stare, she tried to lose herself in the darkness and the crowds. In front of her, or behind her—she couldn't tell which, and was troubled by the confusion—she could hear drums pounding relentlessly. After a very few minutes she felt she could not continue the masquerade of knowing where she was going; she simply must stand still for a minute in order to get her bearings—buy something perhaps, something to eat, the grilled meat she could smell, or some herbs, or cosmetics to take home, show to friends, say, "It was absolutely fascinating."

She stopped short before a snake charmer's mat. Squatting on the mat, the *ghaitah* player coaxed a black cobra into striking position.

Just like that, someone asked her if she wanted to buy rugs. *"Non, non, non, merci,"* she said firmly. But not as brusquely as she might have, for she had been flattered by having been addressed in French.

The snake charmer's moneyman was demanding a contribution. She shrank back abruptly and moved on, holding her head up and squinting as if she were shortsighted.

"You American," she heard. She quickened her pace. "What kind of rugs you like?"

The question, though there could not have been a more obvious ploy, stymied her anew. She saw all at once a way to make it up to Will. Not the rugs but something else—something to calm her down, take the edge off. "Forget the wine," Will had said, dressing for dinner. "Where's the complimentary hash stash?" And now she had a chance to be clever about it, to come through for him.

"Madame, where you going?" said the voice at her flank. "You lost?"

She took an awkward step and tripped. A pair of arms reached out to steady her. On the point of shrieking, Lydia caught the scream in her throat. Dusted herself off and pretended to laugh. "No, no, I'm fine."

"You have bad experience in Maroc, Madame?"

"No." Self-consciously, she lightened her tone. She was being too serious, setting herself up for ridicule. "Everything's been great."

"Then why not talk?"

"I'm waiting for my husband," she said and was shocked to hear the essential falseness in her voice. It was like when she bought vodka at the package store and felt her face go sheepish and guilty when she went up to the counter to pay, knowing the man would card her.

"It is no problem—I am guide for you. You and your husband," he added. Where is your husband?"

"He's back at the restaurant."

"What restaurant?"

"The—it doesn't matter. It's not important."

"The Café Florent?"

"Maybe," she said reluctantly. "Yes, that might have been it."

"We can go right now. Then I show you beautiful mosque—very close Djemaa el Fna. After we buy rings." He introduced himself then—Ahmed. Would he expect her to introduce herself as well? She glanced quickly sideways at him. It surprised her to see that her solicitor was a good head shorter than she and heavy-set, a big torso barreling out over truncated legs. His hair was shaved on both sides in some ingenuous attempt to look contemporary. Then she saw that he was not alone. A second man hung back, letting the other fellow do the talking.

She had been composing in her head a long, surprisingly elaborate narrative to the effect that the second pair of eyes—for she must have sensed the other presence some time ago—belonged to Will; that he had caught up with her but was following at a discreet distance, indulging her in her little adventure. The disappointment that it was not Will was crushing. She gasped for air, unable to stop herself though she knew it gave her away.

"You all right, Madame?"

"I'm fine—fine." She looked at him. "I'm after some hash, not rugs, that's all."

The request did not seem to go down well. As Ahmed hesitated, pursing his lips, the other man spoke to him sharply in Arabic. A feeling of desperation filled her when she contemplated the possibility of failure; the empty-handed, inglorious return to the hotel.

"I mean, if it's a problem—"

"Of course, it's no problem!" He seized Lydia's forearm. "You come with me—I show you."

"Oh!" she said. "I'm sorry," and struggled to remove her arm.

"I don't bother you!" the man—Ahmed—said dismissively, reaffirming his grip. Oh, well, she thought. It isn't a big deal.

Surreptitiously, as he led her away, she tried to keep track of the minaret. The lack of all other architectural points of reference was worrying; she had no context for the haphazardness of an urban space not formed by its flanking buildings.

At the entrance to the souks, Lydia hesitated, casting her eye down the long, covered thoroughfare. "Very close—very close," Ahmed said testily. The second man had vanished.

"Oh, I know," she said. "It's just, I don't want my husband to worry. I said I'd only be five minutes. He doesn't like me to go off alone, you know?"

They passed two large gift shops, an array of silver, pottery, carpets in the window, both dark—closed, she realized belatedly, for the evening. He took the passageway on the right, relinquishing Lydia's arm. But now the gesture alarmed rather than comforted her. She had grown used to its nervous peremptory demand. They walked on a little farther, turned down another alley and then into a small, run-down square. An older, graying American couple appeared from the far side, following their guide back out—laughing on cue at something the man had said, their swollen midriffs protruding between polo shirts and khakis.

Lydia glanced up at the woman as they passed. "Is it down here then?" she said loudly to Ahmed. She thought the woman might at least take note of her, and then, should anything happen . . . but then she met her compatriot's eyes. It wasn't concern she saw in the puffy yet pinched face, but avidity; she blinked furiously at Lydia as they went by—hoping, Lydia realized, to see something alarming.

Across the square the paths were narrower, the layout more arbitrary. The souks were jammed in one on top of another; carpets, then leather goods. "So, soon we'll be at the hashish district, right?" she joked.

Ahmed shook his head. "You don't talk to everyone," he said heatedly. "Very dangerous. Many people try to trick you here."

She dared again to look at him, surprised he was taking such a personal interest in her situation. He seemed pointedly to avoid looking at her, as if he might have liked to but had to keep up the act, staring straight ahead, his face so adamantly solemn she wanted to laugh.

They stopped outside some kind of herbal apothecary. Sacks of herbs and spices sat in rows before a wooden counter. The interior was painted sky blue, like the sides of an old cement swimming pool, lit by a bare bulb. At the back of the small room, three men sat playing cards, watched over by a fourth who was standing, commenting on the play. When Lydia came in with Ahmed, they looked at her and as a group looked away.

The man who was standing came up to the counter, speaking to Ahmed; he was tall, and moved languidly, a tight little smile on his lips. After a minute Lydia recognized the man who had been beside them before—transformed, on his home turf, from the impatient hanger-on to a stance that was altogether proprietary.

Ahmed seemed to warn him with a dismissive gesture against doing something, but it was clear who took orders from whom. "You want—?" he asked her urgently, adding a word she could not understand.

"*Vous avez besoin?*" interrupted the tall one dismissively. "*Vous avez besoin?*"

"*J'ai besoin de quoi?*" Lydia said, matching his tone. She found herself siding, mentally, with Ahmed against the man, feeling protective toward the former: no doubt a delusional position. "I'm sorry." She shrugged. "I don't understand."

Ahmed smoothed his shaved temples in exasperation. "You need—? You need—?" The two of them, short and tall, were shouting the word at her now.

"I need?" Lydia looked at them. "A 'peep'? What? Oh, a pipe! A pipe! Yes. We need a pipe. *Nous avons besoin du pipe.*"

They all laughed then, Lydia with the two men. Ahmed's sounded spontaneous but the taller man seemed to be insinuating something with the laugh. She suddenly was aware that he was going to rip her off.

There was a brief heated exchange between the two of them, and a price was named by the latter.

"Well, it's more than I expected!" she said noncommittally.

Both men's faces went flat with disapproval. "Good price, good price. No bargain here," Ahmed said.

"The pipe—free," said the tall one, his eyes salesman-smooth. Smart, she could see—and more polished than Ahmed—but like most salesmen, not as smart as he thought he was. "For you."

Lydia looked down, stalling for time. Not bargaining was shameful—bargaining was worse. She went to open her purse and her stomach turned over: The bag was already unzipped. Feverishly she fumbled inside it, not raising her eyes, knowing her search would be fruitless. "My wallet's been stolen!" she announced finally, appalled to hear the quaver in her voice. And she really did think that it had been stolen. It was only later that she remembered she had left it in the hotel safe—she never bothered to bring cash when she was with Will.

They didn't seem to have understood: "I don't have any money," she said, and tears came to her eyes. At once Ahmed began to argue, his voice raised, with the other fellow.

Now outside the shop there was some commotion—a group of men were shouting, shoving, in some kind of fight; there was a scuffle on the ground. The men playing cards deserted the back of the shop and pushed by Lydia to see what was going on; one of them, she saw, was no more than a teenager.

"They drink," Ahmed shouted to her, gesturing to the mêlée. "It is against Allah."

"My God, they've got knives!" Lydia cried, pressing herself back against the storefront.

The fight bulged toward them like a living thing. The tall shop owner materialized at Lydia's side shouting, a blade in his hand. The crowd circled close again—closer. Her protest caught in her throat—she was trapped; there was nowhere to go. She covered her face with her hands, leaning away from the shouting, writhing bodies. She was screaming now but she couldn't hear her own voice in the throng. When she looked up, Ahmed had been thrown backward against the wall. She put out her hand to help him and was knocked to the ground. "Ahmed!" she cried, going down. "Ahmed!"

"Lyd! Lyd! Lydia!" Will was beside her, on top of her in his pink oxford shirt and loafers. He dragged her up to her feet as a sharp whistle sounded in the distance. The fight seemed to pause; the men scattered, shouting. Emerging from the dregs of it came the shop owner, putting his knife back into his pocket.

"*Vous n'avez pas payé.*"

"But—I mean—I never got the hash," Lydia said, confused.

"Don't fucking reason with the guy, keep walking."

"*Vous n'avez pas payé, madame.*"

"You don't understand, Will! There was something—you interrupted a business transaction!"

"I don't give a shit, keep walking." But then he stopped and turned, pinning her to his side. "Another day, guys," he said. Another of the men from the shop came running up to join them—the teenager, keyed up, deprived of a fight, perhaps—looking for action. "Sorry, guys—it's not going to happen." The voice, Lydia recognized, Will used for real estate brokers, car salesmen—the lack of conciliation never failed to impress her. But was it smart?

"Where's Ahmed?" she said, alarmed, as Will yanked her forward again. She tried to turn around in his grip. "Was he all right? He's not hurt, is he?"

"Keep walking, Lydia."

"You king?" The proprietor had spoken, addressing Will, the question phrased cordially, as if he were simply making conversation. And now Will, the big man, for whom to turn and run would be beneath him, stopped and answered the challenge: "Look, we're not interested, okay? Sorry about that. Whatever it is you're selling, we don't want any."

"I did, though—it's not fair, Will!" Lydia cried, scuffing her feet as Will dragged her along. Her fear had been replaced with a bristling petulance. She thought she might throw a tantrum if he didn't stop and listen to her.

"What kind of rugs you like, sir?" the young one tried.

"Look, I'm sorry." Will stopped again. "Not tonight."

"You think you big shot, eh?" The shop owner continued to walk companionably alongside them.

"No, no." Will was fed up.

"You have camera?" the young one said suddenly. "You pay us for photograph."

"No. No, we actually do not have a camera," Lydia said. "What terrible tourists we are!" The situation had suddenly struck her as ridiculous in the extreme. "Let's just pay them, Will, and get out of here."

"Yes, you listen to your wife—pay me—hundred dirhams."

"Pay them hundred dirhams, Will." She was biting her lip so as not to laugh, hysteria threatening.

"Ri-ight." Will stopped to confront them. The shop man raised his hand to him—Will faltered, he stumbled.

"You big shot? You think you big shot?"

Paralyzed, Lydia could not speak. The young one began to yell insults, directly at her. The whistle sounded again, in the distance. The two men ran down the way, turning to shout at Lydia and Will, and were gone. Will was bleeding, bent over, holding his temple.

"Oh, God, oh, my God!" Lydia knelt and embraced him uselessly. A few men had come out of the souks to witness the commotion. Her eyes flashed accusingly up at them. "Get a doctor! For Christ's sake, a doctor! The police! Where the fuck are the police?"

Will straightened up, his hand pressed to the side of his face. "What did he hit me with? What the fuck was that?" A flicker of something crossed Will's face as he felt in his pockets.

"What? What's wrong?"

He looked over her head into the depths of the bazaar to where their assailants had vanished. "Fucker got my wallet, too."

"No!" Lydia cried out, hearing the admiration in his voice. She grabbed wildly at his arm, whacking at it with the flat of her hand. "It isn't fair!" she cried, and she burst into tears.

WILL HAD BEEN gone more than an hour at the hotel infirmary, Lydia deprived of even the option of waiting it out with him, shuttled off to the room by the bevy of agitated staff who met the police car.

She was sitting now on the edge of the enormous bed, sipping the complimentary wine. From time to time she shifted her position ever so slightly. She had tried turning on the television but it wouldn't do. Nor would getting into her nightgown. So she waited in her dress, trying not to slouch, listening for his footsteps or some other message the night would yet yield. But as the minutes went by it was as if she were back up at the gas station on top of the mountain, straining to hear what was being said a thousand feet below.

She had lost track of time when she heard the gate open outside. Self-consciously she got to her feet. Will came through the sliding doors in his bedraggled shirt and trousers, his head wrapped in a bandage. He did not speak to her when he came in. She watched him kick off his shoes, begin to unbutton his shirt.

"You caved, huh?" he said when he saw the open bottle on the bedside table.

"I wasn't really going to save it till the last night."

"Uh-huh."

He took the glass she held out and swallowed half of it. She refilled it and placed it on the bedside table: an offering. He took off his shirt, made a ball of it, and threw it to the floor.

"Oh, Will—on the floor? Must you? I mean, you're a grown man, aren't you? Do you have to throw your clothes on the floor? I'm sorry," she said. "I'm sorry, I won't say anything. I'll just sit here—" He emptied out his pockets, tossing cell phone, coins, matches onto the bureau. He looked briefly out the glass doors before coming to stand before her at the foot of the bed.

"Are you really, really mad at me?" Her eyes, pleased and troubled, sought his. "What can I do?" She crawled down the bed to be closer to him, sitting contritely at the end of it. He looked at her. "I'm really, really, genuinely, horribly sorry. I shouldn't have gone off like that. I had no right—" She hesitated. "Were they annoyed we left early? Did they say anything at all when you paid the check?"

Will frowned, watching her. "I never paid it."

"You mean, we skipped out on the bill?" When he didn't deny it, Lydia gasped. "But—we'll have to go back tomorrow and pay it. Thank God I found my wallet. But we'll have to go and apologize. My God—they're probably tracking us down as we speak, Will!" She leaned over and snatched the phone off the bedside table. "Do you know what—we should call right now. How do you dial out on this thing?"

Will walked around to the side of the bed. He stood before her now in his boxers. "I'm sorry! I said I was sorry." She looked up at him. "Your bandage is coming off, you know. You look ridiculous. You look like an extra in *ER*. A head trauma victim." He pried the phone from her hands and tossed it to the floor. "Oh, my God, you've got to be kidding me." His hands under her armpits, he thrust her up the gigantic bed. "You're scaring me," Lydia said sarcastically. She struggled onto her stomach, the dress bunching and knotting around her waist. "It's not funny," she said as Will pinned her there, pinned her hands easily to the small of her back with one of his. "It's not funny, Will." The side of her face pressed into the silk coverlet, she felt her underwear removed from the crack of her buttocks, yanked down to her ankles, where it caught, briefly, on her sandals. "Will!" She struggled under his hold. "For God's sake, they were expensive!"

She writhed, further tangling the dress. The night air whistled up her bare skin. "I can't see," she began to protest, trying pathetically to raise herself on her elbows. A warm, impervious arm went around her midriff. "You're not listening to me! I—" The quickness of his entry made her gasp. She clenched the coverlet as he jackknifed her into position and held her there.

Grunting—outraged—he worked her roughly till he came, not for her pleasure, it was clear, but for something to do with his hand.

Afterward, wearing one of the hotel robes, Lydia sat on the patio outside, her feet dangling in the wading pool. She would straighten her legs so her toes broke the surface of the water, then plunge her feet back down to the bottom. She had pooh-poohed the wading pool, but it was proving a luxury, after all. No doubt she would get used to the hotel and not want to leave. She heard Will moving inside the room and listened to see if he was coming out. Instead of Will, she might have married someone like Ahmed: That thought struck her idly. One always thought of oneself as the stupider, the more desperate, the handicapped—but perhaps it was all a matter of comparison. *She could have been happy with someone short, freakish, penniless* . . . Even tonight: She might have brought her own money to the restaurant. She might have been the one to come through. Instead he had tossed a packet of hash on the bed just now. "Got it off the hotel doctor—can you imagine? Must be one of the 'amenities.' " But still, she might have been, of the two of them, the reliable one, the one to be counted on. That she was not no longer seemed the objective state of affairs, just a circumstantial event, like traveling—the way it cast you into roles. It seemed very important all at once to keep putting herself in situations where she would be reminded of this, viscerally reminded. But there was less than a week left in their honeymoon and she could feel the indolence overtaking her, the tourist's satiety; she'd had enough of authentic experience. She doubted she would leave the grounds of the hotel.

WHEN WILL JOINED her he had reaffixed his bandage. It had a triumphant, jaunty look, like a clever costume.

He lit a cigarette, cupping his hand over the flame—and took an exultant drag. "This is the last one," he warned her. "We'll have to get a pipe for the other stuff." Lydia let this pass. He walked over to where she was sitting and handed the cigarette to her. "Let's get massages tomorrow," he said.

"Okay."

"Hey, isn't that Cassiopeia?" Will said, craning his neck at the sky.

"Is it?" Lydia said. She was very calm, letting him point out the stars.

Acknowledgments

I'd like to thank Laura Ford, who brought the book to fruition, and Dan Menaker, who was a great source of encouragement early on.

David McCormick saw me through the fits and starts of a long project.

I'm lucky to have as my friend Cressida Connolly, whose guidance and good taste I relied on from beginning to end.

SPOILED

Caitlin Macy

A Reader's Guide

A Conversation with Caitlin Macy

Random House Reader's Circle: Each of the stories in *Spoiled* is wonderfully unique, yet there are similar themes running throughout the collection. How did you decide on the subject matter for these stories? Why did you choose to write about what might be perceived as a certain type of woman?

Caitlin Macy: I started writing the stories and the unifying theme came later. An editor of mine at Random House came up with the title for the story "Spoiled." At that point I had written about half of the stories in the book and I thought, *Aha, that's what this book is about.*

RHRC: In many of the stories, you show women and girls behaving badly—acting spoiled. Are we supposed to empathize with them?

CM: Not necessarily! I do care about all of my characters no matter how repellent their behavior, I suppose because I feel that they're ultimately suffering also. Many of them are trapped emotionally and psychologically if not logistically. That doesn't excuse their behavior of course, but for me, it mitigates it a bit. People act out when they are anxious and unhappy.

RHRC: Do you relate to any of the women in particular? Are any of them based on people you know?

CM: I definitely relate to the younger sister in "Bait and Switch," as I'm a younger sister myself. I also empathize with the thirty-something lawyer in "The Secret Vote." The anxieties of contemporary life for my generation are manifold; any decision that represents a break with one's family can be agonizing.

None of the characters map directly to friends of mine though I certainly use details from acquaintances' lives, from conversations I've overheard in the park, from gossip in Starbucks.

RHRC: Your last book, *The Fundamentals of Play,* was a novel. Which do you prefer, short stories or novels? And how is the writing process different for each?

CM: I think I'm more naturally a novelist and I find the longer form friendlier; it's more forgiving to a writer—one can wax on a bit about things, one doesn't have to have to write quite as tightly as one does in a story. With a story, I really have to have a sense of where it's going right from the beginning and how it's going to get there. It's a challenging form: like making up a riddle or a joke, there's very little room for digression.

RHRC: Who are some of your literary influences? And do you see this book as part of a certain tradition of books that explore wealth and class?

CM: My first book was heavily influenced by *The Great Gatsby,* which I reread a thousand times. Nowadays I read a lot of contemporary women writers: Alice Munro, Nadine Gordimer, Tessa Hadley, Rachel Cusk. I'm happy to be included in the tradition of people who write about class. On the other hand, I am fascinated by class not as a study in and of itself but as a particularly illuminating lens through which one can explore the emotional drives of one's characters.

RHRC: We'd love to know what you're working on now. Is it something in the same vein as *Spoiled*?

CM: It's a bit of a departure! I just finished a screenplay, a romantic comedy. Beyond the love interest there is a central relationship between the heroine and a female friend of hers—a bad friend actually—so I'm still exploring women's relationships.

Questions and Topics for Discussion

1. In two of the stories, "Annabel's Mother" and "The Red Coat," Macy writes about a woman's conflicted relationship with her domestic help—a nanny and a cleaning woman, respectively. What do you think a woman's relationship with her help says about her as a person?

2. In "The Secret Vote," a young woman raised Roman Catholic reacts with distaste to the idea of a gay couple having a child with a surrogate mother. But the story ends with the young woman herself having an abortion. What is Macy saying about the woman's perspective? Is it hypocritical?

3. Unlike the United Kingdom, America isn't supposed to have true class distinctions, yet these nuances play an important role in *Spoiled*. Why do you think that is?

4. Are there moral lessons that can be taken from the ways the women in these stories behave? Do you think these stories are meant to be cautionary tales?

5. The women in most of these stories are well-off, some of them very well-off. Why do you think they aren't happier?

6. The subjects of several of the stories ("Annabel's Mother," "Bad Ghost," "Spoiled," "Bait and Switch") are parents and their children, or parental stand-ins—nannies, friends' mothers, a girl's riding instructor—and their charges. Do you think a spoiled child makes for a spoiled adult?

7. This book came out in the middle of a global financial melt-down. How do you think the characters would be doing in today's financial climate?

8. What does it mean to be spoiled?

CAITLIN MACY is the author of *The Fundamentals of Play* and the winner of an O. Henry Prize in 2005. Her work has been published in *The New York Times, The New Yorker,* and *Slate.* Macy lives with her family in New York City.

ABOUT THE TYPE

This book was set in Garamond No. 3, a variation of the classic Garamond typeface originally designed by the Parisian type cutter Claude Garamond (1480–1561).

Claude Garamond's distinguished romans and italics first appeared in *Opera Ciceronis* in 1543–44. The Garamond types are clear, open, and elegant.